HUCKLEBERRY HILL

*For Rod, Tom
Enjoy -
love*

David W. Christner

David W. Christner

MOONFLOWER PRESS

DEDICATION

To my wife Linda, my sister Colleen, my mom and brother John, Christopher and Carrie, and all the grandkids hither and yon, with love.

CONTENTS

ACKNOWLEDGEMENT

I would like as well to express my sincere appreciation to Grace Farrell and the members of the Carolina Fiber and Fiction Center in Richmond, Rhode Island for the their invaluable assistance in the editorial preparation of this edition of "Huckleberry Hill."

1

WAS VICTOR MATURE?

I didn't kill Fanny; you have to understand that. She was dead, or nearly so, when I barged in—before that even. And other than possibly contributing a few gray hairs to her small, pretty head, I had nothing to do with what Preacher called Fanny's "untimely demise." He said the exact same thing about Roseabeth's mother. And he always added that she, Roseabeth's mother, had been called away to do God's work elsewhere.

I reckon preachers are supposed to think like that, part of being a man of God, but, to tell you the truth, I can't see much sense in it. If you ask me—which few people do—seems like God ought to have all the help He needs without the preacher's wife, unless of course, He doesn't have any better handle on things "up there" than He does down here in what Huck Finn called the "territories" and what has since become known as Oklahoma—former home of the red man, now home of the white man.

Seems to me too that somebody other than old *Watakushi*—that's Japanese for I, myself, or just plain old number one—ought to be held accountable for Fanny's demise and Roseabeth's ruin. But no, I'm responsible. Actually, it doesn't really much matter about Fanny. Besides being dead, she had no money or property to speak of, so everybody has lost interest in her and is concentrating their sympathy on *poor* Roseabeth—because she is still very much alive—and I might add, kicking. To hear people talk, you'd think that what happened to Roseabeth, or to put it more accurately, what I did with Roseabeth, is much worse than what happened to Fanny. And from what I understand, Fanny used to make a pretty good living doing the exact same thing! I find the entire reaction to the agony and the ecstasy I experienced on Huckleberry Hill more than a little disconcerting.

If I did kill Fanny, which I didn't, it was an accident. Just like what I did with Roseabeth; that was an accident too. That is to say, I didn't *plan* on doing anything to either of them. It was inevitable, I guess. That's what Doc would have said.

Consider this: If it hadn't have been for the emergency brake failing on Si's old Chevy pickup, that infamous hill in front of Fanny's place, some bad timing on Fanny's part, and a cab full of more nylon net and flame colored taffeta than you'd supposed existed in the world, the whole catastrophe might have been avoided. But I doubt it. It was prom night after all, and something weird was bound to happen. And it did!

I'd been on a libidinal roller coaster with Roseabeth for as long as I can recollect, even though I didn't recognize it for what it was until now. Even so, I never figured to pay the ultimate price for my infatuation, which is what I'm about to do. At least that's the way I see it. What is happening to me shouldn't happen to anyone, especially not to a youth of my peculiar sensibilities and certainly not in the middle of the 20th century. Yet, here, I am, locked up in the steeple of the Free Will Baptist Church (without much emphasis on the "free will" part) and on the verge of being married off to Roseabeth Bascom in a wedding of the shotgun variety. If Preacher gets his way, I will be too—confined for life—and still in the spring of my seventeenth year of existence, to use the term pretty loosely, existence.

Injustice is what I call it. Because it couldn't matter to Fanny what they do me; she's gone to meet her Maker. And as for Roseabeth: She enjoyed it—up to a point, not the aftermath, which is quite understandable. Anyway, I'm being punished for doing something with Roseabeth that she enjoyed. I don't get it. But maybe I *did*, and it is that fact which accounts for the major part of my present difficulty, which, aside from figuring a way out of it, is to get it set once and for all in my own mind just what did happen and why.

That's why I'm going to the considerable trouble, not to mention the humiliation, of filling in the Big Chief tablet Preacher gave me with the necessary background information to reconstruct the catastrophe that took place on Huckleberry Hill. But even if I can't make any sense out of it, maybe somebody else can, and if this information keeps just one poor kid from making the same mistakes I did, I'll consider the world to be a better place to live. Not that I consider it a bad place now, considering the lack of viable alternatives, but it could use some improvement.

About what happened I do know this much: It happened two ways, slowly, over a period of years, and then all of a sudden, in one huge burst of—of—I don't rightly know what to call it. Enthusiasm maybe. No, it was stronger stuff than that. Exuberance? Yeah, for sure, but more powerful still. Mr. Sigmund Freud, whose work I stumbled on quite by accident, would have called it an "excess of libidinal energy." Mr. Walt Whitman referred to such excesses as "pent-up aching rivers." And it *was* that, along with what Doc undoubtedly would have referred to as, "unmitigated lust." There you have it; it was *all* those things. Along with the night and stars and the way Roseabeth smelled and that strapless gown. Great God Almighty! What was I *supposed* to do in a situation like that? Quote her some baseball statistics? Maybe give her a brief synopsis of *The Great Chain of Being*? Hot damn! Roseabeth didn't give a hang about baseball *or* metaphysics.

I will say this in my defense and, I believe, to my credit: I didn't dance with Roseabeth. Even when she insisted I refused, at first, holding steadfastly to my moral conviction that dancing is a sin, even though it isn't mentioned in the top ten that Moses got from the burning bush on the mountaintop. What happened was: Roseabeth danced with me; I didn't dance with her. And nobody seemed to mind all that much. So I don't understand what all the fuss is about. What I do understand is that I have somehow offended the moral sensibilities of a great many good people—*especially* her father's—even if not those of Roseabeth and myself. Maybe that's the worst part of all.

Just how I figured out even that much of what happened will probably be something of a mystery to me for some time. Nobody, with the possible exception of Fanny, ever talked to me honestly and frankly about sex during the explosive years of my early adolescence. And sex almost ruined me on at least two occasions, both of which occurred years before the catastrophe that took place on Huckleberry Hill.

Naturally I have been unmercifully subjected to the locker room banter about girls—those that do (what?) and those that don't—that largely makes up a kid's sex education these days. But not an awful lot of that information seems to be entirely accurate, or even close to being so. It is second hand, sometimes third, and in many cases pure or impure fabrication, depending upon what it is that is being fabricated. This collection of misinformation is what made the task of growing up just so much harder than when such subjects just weren't discussed at all.

The trouble all started, as far as I can recollect, the summer that I turned 13, not a good year by anybody's assessment. That was the year that I began to . . . mature, in earnest. Personally, I didn't give a hang about doing it; didn't even know *how* to do it. But as I understood it at the time, that was beside the point. There was nothing I could do to prevent it. I just had to let Nature take her course, which would have been okay, except for the fact that I was highly satisfied with the status quo. Besides, I recall thinking that everybody who I knew who was mature—adults, I mean—seemed to have all manner of worries: money, food, women, men, kids, everything. If that was what came with maturity, I'd have just as soon stayed a kid who was pretty much certain of where his next meal was coming from, even if it was rice more than half the time.

Yessir! Things suited me just fine. I recall the river being full of catfish; Mickey Mantle was hitting .324 for the Yankees; Silas had hung me a new basketball goal, and, the sky that summer was about as blue as you'd ever hope to see it. The nights cooled down nicely, and I felt as though Silas, Mariko, and Doc would have done about anything for me. I mean I had the feeling that they thought I was an okay kid. And I was, then. Everything changed rather suddenly, though, that morning when I woke up four years ago and had a revelation. Actually, it wasn't a revelation at all. What it was is a hair, a hair where I'm dead certain there hadn't been one the day before. Things started going downhill at that very moment, as you shall see.

"Ezra," Mariko called, "get up. Doc has already left for the river."

"I'm gittin'," I said, but I wasn't. I was just lying there, square in the middle of my bed, staring down at it. It wasn't much of a hair really; one skimpy dark hair sprouting out of what otherwise looked like a barren stretch of desert. After a moment I climbed off the bed and walked to the window where the morning sun poured in like a stream of warm honey. There I could have a look at this development in a different light. Once there I only confirmed what I thought I'd seen only moments before. It was a hair all right. Immediately I started worrying.

Where'd it come from? How many more was I going to get? When? And where else? Preacher Bascom had hair sprouting out his nose and ears, and that was no sight for sore eyes. And what about money? If you were mature you had to have money to buy cigarettes because smoking cigarettes helped you not to worry, and smoking cigarettes was a sure sign of maturity. And *that* worried me too. I didn't want to smoke cigarettes even if it did make you mature.

Why, I just wanted to play ball, go fishing, and listen, up to a point, to all Doc had to tell me about the world and life. As far as I knew Doc was about the wisest man that ever lived, and that includes Solomon and Aristotle and Mr. Albert Einstein, because Doc knew everything about them, but they didn't know the first thing about him. Doc told me all about Plato and Charles Darwin and Ernest Hemingway and George Elliot and Madam Curie and Herman Melville and Mark Twain and the Great Chain of Being and . . .

"Ezra! Come on down now. Your breakfast is almost ready."

"Okay," I said, "I'm comin'."

Forcing this maturity thing from my mind temporarily by thinking about how pretty Roseabeth Bascom was getting, I washed up, pulled on some faded Levis and a pair of PF Flyers, then hurried downstairs. Mariko was waiting in the kitchen with a typical breakfast—rice cakes, green tea, a bowl of cold rice with a raw egg broken on top so the yoke ran into the crevices of the rice so you couldn't get it out no matter what.

Mariko was Japanese, Nisei, and my mom. This breakfast was just one example of the many ways that I was learning that Japanese culture had a lot more to offer us than Pearl Harbor, which seemed to be the *only* thing most people remembered about the Japanese. Mariko was a pre-war bride. My father, who the Navy had stationed in San Francisco, married her before we entered the war. That had kept Mariko from being sent to the "relocation center" where her parents died of dysentery early in 1942. My father's marriage didn't, however, keep him from falling victim to the madness in the North Atlantic where the Navy had sent him after his union with my mother. From what I could understand, I wasn't supposed to feel as bad since my father was killed by the Germans instead of the Japanese. To tell you the truth, I'd probably have felt a lot better if he hadn't been killed at all.

Anyway, Doc naturally took us in after that, and that's how we finally ended up attached to Silas here in the territories with me having rice for breakfast and learning about Japanese culture. Well, I wasn't crazy about this culture business, but I'd learned by this time that kids had to put up with a certain amount of this kind of thing from their parents, and besides, there were lots of worse things in the world than having rice for breakfast.

"Look at you," I heard Mariko say. She was standing across the kitchen from me; her arms were folded in front of her, and she was smiling at me and shaking her head. I took a quick look down and didn't find anything out of the ordinary. So I glanced up and shrugged. She crossed to me, and I let her hug me. She was real big on that, and since it seemed to mean something to her I went along with it. She also happened to be about the prettiest mom a kid could ever hope for—thin, dazzling dark eyes and hair, white straight teeth, and skin as soft as silk. She held me back at arm's length and pushed the hair back from my eyes. She smiled and said, "Ezra, you need a haircut."

"Huh," I said nervously and glanced down at my groin area. I hoped she wasn't talking about *that* hair.

"You need a haircut," she repeated.

"Oh, a *haircut*," I said relieved. "I know." I stepped back, stumbled over my left foot and more or less fell into my chair.

"Goodness, Ezra, I think you're growing too fast for your own good."

"I am," I agreed, having no reason to doubt her.

"It won't be long before you'll be a man."

"How long?" I blurted out, startling her.

"Well, just relax, Son. It takes a little while." She eyed me kind of funny—like maybe she suspected something. Then she said, "Eat up."

I started on the rice, then took a sip of the tea from a small pottery cup that had been in Mariko's family a lot longer than I had. She sat down opposite me and began to study her cup. After a moment I ventured, "Mariko?" Sometimes I called her that. Over the top of her cup she let her eyes settle on mine. "Are—are—Japanese men—ah—hairy?"

She blinked and then sort of intensified her gaze, cocking her head a little. "Hairy?" she said.

I avoided her eyes and started to shift around some in my chair. "Yeah, you know—*hairy.*"

"In what way?" she asked, creasing her brow.

"In—jist the regular way," I said, sorry that I'd brought it up. "Some here, some there."

She shook her head and said, "I don't understand."

"I don't either," I told her. "That's why I asked."

"Ezra, what is it—that you don't understand?"

I shrugged and said, "If I knew what it was that I didn't understand I wouldn't of asked you to explain it to me." I tried to choke down some more rice.

She set her cup aside and glanced out the window, probably genuinely puzzled, thinking nonetheless. When she turned back to me she asked, "Well, what does *hair* have to do with it?"

"Everything, I think," I said passionately.

She nodded, smiled slightly and found my eyes with hers, but not for long. "Ezra, do *you* have some new hair? Is that what this is all about?"

"Me? Why no. No," I said impulsively. Boy she had a way of getting right to the root of things. "I—I was jist wondering if—if Japanese men were as hairy as American men. That's all. And if—if they had to git haircuts as often. You're the one that brought up hair." I gulped down the last of my tea and started for the door.

"That's *all*?" she asked. "You're sure?"

"Mom! It's . . . somethin' you wouldn't understand."

"Because I'm a woman?"

"No, no," I insisted, backing out of the kitchen. It's 'cause—'cause I'm a boy."

"Who's becoming a man?"

"No," I said, "I'm jist a kid who's tryin' to stay a kid. Now I've got to go."

Doc's probably at the river catchin' up all the fish."

"Okay," she said. "But why don't you ask Doc about it? Or Silas?"

"About what?"

She looked a little disappointed. "About . . . staying a kid."

"Okay, I'll do that," I promised. In a flash I'd made it through the back door and leaped off the porch. I filled my lungs with the potent morning air, trying to get hold of myself. I'd never been in such a sweat. And all because of *one* hair. Lord, I hated to think about what was going to happen by and by. As I lit out for the river I heard Mariko call, "Good luck," which would have been okay if I'd known just how she meant it.

Doc wasn't a doctor at all; at least not the kind that makes people well when they're sick. Fact is, he dealt me a nearly fatal dose of metaphysics before I had a real clear understanding of *The Hardy Boys*. Doc was what's called a Doctor of Philosophy,

a Ph.D., and his particular field of specialization was literature, American and otherwise, which he'd taught for some
thirty-odd years at the university in Norman before retiring,
five, maybe six years ago. I had been his only student since his
retirement, and the job of removing "ain't" from my vocabulary had become what Doc termed an "arduous task" for both
of us. Bad grammar, you see, was one of the two things that
Doc couldn't hardly tolerate. Injustice was the other. And I
was forever trying not to unconsciously split my infinitives for
Doc, but I couldn't see much future in it. He was the only one
who noticed, and when I did find words like "aren't" creeping
into my working vocabulary when "ain't" would have worked
just as well, my cronies came down on me real hard like. So
I had to try to keep everything that Doc taught me under
wraps. From what I could tell, there was nothing tougher on a
kid than trying to be grammatical in a largely ungrammatical
world. Of course it was no picnic being evenhanded either; I
had both cheeks busted more than once for trying to see that
"justice prevailed." Another one of Doc's notions. But I hung
in there because it was important to Doc for me to become a
decent and grammatical human being. But at 13 it was clear
that I had a ways to go on both counts. I could express myself
decently when I put my mind to it, but it was a powerful lot of
trouble.

Doc also, aside from Mariko and Silas, was the only religious liberal in Mansfield, and, I suspect, maybe the only
practicing freelance minister of that description in the territories, a factor which bore directly, if not favorably, upon my
upbringing, my religious education in this case. According to
Doc, I, too, was a religious liberal but also an occasional Free
Will Baptist. From the Baptists I learned what a sin it was to

dance, and from Doc and all his books came my introduction to Plato and the roots of Western ethical thought, the foundation, according to Doc, of my becoming a decent and grammatical human being.

Of course I never let on to anyone else that I was fully aware of the fact that Doc was unopposed to dancing. *That* would have ruined his good name; it was enough that he was a religious liberal. Few in Mansfield knew just what that entailed, and nobody bothered to find out by attending the services that Doc held religiously every Sunday, even though Silas, Mariko, me, a handful of Kiowa Indians and occasionally Fanny Boltwood were his only takers.

I split my time between Doc's lectures and the Baptist meetings because Doc wanted me to hear more than his side of the story. Seemed to me, however, that rather than hearing different sides of the same story, I was hearing two stories that weren't even remotely related. Preacher Bascom went on and on about God and his boy, Jesus, while Doc kept harping on the ancient Greeks to begin with and later a bunch of other foreigners like Hegel, Kant, Galileo, Descartes, Sartre, Hannah Arendt and only God knows who else. But people in Mansfield had never heard of *any* of them, and, in my opinion, may have been better off for it. Now Doc was real high on Jesus too; said Jesus was the most decentest man who ever lived and I ought to try and . . . "emulate" him I think it was. Doc might not have thought that Jesus was everything the Baptists had him cracked up to be, but he thought Jesus was a far sight better than the rest of us.

So, I naturally thought Doc most surely was about the wisest man since Solomon, and that's why I was sure he could help me get this maturity business straight. I just hoped that he could do it without bringing Aristotle or Plato into the conversation. Doc, with all his knowledge, I have to admit, had a way of making a simple thing seem downright impossible.

Why, those stories about Jesus the Baptists told were so simple that even a kid my age could understand them; you hardly had to think about them at all before the point would leap right out of the story and knock you smack out of the pew. But the stories Doc told were altogether different; you had to get your old mind working overtime to make any sense of them at all. For Doc, and consequently, for me, nothing could be simple. It was as simple as that.

Doc didn't look complicated though, not dozing under a big cottonwood tree set alongside the left bank of the Washita, not much of a river by Mr. Twain's standards, but a moving body of water nonetheless. And a river of, "uncommon historical import," according to Doc. I'll tell you why it was an important river when it comes to me.

Up through the branches of the cottonwood I could see the sun flickering like some huge gem in that scorching yellow-blue sky. Here in the shade with a slight breeze being funneled between the high banks of the river the heat wasn't too bad. The river was rolling by ever so lazy and peaceful like, and our bobbers were dancing just slightly in the current. I was sitting there next to Doc trying not to think about not thinking.

Part of my Japanese cultural education had to do with, God forbid, Zen Buddhism. And the idea, Mariko told me, was to reach a state of nothingness. I wasn't all that keen on the idea to tell you the truth, but I'd promised Mariko that I'd give it a go, and I was hesitant to wake up Doc to find out about the maturity thing just yet. Squeezing my eyes shut real hard I tried to clear my mind of all thought, something I'd been accused of doing more than a few times at school. But this time it didn't work. I found that by trying not to think about not thinking about nothing, I couldn't help but try to think of what, if anything, nothing was. I mean, everything was something; even the black hole of space without a molecule of anything in it was a black hole in space, which was something.

I guess it was like Mariko said: You couldn't do it consciously. You had to let it sneak up on you, and then as soon as you were aware that you had it, you lost it. As far as I could tell, there was just no way of being dead certain of whether you had it or not. Such a line of thought was getting me nowhere so I gave up on it. I still had this maturity business to get settled, and I'd done some thinking on it since I'd left Mariko. I thought that maybe I was on to something, and if Doc wouldn't turn a simple question into a lecture on metaphysics, I could probably benefit from his expertise. And maybe even from my own experience of getting mature. I sure hoped so because the whole thing was getting to be real aggravating to me, and I don't think so good when I'm aggravated. Who does?

Doc was beginning to stir some; his eyes were twitching, and he was making funny little sounds in his sleep and sort of smacking his lips. It was kind of disgusting, but the sort of thing you overlook in people you love. I mean, if you didn't or couldn't, I don't see how anybody could or would ever love anybody else. I didn't want to wake him yet, so I reeled in my line to check my bait, a juicy night crawler that looked none too happy with the lot that fate had dealt him. I didn't blame the poor thing; seemed unjust to me, but Doc said that with worms justice didn't carry a whole lot of weight. So I threw him back in the river, way over to the far side where some roots hung down covering the undercut bank. Catfish got up there in the shade on these hot days and dozed just like Doc was doing.

Glancing down at my grandfather I couldn't help but smile and at the same time cock my head and look at him with some kind of vague notion of something that went well beyond admiration. His rod was resting in those huge hands, hands that had seen a good deal of wear from more than just flipping pages of all those books he'd studied. They were all gnarled and puffy, and the little finger on his left hand was missing, bitten off by a catfish years ago, he'd told me. He just told me that, I think, to tease me because I'd been having such a tough time with *Moby Dick*; for years I'd been struggling with *Moby Dick*. But all Doc would say is that I would understand and appreciate it fully when I was more mature. It was an okay story, a little heavy here and there on symbolism for a ten-year-old, which is when Doc started me in on it, but it was real exciting and adventurous. That wasn't enough though. Doc told me I had to, "get something," out of it. He wouldn't tell me what though; said I had to get it for my own self, and when I did I'd know it. Sounded a little like Zen to me.

Anyway, that's the reason I decided not to fight this maturity business, to go ahead and get mature. It would be terrific, I thought, to finally get something out of *Moby Dick*, even if it did seem like a powerful lot of trouble to put a kid through just so he'd understand a book.

Doc's chuckling broke into my already unsettled peace of mind. When I looked I found him staring at me, smiling, and laughing to himself like—like maybe he *knew* what I was thinking. I suppose he may have. Still he asked: "What's going on in that head of yours, Ezra? You look mighty bewildered." I shrugged and squinted at him as a shaft of sunlight slanted through the swaying limbs of the cottonwood. "You considering nailing Old Blue?"

"Naw," I said. "Old Blue's for you to catch. He didn't eat my finger. Actually, I was—was thinkin' 'bout—'bout gittin' mature."

Doc reflected momentarily, taking a few turns on his reel to get the slack out of his line. "Maturity, huh? What about it?"

"I'm not sure," I said. "That's why I'm thinkin' 'bout it."

He nodded, digesting that, and then rubbed the back of his leathery neck with a bright red bandanna. Doc made it a habit to think before he spoke, and he encouraged me to do the same. But I'm afraid my mouth worked a lot faster than my brain, as was the case with the vast majority of folks. "Maturity, huh?" he said again.

"Yessir, why don't you tell me 'bout it?"

"Maturity?"

"That's what we're talkin' 'bout," I said. Then added: "It would save me a powerful lot of thinkin'."

"Now don't you get down on thinking, Son. There's nothing in the world wrong with thinking, except that too little of it goes on. Now where would Plato be if he hadn't been such a thinker?"

"Exact same place he is anyway," I said, "a hole in the ground."

"Well, you've got yourself a point there, Ezra, but we never would have heard of him if he hadn't been such a thinker. *That's* the difference."

"I didn't mean to git down on thinkin'," I said, thinking we seemed to be getting off the subject of maturity. So I persisted: "I've *been* thinkin', but I can't seem to make much sense out of it—maturity."

Doc reeled in his line and inspected his now empty hook with the careful eye of a surgeon. "Hand me the worms," he said and reached for the can with a wiry arm. I opened the can and handed them to him. "Fine specimens here, Ezra," he said, holding one to the hook. Doc was slim, his skin the color of leather, and his hair a ghostly white like the bushy eyebrows over his dark, sad eyes. "Fine specimens. Where'd you say you got them?"

"I didn't," I told him.

"Who did? Doc asked"

"Who did what?"

"Who got the worms?"

"*I* did!"

"You just said that you didn't."

"What I meant was that I didn't *say* where I got 'em Doc, not that I didn't git them. I did."

He looked me straight in the eye and said, "Say what you mean, Son."

"I thought I did."

"Where *did* you get them?"

"Behind the feed lot," I explained, wondering what the devil was going on, "where the troughs drain into the ditch."

"Ah, yes. Prime area," Doc said, "prime area." He baited up and cast his line out into the middle of the river.

"What's hair got to do with it?" I asked before he could get settled.

He scratched the back of his head and said, "What's hair got to do with what?"

"Gittin' mature," I said as patiently as I could.

"Oh, you're still on that, huh?"

"Yessir. I never got off of it."

Rubbing the white stubble on his chin he narrowed his eyes at me. "Tell me, Ezra, how do you feel about . . . *females* these days?"

"Girls, you mean?" He nodded. I just knew he'd do this. "What's *that* got to do with it? Come on, Doc," I protested, "I asked you a simple question, and you havta go and drag girls into it."

"It's not a simple question; there are very few simple questions," Doc said. "And females—girls as you call them—have a great deal to do with it. Now how do you feel about them?"

I started to wiggle around some and noticed the heat was getting pretty intense, even under the shade of that cottonwood. The fact is I had just recently begun to look at girls in a different light, not that I ever had anything against them. But aside from somebody to play ball with or chase around the schoolyard, I'd noticed lately that girls were—well, kind of—pretty, different even. Especially Roseabeth, Preacher Bascom's daughter and Fonda Peters, daughter of the minister over at the Methodist Church.

"Well?" Doc said.

"I like girls all right," I told him and was suddenly struck by the thought that girls had more *hair* than boys, a lot more. *That's* what they had to do with it! I could hardly contain my enthusiasm. "Are girls more mature than boys, Doc, 'cause—'cause they got more hair? Is that it?" I sat back smiling then and waited for his response because he was always so proud when I figured out something for my own self.

But this time he just stared at me with a kind of funny expression, a troubled one I'd say. "Ezra," he finally said, "hair has got very little, if anything, to do with it. Girls—females of many species—*do* mature earlier than their male counterparts, but not because they have more hair. It's . . . biological."

"Oh," I said quietly, trying to hide my disappointment and because I wasn't dead certain of what he was driving at. I was *sure* hair had something to do with it. "But I'm gittin' more hair; doesn't that mean that I'm gittin' more mature?"

Doc nodded. "Yes, that's true . . . physically, but—"

"I *see!*" I said. "It's like—like *Samson!* He had all this hair, and he was the strongest and the most maturest man who ever lived. And—and he killed a lion and a jackass and all them Philistines—"

"*Those* Philistines."

"Yeah, them too," I said and hurried on. "And then—then Jane cut off all his hair, and he got all weak and—and *immature* because he didn't have all that hair anymore."

"That was Tarzan," Doc said.

"Tarzan! He got weak too?"

"No!" Doc said. "Jane didn't cut off his hair; Delilah did."

"Delilah didn't even know Tarzan."

"Ezra, *I* know that, but you said that Jane cut off Samson's hair. But she didn't. Delilah did!"

"Oh," I said and scratched the back of my head. "Well, what did Jane cut off?"

Doc suddenly ripped the bandanna from his neck and began mopping his brow. "I don't know that Jane cut off anything! We were talking about *Samson!*"

"Then why'd you bring up Tarzan?"

"Because you brought up Jane."

"But I meant Delilah. *She's* the one who cut off all Samson's long hair."

Doc just nodded and began gnawing on his lower lip; he was ordinarily about the patientest man in the world, but even he was sometimes unnerved by what I told him. "Now what were we discussing *before* Tarzan got involved?"

"Maturity," I reminded him, "'bout how Samson got all weak and immature because *Delilah* cut off his hair." I was real careful to get it right this time, but I don't see what difference it would have made. From what I understood he'd of gotten just as immature if Jane had been the one.

"Okay," Doc said, "I'm with you, I think, go on."

"Okay, so that means that when you lose your hair, re-gardless of who cuts it off, you're not mature anymore, that you git all weak and can't whip *those* Philistines anymore. Right?"

"Ezra, there are any number of things that can make a man lose his hair, not any one of which necessarily means that a man is becoming *less* mature. When you lose your hair as a natural consequence of the aging process it isn't so much a matter of becoming immature as it is one of becoming . . . overripe. You understand that?"

"No sir."

"All right then, take an apple."

"I ain't got one."

"I *don't* have one."

"I don't either."

"I was making an analogy."

"I'd sooner have an apple," I told him and smiled.

"*Consider* the apple," Doc said, raising his voice just enough to let me know his patience was wearing a little thin.

"Now if you let an apple stay on the tree without picking it, what happens?"

"Birds git it?" I guessed.

Doc shook his head. "Okay, yes, that's possible, but that's not what I had in mind. What else might happen?"

I thought about it until I spotted our can of bait. "Worms," I said. "Worms will eat it."

Doc just looked out across the river for a considerable long time; he was working pretty hard on his lower lip. Finally he turned to me and said, "Assuming that neither the birds nor the worms get the apple, what else might happen to it if left on the tree?"

I ventured another guess. "It'll . . . rot?"

"Hot damn, Ezra, that's right! It will rot!" He sure seemed relieved. "I knew you'd get it, sooner or later. Okay, it will rot. And why?"

"'Cause—"

"Never mind, I'll tell you; I've given the Socratic Method a fair shake. It will rot because it's *over*—ripe; that is to say, because it passes its prime. It starts out as a bud you see. Then it's small, a little green apple, right?" I nodded. Kids who weren't mature were called green too. "Then as it matures, what happens?"

"It . . . grows."

"Exactly! It grows, big and red and juicy and delicious and finally it's fully mature, but . . . nobody picks it."

"Why not?"

"Why not what?"

"Why don't somebody pick a nice apple like that?"

"Because it's not an apple, Son, it's an analogy."

"That's right," I said. "I forgot."

"Okay, so, we've got this beautiful ripe apple, but nobody picks it—and the birds don't get it, or—or the worms either."

"They don't give a hang about analogies."

"Right," Doc agreed. "So . . . it begins to shrink, to shrivel up, wrinkle, to turn yellow and finally . . . to die. Just like human beings. You see that, Ezra?"

Doc was always doing that, talking about one thing when he meant something entirely different. Sometimes it made me wonder whether he was wise or not. If he meant people I don't know why he kept harping on apples.

"Ezra, do you understand what I'm saying?"

Scratching my head I said, "But apples ain't got any hair, Doc! Can you tell me the same story with peaches; they at least got a little fuzz."

"Dammit, boy," he snapped, "When you get home tell Silas to explain it to you. I obviously have neither the intellectual capacity nor the patience required to take on such an arduous task. Peaches have hair! Lord is Socrates had ever had to deal with the likes of you . . ." He turned away, locking his gaze on the far side of the river, still mumbling to himself. I didn't know what I'd said to upset him. Peaches did got—*have* hair. There I was being ungrammatical again; no wonder he got so upset. I knew he'd cool down in a while; he always did. So I just watched my bobber and got to thinking, and something occurred to me.

Not long before, I'd seen the movie version of *Samson and Delilah*. According to Doc, it was a Cecil B. DeMille epic that was vastly over-produced and under-rehearsed. The beautiful Hedy Lamar played the role of Delilah. She had this dark silken hair that cascaded over her shoulders like a waterfall and ran all the way down her back. Some hunk of a man played opposite her in the other title role, and he actually had a fuller head of hair than Hedy had. That was okay; after all, he was Samson. But what I found to be somewhat troubling was the actor's name: Victor *Mature*!

2

TRAINING THE GORILLA

I still haven't figured out where I went wrong with Roseabeth. If that's what I did, which seems to be the general consensus, so I'll keep this journal going for what I hope will turn out to be our mutual benefit. What you have to understand first off, I suppose, is the catastrophe. And to understand that you have to understand what happened during the early years of my sexual and intellectual maturation; I suppose that's the story I'm trying to tell—that of my "awakening" as Kate Chopin would have put it. Doc introduced to her not long after lumbering me with "Moby Dick." In the Chopin story, soon after the heroine is *awakened*, she wanders off into the Gulf of Mexico and drowns herself, and I can't say that I blame her. Maturing is a grueling task. That's for sure.

As I understand the sexual part of it, given a willing and knowledgeable partner, the entire process should take, at the very most, no more than thirty minutes. As it is, however, I've been maturating now for some four years, since the day I discovered the hair that I already told you about. And I don't think I'm through yet. Nor do I have a clear understanding yet of what happened during those years, and as you know I certainly don't fully comprehend what happened prom night with Roseabeth, the night for which I am about to pay so dearly. In some countries they get the whole thing over with in a single night. I know because I heard Brinton Turkle say so, and Brinton's the smartest kid in my class. Well, he's not on par with me when it comes to metaphysics, but he knows about *life*. Where I'm grammatical, he's clinical, because he's the son of our town's only doctor, and Brinton knows about sexual maturation because he read a book called *Coming of Age in Samoa* by a woman who'd been there and watched them. Well, he probably didn't read the book himself, because kids can't get that kind of book in Mansfield, but he'd heard about it and told me.

Over there, in Samoa, when they think kids are ripe—have enough hair and in all the right places—they take and throw them in a pit with a bunch of kids of the opposite sex that are also ripe. They give them a quick idea of what to do and how to do it; then they throw in some coconut oil, a few palm leaves, some breadfruit and sea shells and leave them there overnight, preferably under a full moon. In the morning when they open up the pit, all the kids crawl out, but they aren't kids anymore. No sir! They're adults, fully maturated, mature, of age, experienced, and highly satisfied to boot. How's that for efficiency? *One* night!

Sounds simple enough, and whether those kids understand *Moby Dick* or not probably doesn't make an awful lot of difference to them. They get the thing over with in short order, and, I'm sure, are glad of it. Not so with us kids here in the territories. We have to figure it out for our own selves, and if we don't do it right, which few of us probably do, it's nobody's fault but our own. As far as I'm concerned, you might just as well lock a kid up in a closet with an algebra book and a gorilla, and tell the kid to learn algebra. He can do it, but *first* he'd better train the gorilla. That's the way sex is I think: you have to train the gorilla. Of course the gorilla might help the kid with his algebra *if* it knows anything about algebra, but I haven't seen a gorilla yet that can solve even the simplest quadratic equation.

That's just the way most adults are about sex. They don't know anything about it. Or, if they do, they aren't about to share any of their knowledge with a kid because that would be corrupting the kid. So, are the adults that do have some basic understanding of sex, like Fanny Boltwood, headed straight for hell like Preacher says? Must be. Look what happened to Fanny. I have to admit that Silas was no great storehouse of knowledge on the subject of sex either.

It wasn't long after my conversation about maturity with Doc that Silas got me real confused, or maybe I got him confused. Anyway, I was still wet behind the ears and just recently a few more places too and more determined than ever to get mature as soon as possible so I could understand—get something out of—*Moby Dick*. As I recollect, my encounter with Silas went something like this.

I was in the backyard weeding the garden and wrestling with Mr. Melville's metaphysical scheme of the universe when I heard the gravel crunching beneath the squeaky wheels of Si's beat-up Chevy pickup. He'd probably been out doing some research for his next novel; Silas would go out and sit on the mountainside waiting for an idea to smack him up against the side of the head and then hurry home and write up a pot-boiler western in about three weeks. It drove Doc crazy, him being a man of letters and all, but Silas made a decent living at it. And I was proud of him because he could sure tell a good story. And the best part was that Silas' characters never used a gun to solve their problems, although they all carried guns. Had to in the Old West because you never knew when a snake might turn up.

Silas, you see, was my stepfather *and* my father *and* my uncle. It was little wonder I was having such a time trying to figure out where I came from. First, he was my uncle, the younger brother of my father. Then, when Silas married Mariko after my father was killed in the war, he became my stepfather. Later, he legally adopted me, and that made him my father. And I was glad of it, most of the time.

I waved as the pickup rolled to a stop, then I turned back to the garden, jerking a clump of milkweed out of the peas. There's nothing worse than milkweed in peas, except for injustice of course. "Hello, Ezra," Silas called, moving up behind me.

"Hi!"

"How's it goin'?"

"'Bout done," I said.

He surveyed the garden, reaching down every now and again to pull a weed I'd missed. "Looks good," he said. "Why don't you pick some of those tomatoes for supper?"

"Already did," I told him. "They're in the house."

"Okra?"

"That too."

"Boy, you're on the ball today, aren't you?"

"If you say so."

"What else your mom fixin'?" I just looked at him and he said, "Rice, huh?"

"Long stem, white, steamed."

"Anything else?"

"Fish," I told him. "I filleted a batch of bluegills I caught out at Taylor's Pond."

"Bluegills? No bass, huh?"

"Nope, bass were sleepin', I guess." I stood up for a minute to stretch my back and neck. "Did you get inspired today?"

"Did I ever!" Silas said, his eyes starting to just sparkle. "Listen to this: There's this buffalo see, a great *white* buffalo and . . ."

"Already sounds familiar," I said.

"No, now wait a minute. You've got to hear the whole story. This pioneer, or scout it was, is out hunting early one bright winter morning when he comes up the side of a mountain, and suddenly there it is, materializing out of nowhere. 'Course the scout hasn't read any Faulkner, so he doesn't know where it comes from. But it's there, jist the same—the great white buffalo of the Kiowa legend. The scout doesn't want to kill it, but he has to. He has to feed the starvin' settlers."

"What starvin' settlers?"

"The ones I forgot to mention."

"Aw, Silas, come on," I protested. He was making this up as he went along; he did it to me all the time and could go on for hours. Part of our Irish heritage I suppose.

"Lemme finish." I rolled my eyes back in my head, and he went on. "The scout has to kill it—has to feed the settlers—but he knows he can't kill it with a gun or a knife. It's a legend so he has to kill it with his *bare* hands; legends, you see, don't die with the help of any mechanical devices. He starts at it, throwin' his Winchester and hunting' knife aside. That buffalo just watches him, stares at him, then when they can see the fire in each other's eyes the buffalo charges, snortin' and rippin' at the frozen prairie turf like some rough beast slouching toward Bethlehem. The pioneer—"

"Scout," you said.

"It don't matter. Now don't interrupt me durin' the climax of a story."

"Sorry, I just want it to be right."

"It's okay. So—the buffalo's chargin', and the *scout* tries to jump aside, but the buffalo gores him in the leg, tearin' it all to pieces, shatterin' the bone, and then disappears off into a white cloud on the horizon."

"Aw, Silas," I said, "I know what's gonna happen. The pioneer—"

"Scout."

"Okay. The scout's gonna lose his leg and hunt for the great white buffalo for the rest of his life from a prairie schooner. It's been done."

"No, sir," Silas said. "The Kiowas find the scout, take him back to the camp of the settlers, and there he dies in the arms of a lady friend he'd met in a saloon in Dallas some years before. "It's going to be kind of a cross, you see, between *Moby Dick* and *The Snows of Kilimanjaro* with a little Faulkner thrown in. Doc's going to love it."

"Doc's gonna *hate* it. He—." I stopped when Silas winked at me.

"No. I didn't come up with a new story idea today. But don't you worry; there are plenty of them out there. What have you been up to?"

"Workin' out," I said. "I ran five miles this mornin', lifted weights, and shot some baskets, went fishin'. Before I started weedin' the garden I was readin'."

"Readin', huh? What?"

"*Moby Dick*," I said.

"Great literature—*Moby*. Doc helpin' you?"

"Not much; says I have to get it for myself." I uprooted some goat heads and turned to Silas. You ever read *Moby Dick*?" I knew Silas knew the story—everybody did, but I didn't know if he'd actually ever read it for himself all the way through.

"Did I ever have what?" he asked, laughing.

I looked at him, puzzled. "Not *have*. *Read*. Did you ever read *Moby Dick*?"

"Oh yeah," he said, "I read it all right. Saw a movie about it too."

"The one with Gregory Peck?" It had just come out and was the rage in Mansfield's literary community, a community that was pretty much limited to Doc, Mariko, Silas and ole *Watakushi*.

"No, I believe this one had his pecker," Silas said and poked me real good in the rib cage. "It was a trainin' film I saw in the army."

I just knelt there, forced a confused smile, and said, "I don't get it."

Silas widened his grin, laughed and said, "I hope you never do." He started laughing all over the place then.

"Did I say somethin' funny?"

"No," Silas choked, mussing my hair, "I did."

"Oh," I said vaguely.

"It's an *inside* joke," he said and just howled. Finally, when he got hold of himself, he said, "You see, Ezra, it has to do with—with a condition that—that . . . how old are you, Son?"

"Thirteen," I told him.

"Yeah, well, thirteen. Huh, you don't happen to know what—VD is, do you?"

"Valentine's Day?" I guessed.

"I didn't think you did," Silas said.

"Victory Day?" I guessed again, thinking that maybe it had something to do with the army.

"No, no, Ezra. It's somethin' else entirely."

"What?"

"Well, in order to understand the joke, you have to understand—a whole lot more, much of which I'm not entirely certain that *I* fully comprehend."

"Well, why don't you tell me what you *do* understand?"

"Because I don't reckon you'd even understand that, Ezra, not until you're more . . . mature."

I sort of fell back with a sigh, staring into the ripening oblivion of the garden; the green tomatoes caught my eye, and I gladly would have traded places with any one of them. This maturity business was beginning to depress me. Not only could I not understand the book, *Moby*, until I was more mature, I couldn't understand Si's joke either. Suddenly, in a fit of frustration I turned on Silas and almost pleaded, "Well, for God's sake Silas tell me *somethin'*!"

"Now just settle yourself down, Ezra. It's not all that easy to explain. It's not, in fact, the kind of thing that you can tell someone about anyhow. It's somethin' you have to git for yourself, and when you do git it, believe me, you'll know it."

"You mean it has somethin' to do with Zen?"

"No, believe me; Zen's got nothin' whatsoever to do with it."

"Well, then where do you git it, and how will I *know* whether I've got it or not?"

Silas thought for a minute, kicking at the sandy topsoil. "Actually, it's more a case of it gittin' you than of you gittin' it. And when it does, you just *know*."

"Then it *is* like Zen!"

"No, it ain't nothin' like Zen," Silas insisted. "It's more like—like fruit ripenin' and apple say—"

"Oh, no!" I protested. "Don't even start on me with the apples. Doc already told me all about them, and I still didn't git it."

Silas rubbed his chin and smiled. "I didn't either," he said, "at the time." Then he knelt down, picked up some dirt and let it run through his hand. When he looked back at me, he asked, "Ezra, do you know what a—a metamorphosis is?"

"A what?"

"I didn't reckon you did." He pushed his hat back, and I could see beads of sweat forming on his brow. "Well, a metamorphosis is a . . . process of change from one thing to another. It's what happens to a caterpillar as it changes into a beautiful butterfly, you see. Now, the exact same thing is happenin' to you at this very moment."

"It is?" I said and gulped. I had been feeling kind of strange, but to tell you the truth, I didn't much cotton to the idea. Butterflies are mighty pretty and all, but I couldn't see much sense in looking like one.

"Now I don't mean to say that *you* are going to change into a butterfly; you didn't think that, did you?"

I was relieved to hear it. "'Course not," I said. "I'm not stupid."

"Okay, so don't misunderstand me. But what's happenin' to you is the very same thing that happens to a butterfly. A change, you see, is takin' place inside your body."

That reminded me of somethin' I'd heard being kicked around the locker room on this very subject. "Is this what you call a—a—change of life?"

"Where'd you hear that?"

"Locker room."

"I thought so. Well, this is *a* change of life, yeah, but it's not *that* change of life. The difference here is that when you finish this—metamorphosis I was tellin' you about, you'll be able to have a baby. And when you finish the other, you won't, if you went through the second, which you don't."

What he'd just told me had me worried; you probably understand that. I didn't want to have a baby, had no intention of having one, whether I was mature or not. I'd seen them. Minabell Parsons down the street had one, and it was a frightful lot of trouble.

"Ezra, again now, don't git confused. You, *personally*, won't be able to have a baby; women have babies—."

"After they've gone through the change of life," I interjected.

"No," Silas said, "before."

"Oh, but you just said—"

"Never mind that! What I'm tryin' to tell you now . . . is that when you're mature, have completed your metamorphosis, you'll be able to make girls—*women* have babies."

"Now why would I want to go and do a thing like that for? I don't want to make anybody do anythin'. And if a girl wants a baby, I figure she can git one her own self. I don't want to git involved in that kinda deal."

"Well, you will," Silas told me.

"I bet I don't," I told him right back.

Silas gazed up into the blue sky, studying the clouds like maybe the answer was up there in the sky somewhere. Then he said, "Ezra, there's somethin' you don't understand."

"You mean somethin' other than *Moby Dick?*"

"Yeah," he said, "a whole lot more than ole *Moby.*"

"Well, you gonna tell me?"

"All right," he said and took a swipe at the sweat trickling down his temple. "I'll try to explain it to you. Let's go sit down over there on the porch; that sun's still powerful hot." We got up and moved into the shade of the porch; it was cooler there and quiet except for the wind chimes Mariko had hung outside the kitchen window. They were just tinkling ever so slightly in the soft evening breeze. Silas sat down beside me on the steps, but kept shifting around like he couldn't get comfortable. "Now, Ezra, what's happening is this . . . no, no . . . what you have to understand is . . . no, no." He thought for a moment then said suddenly, "Remember last spring when that old red cow of Joe Levy's was calving?"

"Is that what she was doin'?"

"That's what you *call* what she was doin'. Calving."

"Yessir, I recall that."

"Well," Silas said, what'd you think of that?"

"It was—kinda disgusting actually. But I was real curious about it."

Silas found a piece of straw on the porch and started chewing on it. "Curious, huh?" I nodded. "How's that?"

"Well," I explained, looking him in the eye, "I was curious 'bout how fast that calf was goin' when he hit."

Silas all at once just exploded with laughter, sending the straw out toward the garden like a rocket. "How—how fast he was goin' when he hit? Great God Almighty, Son! Where'd you ever git a notion like that? How fast he was goin' when he hit!" He was just coming all to pieces. "You mean you thought that calf ran up that—" He looked at me and stopped laughing suddenly, taking a huge gulp of the evening air. "Damn, Ezra, are you serious?"

I shrugged and said, "Yessir. I just acted like I knew what was happenin' 'cause I didn't want to look like an idiot." He nodded and squinted into the fading sun. "How *did* that calf git in there?"

Silas cleared his throat, or tried to, and sort of cocked his head. "Well, sir, now that's a very interestin' story."

"I love a good story."

"I know you do. What'd you think: one fine mornin' Miss Cow wakes up, blinks at the morning sun, and there standin' right next to her is a new calf waitin' for breakfast?"

"I didn't know what to think," I told him.

Silas put his arm around me and said real serious like, "Now, Ezra, surely you must have heard somethin' about— 'bout sex. Don't you boys talk about it in the locker room?"

"Sex?"

"Yeah, sex."

"Sure we do," I admitted, "some. But...what's sex got to do with cows?"

Silas nodded, took off his ball cap and ran his hand through his dark hair, repeating the question. "What cows have got to do with sex, Son, is *how* the calf gits into the mother cow. Okay?"

"Okay."

"Okay." He put his cap back on and gulped real hard. "Now, did you ever notice that cows, that is, *bulls* or *male* cows—cattle, have testicles?"

"*Huh?*"

"Testicles," he said simply. "Bulls have testicles!"

"Where?" I asked. "I never saw them."

He looked at me with a kind of pained expression and said, "They keep them in a bag—the—the ... scrotum."

"In a bag! What good are they in a bag? Can't catch nothin' with them in bag."

"Goddammit, boy, what the hell are you talkin' about? You can't catch anything with testicles anyhow!"

"Course not, if you keep them in a bag. But boy those octopuses can sure catch stuff with them."

"Octopuses? *Octopuses!* Those are *tentacles*, not testicles. I'm talkin' about ... *balls!*"

"Balls!" I yelled. "Well, why didn't you say so? I know bulls got balls."

"The scientific name is testicles—testes."

"You don't have to git technical on me."

"Ezra, testicles isn't gittin' technical. I just assumed you knew that bulls didn't have tentacles."

"I *did* know that. I jist didn't know that's what you call them." We both tried to settle down by taking deep breaths of the evening air. The smell of the earth was strong and rich, and unless I was mistaken, I caught the faint scent of manure, probably being carried over from the feed lot. "So, I guess octopuses got both tentacles *and* testicles," I said as a peace offering.

"Well now I assume that's the case," Silas said, "with male octopuses. But that's totally irrelevant to this conversation because I'm talkin' about bulls, *not* octopuses. Okay?"

"Okay. You don't have to git sore."

"I'm not sore. Okay?"

"Okay."

"Okay. So . . . all male cattle have testicles . . . no, I take that back, jist bulls."

"Aren't all male cows bulls?"

"Well, yeah, to begin with, but in some cases, bulls have their testicles—removed, and that makes them what we call steers."

"I know 'bout that," I said energetically, "some bulls are— are—*circumcised*." I knew that because I'd been, but then that's not quite what they did to me, I don't think.

"No, Ezra, that's somethin' entirely different. Bulls don't need to be circumcised."

"But people do?"

"Some."

"Why jist some? Why not everybody?"

"Because—because of their religious beliefs," Silas explained wearily.

"'Cause of their religious beliefs!" Poo! Why, they did it to me when I was a baby; I didn't even *have* any religious beliefs."

"No, no. They do it because of your parents' religious beliefs. It's a religious rite."

"Well it sounds like a religious wrong to me!" Silas just shook his head. "You mean Buddhists and religious liberals believe in circumcision?"

"No, that's not what I mean!"

"Then why was *I* circumcised?"

"Probably because you were delivered by a Jewish doctor."

"Delivered?"

Silas buried his hands in his face. I knew I'd come from San Francisco, but I didn't know that I'd been *delivered* there. "Jesus, Ezra, how'd we ever git off on this subject?"

"Preacher says that Jesus—*delivered* us from evil, from . . .
the den of iniquity. Do Jewish doctors do that too—deliver
us from evil through the religious rite of circumcision?" Silas
was staring at me; I think I saw a hint of fear in his eyes. And
I was just warming up. "Jesus was Jewish, right? And a doctor
too, cause he went around healin' all the sick people all the
time and deliverin' them from evil. So maybe he did a few
circumcisions on the side, huh? Huh?"

Silas stood up, turned and grabbed me by the shoulders.
"Ezra, I'm tryin' my best to explain to you how the calf got
in the cow, and you're sittin' there tellin' me how Jesus was a
Jewish doctor who was deliverin' people from the den of iniquity and performin' circumcisions two thousand years ago. Is
that what you're tellin' me?"

I shrugged and said, "It's jist a theory."

"Yeah well that's jist what Mr. Einstein said about relativity.
Let's jist forget Jesus for the time bein' and concentrate on
how the calf got into the fatted cow, to put it in terms you'll be
familiar with, okay?"

"Okay, but Preacher said you should never forget 'bout
Jesus."

"We're not gonna forget him completely; we're jist gonna
set him aside temporarily. I don't think Preacher would mind
that."

"No, I reckon not. People do it all the time—whenever he's
not convenient."

"All right then. We were talkin' about bulls—"

"Balls."

"Bulls' balls, right. And we established the fact that you
are aware of the fact that bulls do, in fact, have balls."

"Yessir, we did establish that fact."

"Well, good, because that's where the calf is ... in the bull's testicles—balls."

"Not the calf I saw. Wouldn't fit."

"Hang on there, Ezra. I'm not through. The whole thing isn't in there, you see?"

"No?"

"No."

"How much is?" I asked. I thought it was a reasonable question.

"Half," Silas said.

"*Half?*"

"It's not exactly a whole half, you see. Most of the other half is in the mother cow."

"Other half?!"

"That is to say that the *egg* is in the mother cow."

"*Egg?* I ain't stupid, Silas! Cows ain't got eggs. Birds got eggs, and—and—alligators, and chickens, but not *cows*! I want the truth!"

I leaped off the porch, startled when Si's cap plopped down on the board beside me with a bang. When I looked up, he was already halfway in the house, grumbling to himself and sticking pretty much to the vernacular from what I could make out. "Dammit boy, I never ..."

"Hey, Silas, wait a minute. It's okay if cows got eggs. I believe you; I've jist never seen one. Where do they lay'em?" Silas. Silas! Who's gonna tell me this stuff? How will I ever git mature unless someone tells me how to do it?"

"Git a book," he yelled from the kitchen. Then the back door flew open; Silas stormed out in about the biggest sweat I'd ever seen, grabbed his ball cap off the porch and disappeared back through the door before it even had a chance to close. Then from inside I heard him yell, "Don't ask me about it again, okay? Okay!"

"Okay," I yelled, "I'll look it up." And that's just what I did as soon as I got nerve enough to go to my room. Here's what Mr. Webster had to say on the subject:

> maturation   a: the process of becoming mature. b: the final stages of differentiation of cells, tissues, or organs. c: the entire process by which diploid gonoclytes are transformed into haploid gametes that includes both meiosis and physiological and structural changes fitting the gamete for its future role.
>
> mature   a: having undergone maturation.

After reading that I nearly gave up on the idea of getting mature; I figured that Mr. Webster had probably had as much trouble with it as I was having. At least I knew that hair had something to do with it.

3

A LITTLE LEARNING

My first few awkward attempts to make some sense out of sex, as you have seen, were not altogether successful. You probably understand that. What you probably don't understand is how things could have gotten any worse. Well, I don't understand it either, but they did, a whole lot worse. The catastrophe on Huckleberry Hill was, without a doubt, the worst thing that happened, but both the incident and the disaster seemed as bad at the time when each of them occurred.

Had Doc introduced me to Mr. Alexander Pope a little sooner, maybe the incident could have been averted. Or if Silas or Doc would have finished what they'd started to tell me about maturity. Or if Mr. Webster had provided a little more meaningful explanation of maturity. If *any* of that would have "come to pass," as Preacher would put it, the incident might not have happened at all. What happened, though, is that when Doc *did* tell me about Mr. Pope, it was too late.

Mr. Pope, Alexander was his given name, you see, wrote in *An Essay on Criticism* that, "A little learning is a dang'rous thing." Well, there you are. And I have absolutely no reason whatsoever to doubt the wisdom of those words. Because it was just that—a little learning—that nearly ruined me before I'd had a chance to ruin myself. The incident, you see, came about as a consequence of my knowing what something looked like, but not knowing exactly what that something was used for.

I tried to get it—learning, knowledge—but, like I said, nobody that knew anything about sex was willing to give it to a kid straight. Kids, on the other hand, as soon as they found out *anything*, or thought they did, told everybody, but nobody ever got anything completely accurate. And if there's anything worse than not knowing anything, it's being mistaken about what you think you know. With my little bit of learning I was an absolute terror at first primarily to myself, and finally to Roseabeth. At least everyone seemed to think that what we did was terrible. I wasn't so sure myself.

For the time being though, I'm safe from myself. Nor am I in a position to unleash my pent up river of desire on any of the local belles, not from this height anyway. I will have to, eventually, if I'm to carry on the family name; I do have that much pretty well set in my own mind now. And I'm the only one left to keep the Casey line in operation. It would be awful to see the line end with the likes of me, because while all that good that Doc did will most likely remain interred with his bones, just like Mr. Shakespeare said, the evil that I accomplish will probably live on for a considerable long time. My predecessors had a very unique background, and I'd sure hate to see the line end with me.

I told you my name already—Ezra Nori-Thorpe Casey; Ezra from my father and the Old Testament prophet; Nori from Mariko's dad; Thorpe from the family of Doc's wife, my grandmother, and Casey from Doc himself. That makes me part Japanese, Native American, and the rest Scotch-Irish. According to Doc, his antecedents were *all* Irish, but after making the Atlantic crossing on a ship called the Cutty Sark, they were Scotch-Irish when they got to the new world and all settled in colonial Newport, RI.

Doc also claimed to be a direct descendent of Huckleberry Finn; I'm not kidding, that's what he said, and his people did move on to Missouri in the first quarter of the nineteenth century and subsequently on to the Territories. But I know Doc couldn't have been descended from Huck; that was pure fabrication on his part, but a sure sign that he was derived from a prodigious line of Irish story tellers, a line of which I am the end, so far.

From this you can see that I have the best of three cultures running in my veins. With all that good blood in my background it's hard to understand just where I went wrong. One explanation is that the good people of Mansfield have such great expectations for kids that you can't help but wander astray every now and again. Okay, maybe I do more than my share of wandering, but such is my nature. Maybe I am descended from Huck after all.

Still, I earnestly tried to do good because "the Good," Doc taught me, is at the very core of the universe, at the core of human existence even. That's what Plato said, and Doc was crazy about Plato. Doc explained to me too that the idea of the Judeo-Christian God came from Plato's original conception of "the Good." I suggested to him one time that maybe God then was just the result of a typographical error, but Doc got all flustered and said there was more to it than that. Besides, moveable type hadn't even been invented in Plato's time. Doc just left it at that, kinda hanging. I suppose he figured that I wouldn't get it if he explained it in any more detail. It was like the maturity business: I had to get it for myself.

But the damage was done. Doc and my more "knowledge-able" cronies had sown the deadly seeds of a little learning, and I watched those seeds blossom into a number of illogical conclusions. One being that the incident was Plato's fault. Or God's. Or even Mariko's. Yeah, Mariko, that's whose fault it was. Or at least if it wasn't for Mariko it never would have happened. But then Silas was the one that put me up to it. He wanted them, but he didn't want them for himself. So what happened was that I got blamed for it by Rufus Ruffin, the local constable, while Silas got off scot-free—he and Plato.

It all came about from my doing a good deed; I told you I tried to do good. For Silas. But good deeds, I've found have a way of coming back to haunt you. Seems like every time I try to do something decent, I get it right back in the face. Or the rear end. Made me wonder about the value of doing good. Remember Jesus? Did nothing but good all his life, so the story goes, although there is a gap there of some twenty-odd years when we don't know exactly what he was up to, and I think it's highly significant that that period includes the time when he would have been . . . maturing. But, assuming he *did* do nothing but good, what good did it do him? Why they stretched him out on a couple of two-by-fours and hammered railroad spikes through his hands and feet. Now is that any way to treat another human being, good or bad? I wonder what they'd have done if he'd been evil; if he'd done what I did. Jesus! Well, I don't suppose that they had them then. Or drug stores either for that matter. Which are two reasons why things are so much tougher on kids these days. Jesus probably never had to face the issue; of course, he didn't have an Uncle Silas either, that I know of. Silas! Right! *That's* whose fault it was. Or was it?

The plain fact is, I don't know whose fault the incident was. I'll let you judge for yourself once you've heard the story. I don't know whose fault it was, but I do know this: The incident was the third most embarrassing thing that ever happened to me. And I aim to show you why.

"Ezra," Silas called, "come in here would you?"

I was in my room reading a book Doc had given me. From the title I thought it was going to be Mr. Hemingway's autobiography. But as it turned out, *The Importance of Being Earnest* by Mr. Oscar Wilde didn't have anything at all to do with Papa Hemingway. What it did have to do with was a kid that was found, now get this, in a *bag* at a railway station. I closed the book and said, "Comin'." Then I slipped on a T-shirt and started for the kitchen, but none too fast. Mariko was feeling poorly so I was careful not to make any racket. Silas was sitting at his typewriter at the kitchen table, sipping a glass of iced tea and cranking out another potboiler western. He looked up and smiled.

"What are you up to, Ezra?"

"Readin'," I allowed.

"One of these day you're gonna quit readin' 'bout life and start livin' it," Silas said. "What do you do for fun?"

"Play ball, run, ride my bike, go fishin' with Doc. And I think readin's fun."

"Well, I guess there's worse things than that. As long as you're readin' good books."

"Doc gives them to me," I said and watched as he pushed himself away from the table. "What'd you want?"

"Oh, I've got a little somethin' I want you to do for me." He got up, crossed to the sink and dumped what remained of his tea. He seemed—a little jumpy, I guess you'd call it. He'd been that way ever since our discussion about maturity some weeks before. "I'd do it myself, but I've got these dishes here to wash up."

"I'll wash them!" I don't know what made me say it; some deep foreboding about the little task Silas had planned for me.

"Oh no, I will!" he insisted. He seemed a little over anxious himself. Ordinarily neither of us would knock ourselves out to do the dishes. He looked out the window over the sink for a second then started running the hot water and squirted some green liquid soap into the dishpan. "Ezra," he said absently, still looking out.

"Yessir."

"How old are you now?"

"Fourteen—almost, according to Mariko."

"Fourteen."

"Almost."

"Right—almost." Silas turned from the window and nodded. "That's old enough, I reckon."

"For what?"

"I'm gonna be frank, Son; no beatin' 'round the bush this time. Do you—do you know what a—what a sanitary napkin is?"

I didn't—*know*, but I did have a notion. I decided to fake it until I was sure. Of what, I didn't know. "Is—is that one that's *extra* clean?" I asked and squinted up my eyes so I'd look real confused. Silas started shaking his head. "Like—like it's been washed in *Holy* water or somethin'," I added for good measure.

"No, no, Son. That's not it." He thought for a moment and kind of screwed up his face. Then he said: "How 'bout . . . tampons? You know what they are?"

The fact is: I knew what they looked like, I think, but I couldn't honestly say that I was dead certain of what they were or what they were for. But I was pretty sure where they went because Brinton Turkle told me so. I shuffled around a little uncomfortably and said, "Don't you?"

"I asked you first," Silas said nervously. By now we were both in a pretty good sweat.

"I know what they look," I told him.

"How's that?"

"Well, they're 'bout yea long," I explained and held up my hands to illustrate my point, "and they—"

"Hold on there, Ezra! *I* know what they look like. How do you know?

"Oh." I scratched my head and stuffed my hands way down deep in the pockets of my Levis. "One year before Christmas, I must of been 'round eight, maybe nine, no, eight—."

"It doesn't matter."

"I guess not. Anyway, it was *nine*, I was jist snoopin' 'round, seein' if I could find out what Santa was goin' to produce that year . . . I wouldn't do that kinda thing now."

"I know you wouldn't. So . . . ?"

"Well, way up high on this shelf where I couldn't reach it, I saw this box with what looked like a—a little—*telescope* on it. So I figured I was gonna git a telescope for Christmas." I shrugged and then added, "Never did git it—the telescope."

Silas started chuckling, then laughing pretty hard. He was real keen on finding the humor in even the worst of situations, which this wasn't by a long shot. "Well, when did you— find out that . . ."

"Brinton told me, but that was jist recently. For the longest time I thought you'd given my telescope to somebody else."

"Telescope!" I just let him laugh; there was nothing else I could do, and there was really no harm in it. When he finally stopped he looked at me real serious like and said, "Ezra, you do this one little thing for me and I'll get you a telescope."

"Don't want one now," I said. "Got no use for it." Silas himself always told me never to bet another man's trick, and that's pretty much what this amounted to.

Rubbing the stubble on his chin with the back of his hand he glanced at me. "Well, you're gonna have to do this whether you want the telescope or not. So you might just as well accept my generosity."

I couldn't see that I had a real clear option, being that he'd cared for me for such a long time, almost ever since I'd been delivered. "What do I havta do?"

"Don't put it like that, Son. You make me feel like a parent or somethin'."

"What can I do for you, Pop?" I asked, forcing a thin smile which he returned in kind.

He took out a couple of dollars from his front pocket and pressed them into my palm. "Run down to Yeager's and git me some."

I faltered some but finally managed to say, "Some what?"

"You know what," he said.

"Tampons?" He nodded. "Silas, I ain't *hardly* goin' down to Yeager's to buy you any tampons!"

48

"Yes you are."

"Oh, Silas!" I moaned, but my protest fell on deaf ears. I couldn't believe it. All of a sudden I felt kind of itchy all over and unsettled. I stretched my neck all around and tried to swallow, but there was nothing there to swallow. I naturally had never anticipated being put in just this position; if I had I might very well have come up with a decent defense. Could have pleaded ignorance. Or innocence. Or insanity. *Anything!* But my mind just wouldn't work; it often seemed to desert me when I needed it most. Shock, I guess it was. All I could manage to say was: "A box of tampons, huh?"

Silas turned back to the dishes and nodded, "One box."

"What—what color?" I'd have said anything to delay it; I didn't even know if they came in colors or not. If they did, I'd of preferred a pastel blue.

"I don't see where color would make a whole lot of difference, Ezra. But I reckon white will do about as well as any," Silas told me.

"Okay," I said, defeated, "one box of white tampons." I left the house just sort of nodding and trying to remember the Twenty-third Psalm. I couldn't get past the "Yea though I walk through the valley of death" part though. What could I say? Or do?

There was nothing wrong with tampons, as far as I knew, other than the fact that they were tampons, and you couldn't blame them for that. All I know is that I'd never known anybody else that ever had to buy some—men, I mean. And I don't mean to imply by that that I was a man; I wasn't, yet. But that metamorphosis or menopause or whatever the heck it was, was still going on. So I was in the process of becoming a man, and I'd never heard of a man, or a boy in the process of becoming one, that had ever had to buy a box of tampons for his uncle. Or anybody else!

I ruminated on my dilemma while kicking an empty Falstaff can in the general direction of Main Street where the stores in Mansfield, about 20 of them in all, were clustered on the four corners around our only stop light. I asked myself what Plato would have done in this situation, a smart man like that. I figured probably that he would have reasoned or deduced his way out of it, but I couldn't do that because I'd run plum out of people to reason with. Or with whom to reason, as Doc would have put it. I was on my own. I thought for a while longer and finally made what I considered to be a rational decision: If by some stroke of luck a freight train should come rumbling through town before I got to Yeager's drug store, I'd get on it and ride until I either fell or got thrown off. If not, I'd accept this chore as a Divine Providence and get the tampons, because God, in His infinite wisdom, had willed it. To what end, I didn't have even the slightest notion; that I'd leave in His hands, because if He was sculptor of the universe He probably couldn't mess me up too badly. I mean, one kid with a box of white tampons could hardly pose a threat to society, unless maybe you could somehow play them and sing some rock'n'roll. Preacher was real sensitive about that.

Thinking all that I meandered on towards Main, knowing that every time I kicked that can I was drawn a little closer to that old devil fate, just like I was being pulled along by one of those huge magnets that have electricity and can pick up cars and buses. I knew I was getting closer because there was no sign anywhere of a train. Rather that the low comforting rumble of a heavy diesel engine, I heard only the empty clanging of a tin can along a deserted street, a might lonely sound it was too.

Even though it was getting on towards evening it seemed to be getting warmer. Every so often somebody would drive past, a teacher or somebody's folks. We'd wave at each other; then I'd try to keep the dust from settling on me by running a ways, keeping the can in front of me like I was herding a calf. You couldn't help but know everybody in a town like Mansfield and everything that everyone did. That last part is what had me worried. *Everyone* was going to know that I was down at Yeager's buying tampons. How could I ever face my cronies with a thing like that in my background? I couldn't! Even though chances were pretty good that they didn't know exactly what they were either, except for Brinton. Even so, I decided I couldn't do it; I could never live it down.

Now I still had to get them, but I wasn't going to buy them, not directly anyhow. I wasn't sure just how I'd work it yet, but I felt my mind grinding away, could feel the gears sort of clanging around up there. My mind didn't work all that often, so when it did, I was well aware of it. And it always made me feel kind of powerful, like I could somehow control my own destiny or something, never mind the immediate evidence to the contrary.

To my relief I found Main Street pretty much empty, which was the normal state of things, except for Saturday night and when the high school was playing ball of one variety or another. So much the better for carrying out a Divine Providence. In front of Yeager's I gave the Falstaff can a final kick in the general direction of the town's single litter barrel, it faded off to the left and landed about a yard short. I retrieved it and flipped it behind my back into the barrel dead center.

Amy Steinmeyer, old Oscar Steinmeyer's youngest, a real brat of an eight-year-old, was sitting at the fountain, sipping on what looked like a cherry-limeade. Mrs. Yeager, a big-boned woman of about thirty or forty, maybe fifty, was keeping pretty close tabs on Amy. And for good reason. Amy was what you called "accident prone." Which would be okay, except her accidents usually involved some poor unsuspecting bystander as well as Amy her own self. Personally, I was real happy to see her there because I figured she'd keep Mrs. Yeager pretty much occupied while I was carrying out God's will.

Over by the stationery I saw Hilda Fartok, Rufus Ruffin's widowed sister, and the organist at the Baptist Church and secretary at the high school. She could be trouble because she was forever involving herself, on the Lord's behalf, in other people's business. But since I was already doing the Lord's business, I hoped she'd leave well enough alone. "Hi, Ezra," Hilda called. "Lookey who's here Amy, Freda." So much for that theory.

"Hello, Ezra," Mrs. Yeager said, "how's your mom?"

"Why has your mom not been well, Ezra?" Hilda asked.

"She looked jist fine yesterday; 'course, with her colorin', sometimes it's hard to tell."

"It's when she's *white* that she don't feel so good. Right now she's fine; jist a little headache or somethin'."

"Well, that's good. Lord knows there's enough sufferin' in this world."

"Yes ma'am, if anyone knows, I reckon He's the one." She seemed satisfied and turned back to her own business. When Mrs. Yeager went back to tending Amy I moved past them, letting on that I was headed for the rear of the store where Mr. Yeager kept all the back issues of *Sports Illustrated* in a box so us kids could keep up on how the Yankees was doing. Mickey Mantle, hailing from Commerce, was our native son, and next to Ishmael, my idol. I liked Mantle because he could whack the cover right off a high fast ball and Ishmael because he was the only one clever enough to get out of *Moby Dick* alive, besides Moby. At least Ishmael was alive when the book ended, which is better than most of us do.

The back issues of the magazine were a pretty good deal, free, and we didn't mess up all the new issues that way. Naturally, we were always a few weeks behind what was really happening in the world, but for Mansfield, a couple of weeks wasn't too bad.

"Aren't you gonna speak to me, Ezra?" Amy called in the sing-song voice of one of God's own angels. But I knew better.

"Hi, Amy," I said, tight-lipped. I wasn't what you call long-winded, even under ideal circumstances, which these weren't. You probably understand that.

Now the aisle off to my left was a no-man's land. Only around Christmas did you ever see any men over there, buying some toilet water or dusting power for their wives or sisters or girlfriends or maybe their Aunt Gertrude; I don't know! Towards the end of the aisle was an area labeled, "Feminine Hygiene." That's all it said, but that was enough for me. It might just as well have said "Posted—Keep out." And I would have gladly. I'd never been in that area, didn't know of anybody who had—men I mean—which isn't to imply that I . . .

Anyway, I'd have just as soon entered a mine field as to place a solitary foot in that other area, but that's what happened; faster than you could say "Helena Rubenstein," there I was, fulfilling what I was now certain was a Divine Providence. God, Plato, and my Uncle Silas all ganged up on thirteen-year-old; hardly seemed fair. I gulped about as hard as I ever had, and my eyes opened up real wide all by themselves. You should have seen the stuff they were hiding under the guise of feminine hygiene.

Both sides of the aisle were loaded with stuff that I doubted if even God knew about. Could have been why He sent me. There were a few things I'd heard of, but most of it I hadn't and was glad of it. I just stared at it, taking deep breaths and catching the scent of dusting powder and a few scents that I couldn't place, exactly. I found all those feminine smells together like that *real* bothersome.

"Could I help you find something, Ezra?" It was Mrs. Yeager.

Good God! Crept up on me like a cat. "What—ah—ah, no ma'am. No! I—I'm jist lookin'." That response didn't settle too well with her, I could tell right off. She was a nice lady, a little on the hysterical side maybe, but otherwise, okay. Even so, I didn't figure she'd understand my mission. I mean, I couldn't hardly tell her that Plato had sent me. Or God. Her smile, a little forced to begin with, I'd say, was beginning to fade when I said, "I—I'm lookin' for a gift, I mean. For Silas. For Christmas." Did you ever notice how lies seem to feed on themselves? Even the smallest white ones can take on a life of their own by the second telling and evolve into a monster. Anyway, Mrs. Yeager was none to satisfied with my explanation.

"Oh," she said, "a gift for Silas. I see." She tried to smile but failed pretty miserably. Then she just walked away shaking her head.

I did it impulsively. When her back was turned I grabbed a box of tampons and stuffed it under my shirt; it didn't set too well, needless to say. I threw the two bucks on the shelf in the general vicinity of the tampons and started sauntering out kind of sideways-like with my back to the fountain. I knew I'd never make it out, but then I thought I just might, this being a mission from God and all. If only Amy would keep Mrs. Yeager and the Hilda occupied for another six steps or so.

"Ezra, why you walkin' like that?" It was Amy all right. Cute kid.

"Like—like what?" I asked and flashed her my best smile.

"Like this," she said, climbing down off the stool with her cherry-limeade and doing a pretty fair imitation. I noticed, too, that Amy had managed to spark the interest of Mrs. Yeager and Hilda. Bless her heart.

"Want an ice cream, Amy? I'll buy." Brats are invariably fond of junk food.

"Jist had one."

"That's a cheery-limeade, ain't it?"

"Yeah, I already finished the ice cream." What'd I tell you? She started towards me, tripped and fell in my direction preceded by the remains of her cherry-limeade. The drink drenched my shirt and a few cubes of ice slipped down the back of my pants even as I turned to catch poor little Amy. She didn't even thank me; she just pointed to the bulge in my shirt and said, "What's that?"

She meant the tampons. My mind had quit on me again; couldn't even think of a decent lie to tell her, not that I made a habit of lying. But I knew that Amy told so many herself she'd be hurt if I didn't at least try one out on her. But before I could conjure up something very creative I noticed some right heavy footfalls, falling in my direction. Mrs. Yeager! And right behind her I heard Hilda's unmistakable pitter-patter.

"Ezra, what *is* that under your shirt?" Mrs. Yeager inquired.

I noticed an element of concern in her voice and hoped she'd recognize the same in mine when I answered, oddly enough, with truth, because, like I said, I couldn't think of a decent lie. And I doubt that even old Huck his own self could have lied his way out of this one. "Tampons," I told her. "One box of white tampons."

"What's tampons?" Amy inquired curiously as Hilda kind of started to wheeze some.

"Amy! You leave this place immediately," Mrs. Yeager snapped. And Amy was gone. "And as for you, Ezra Casey, I will not stand here and be ridiculed and humiliated by a—a— common thief! Now what do you have under your shirt? I want the truth."

The truth was actually pretty far down on the list of things that she really wanted. I discovered at that moment that, for the most part, people would just as soon not hear the truth, especially if it was a little on the unpleasant side, which this was. A lie you can handle is really a lot easier to live with than the truth when it isn't what you wanted to hear. "Mrs. Yeager," I said with as much sincerity as I could possibly muster, which was considerable. "I—I'm not tryin' to—to—what'd you say?"

"Ridicule and humiliate!"

"No, ma'am. Neither," I told her.

"Then why in heaven's name did you stand there and tell me a boldfaced lie about what you're stealing?"

"That's no lie; I am stealin' tampons!" I lifted my shirt and the box tumbled out and hit the floor about the same time Hilda did. "But I'm not stealin' them."

"Oh! Oh, my God! Harry! Harry! Call Rufus quick. Ezra Casey's done the . . . most *awful* thing! I remembered the spring before when Mrs. Schroder, the English teacher, was trying to teach us about exclamatory sentences. I knew what she was talking about now.

It didn't take Rufus long to arrive.

"Goddammit, Boy!" Rufus yelled, "You outta be taken out in the town square and horsewhupped. Of all the lowdown, vile, perverted, disrespectful, mean, ungainly—

"Ungainly?" I said.

"Don't interrupt me, boy," the constable demanded and went on, "ungainly, unlawful, foolish, stupid, deviated things to do." I was impressed; pretty near three complete sentences and Rufus Ruffin, the town law and undertaker, had only cursed once. Some kind of record. "Hell, I'd call that good-for-nothin' father or whatever he is of yours if I thought it'd do any good. But shit-fire, he wouldn't give a rat's ass about it." That wasn't true, but, under the circumstances, I don't think Silas would have done me much good. "So what I done was to call your grandfather. He's a good man and will know jist what to do with the likes of your young ass." Rufus looked at me real disgusted-like, and then launched a wad of tobacco toward the spittoon in the corner. It splattered against the wall behind the spittoon and began to ooze down the wall, pulled by the forces of gravity. Some flies found it in short order and began their feast. Now you can say what you want about tampons, but that was what I considered disgusting. "If your granddaddy can't straighten you out, Boy, I sure as hell don't know who can."

"Plato," I suggested, "he's the one that got me into this mess."

"A *dog*!" Rufus said, and I dropped the subject.

I glanced at the mess over the spittoon. "You jist gonna leave that?"

"The flies 'ill git it."

"That's filthy."

"Don't talk to me 'bout filthy, boy. I'll take and rub your face . . ." He changed his tune when the door swung open behind him. "Why, hello there, Doc. Sorry I had to call you down here, but here he is; caught him red-handed stealin' down to Yeager's. No shit!"

"I appreciate your concern, Rufus. But could I just talk with Ezra alone. I think we can get to the bottom of this."

"Damn straight. I intend to leave right now, but if he gives you any trouble don't hesitate to lock him up," Rufus told Doc.

"I don't anticipate Ezra giving me any trouble, Rufus."

"You can't never tell 'bout kids these days, Doc. Not even your own kin; they get ta listinin' to that rock'n'roll trash and sometimes they jist go plum loco. Take my word or it. Or you can ask Preacher 'bout it. He knows what's what."

"I'll do that," Doc said patiently. "Now if you could just let me have some time with Ezra."

"Okay. Key to the cell's in my desk," Rufus said and then sent a flying wad of tobacco across Doc's path before he walked away.

Doc just smiled and nodded until Rufus was gone. He turned his attention to me then and gave me his, "I want the whole truth and nothing but the truth so help you God," look. But I knew he just thought that's what he wanted. He didn't *really* want it any more than Mrs. Yeager did. "Don't understand why anybody chews that nasty stuff," Doc said.

I nodded in full agreement. Doc was as kind a man as you'd ever hope to see; his heart was big enough to share with all humanity, but, he didn't, according to Silas, know *anything* about women. Silas told me once that he'd forgotten more about women than Doc had ever known, and that he (Silas) didn't know anything about them and never had. I found that to be a curious kind of remark, but I didn't doubt it because Doc had certainly become an isolationist in the matrimonial sense since he'd lost his wife many years before. He was still mighty high on marriage as an institution, for his fellow brethren of course, but when it came to marriage counseling and female problems he wasn't of much practical value as far as I could tell. Plato didn't deal much in those areas either. That's why I was skeptical about Doc understanding the immediate problem. He smiled at me again.

"Hi, Doc," I said.

"Hello, Ezra. Hot out, huh?"

"Yep." Like I said, I wasn't in the habit of dragging out a conversation.

He walked over to me and laid a hand on my shoulder. "You want to talk about it, Son?"

"The heat?"

"That's not what I had in mind, Ezra." He cleared his throat and said, "I was referring to the . . . incident."

So that's what it was—an incident. The "tampons incident." Certainly one I'd never forget; sort of like the Gunfight at OK Corral, without the guns. "At the drug store, you mean?"

He looked worried. "You mean there's *another* one?"

"Oh, no," I told him. "That's the one."

"Well," Doc said, relieved, "that's good."

"Yessir," I agreed, "terrific." You have to look on the bright side of things.

"Mrs. Yeager," he said patiently, "was of the opinion that something terrible happened, but she wouldn't or couldn't tell me just what it was. And when I asked Hilda about it, she passed out, evidently for the second time. I was able, however, to gain enough information to surmise that you took some-thing…without paying for it." He squeezed my shoulder gen-tly. "Is that so, Son?"

"No! I just didn't pay *her* for it."

"Now she is the one you're supposed to pay, Ezra. She owns the store."

"I mean, I didn't pay her *directly*. I threw the money on the—shelf on my way out."

Doc let out a long sigh. He looked relieved. "What shelf?"

"The one right there where I got the—" The word just hung in my throat; I couldn't say it, not to Doc. He wouldn't understand.

"Where you got the what?" Doc asked.

"The stuff," I said.

"What stuff?"

"The stuff that I took."

"Which was?"

"What?"

"Which was what? That's what I want to know," Doc insisted.

I still didn't know exactly how—to phrase it. I didn't want to tell Doc at all even though I knew I'd have to even-tually. I figured that if I waited long enough, even if it took years, maybe that sort of thing might become more socially acceptable—*buying* tampons, not stealing them. I looked Doc straight in the eye and said, "Doc, I don't think you'd understand."

He stared at the floor a minute, then he looked up and scratched the back of his head. "Ezra, did you ask yourself what Jesus would have done in this situation?"

"No sir, I only got as far as Plato, and I figure he'd of deduced his way out of it. As for Jesus, I reckon he'd of parted the Red Sea or somethin' to git out of it."

"Jesus was no coward, Ezra."

"He was no fool either; he wouldn't of—"

"Wouldn't *have*," Doc said, correcting my grammatical mistake.

"You bet he wouldn't have," I agreed.

"Wouldn't have what?" I still couldn't say it. Doc watched me for a moment; then he shook his head, smiled and I think even chuckled a little. "Ezra," he said, "this may surprise you, but I know what—what . . . prophylactics are."

Well, I was real happy that one of us did; few things I hated worse than a conversation when *neither* party knows what they're talking about. Too much of that kind of thing going on in the world. "You do?" I said tentatively.

Doc seemed to relax some and went on boldly where no man had dared to go before: "Of course, and I might add that I know what they're for. I think every boy at some point has to buy, beg, borrow, or perhaps even steal, if it comes to that, his first box of prophylactics."

Funny, I'd never heard tampons call "prophylactics" before, but then there was a lot more of the jargon I'd never heard either. "They do?" I said, and tried to imagine *why* every boy would want a box of tampons.

"Now I must admit it seems a bit early in your case, but, in view of the interest you've developed recently in becoming a man, I suppose I shouldn't really be all that surprised. Now, Ezra, if you remember, there was a time in my life when I needed them."

I just looked at him and said, "There was?"

"Why, *yes*, Son, you must know that."

"Oh, yeah," I said, "you mean when you were married. Your wife, she used them."

"My wife? No, Ezra, *I* used them."

"Well, what the devil for?" I'll admit it; he had me buffaloed. I had no idea that men needed them too, and I can tell you I was none too high on the idea of using them myself. Doc seemed to be somewhat confused, but he went on tolerantly. He was a very patient man, and it was a good thing.

"Now, Ezra, I though Silas had—had . . . talked to you about—*things*."

"He did talk to me 'bout *some* things—'bout butterflies and bulls and balls—but he never finished. And he never mentioned—what'd you call them?"

"Prophylactics."

"Yeah, he never mentioned *them*."

Well—well . . . didn't he tell you where you came from?"

"He sure did—San Francisco. But I already knew that."

Doc shook his head began to gnaw on his lower lip. "What I mean is: did he tell you how you got here?"

I jist stared at him. "Mariko brought me on a train, Doc. You met us at the station in Chickasha; don't you remember?"

"Of course I remember that, Ezra. But what I want to know is: didn't Silas tell you how you got to San Francisco?"

"Yessir. I was delivered there by a Jewish doctor."

Doc squinted at me real hard and cocked his head some. "Ezra, do you know—know where—where *cows* come from?"

"Well, 'course I know *that*, Doc. I'm not stupid. I even saw one that was—calvin' once—Joe Levy's old red cow."

"Good. That's *good!*" Doc said enthusiastically. "Because people come from the same *place* as cows."

Well, my jaw just about dropped over the face of the earth on hearing that; it was the most ridiculous thing I'd ever heard. Milk, of course, came from cows, and eggs, according to Silas, but people? I couldn't believe it. Doc had to be pulling my leg, but he looked so serious. All I could say was: "Well—how do they git in there?"

"Ezra! *People* don't come from cows!"

"But you jist said—"

"No. *No!* *People* come from people, but from the same *place* as cows! What in tarnation he was driving at I didn't know. People? Cows? I was real happy I'd come from San Francisco; seemed a whole lot simpler. "I'm afraid, Ezra, that you've missed the point entirely."

"Of what?"

"Of—of—the origin of the species!" He was kind of losing control now. "You see, Ezra, when you don't want to have a calf—a *child*, a baby, you see, you use a prophylactic."

I blinked and tried to get it straight in my own mind, but something was very wrong here. "What I want to know is: where do you put it?"

He took a deep breath, but that didn't keep his left eye from twitching. "You put it on . . . your *member.*"

"My member!" I stared hard at him and glanced down. "Do you mean ...?"

He began nodding and said, "Your ever-present congregation of one."

"Ohhhh," I said, then it dawned on me that he was talking about what I called "rubbers," things that seniors got at filling stations to prevent the spread of disease, not babies. "Rubbers, Doc. You're talkin' 'bout *rubbers*."

"Of course I'm talking about rubbers. What the devil are *you* talking about?" he almost yelled and grabbed my shoulders with both hands.

"*Tampons*," I told him. "That's what I took from Yeager's."

He watched me closely, and his expression changed to one of . . . I don't rightly know what to call it. Then he jerked his hands away from me like I was a hot oven and stumbled backwards a few steps. For the second time in an hour I saw what a powerful brew the truth was. "Wha—tam—what?"

"Pons," I told him again. "Tampons."

"Not—not the little *telescope* things?"

"Yessir," I said, "the same."

Doc started pacing back and forth, shaking his head. "Ezra! My god, son, what—what were you going to do with them?"

"They weren't for *me*!"

"No? Not you?"

"No sir."

"Good. That's *good*!"

"They were for Silas."

Funny how you could bring a man down with just a few simple words. "For Silas? My god, where did I go wrong?"

"To give to Mariko."

"Oh, oh, a gift for Mariko. I see," Doc said.

"Not a *gift*. She jist needs them 'cause she's got a . . . headache or somethin'."

"A headache?"

"Or somethin'." I don't think he was much clearer on what was going on than I was.

"Now let me get this straight: you took the—the—"

"Tampons."

"Exactly. For Silas to give to Mariko because she has . . . a headache? Or something?" I nodded. "And you took them from Yeager's, but you didn't *steal* them because you left the money on the shelf because . . ."

"I didn't have the guts to buy them from Mrs. Yeager. Hilda Fartok was right there along with Amy Steinmeyer. It would of been all over town in about three seconds," I explained in my defense.

"Yeah, well. I understand that perfectly," Doc allowed, "and I probably would have done the same thing myself." He thought for a moment then let out a deep sigh, relaxing somewhat. "I'll go down to Yeager's and explain the situation. I'm sure Mrs. Yeager will understand."

"Maybe you should pick up some aspirin too?"

"What for?"

"Mariko's headache."

"Yeah, good idea. You can run on home now; I'll be along directly."

"Great, Doc, thanks," I said and bolted for the door.

"What's your hurry?"

"Gotta git home," I said, "to kill Silas." Then I was running down the streets of Mansfield like Mickey Mantle rounding the bases after hitting one out of the park. I was almost home when I remembered that I'd forget the tampons.

4

BULLSHITO: THE CODE

Where I'm locked up is in a room just beneath the towering steeple of the Free Will Baptist Church. Old Ernest would love it: a clean well-lighted room it is, with a view. I'm not all that high on it though, to tell you the truth. From such a high vantage point I could be Billy Budd or even young Ishmael atop the mainmast of Pequod, gazing down on Nantucket or some distant port in the South Seas. But I'm not either of them. I'm Ezra Nori-Thorpe Casey, and I'm about as likely to see the South Sea islands as I am to be pardoned for ruining the preacher's only daughter. And the town I'm looking down on is decidedly un-exotic—Mansfield, Oklahoma, where I've lived most of my life.

Mansfield occupies a level plain nestled between the Washita River to the north and east and a row of ragtag granite outcroppings known as the Wichita Mountains to the south. The town was established in 1895, twelve years before statehood in what was formerly Indian Territory. I'm sensitive to such outrages because Doc told me all about the real estate deals that our government made with the Indians in the nineteenth century and because of my own Indian heritage. My grandmother, you see, Doc's wife, was a member of the Sac Nation and a close relation to Jim Thorpe, a fact which provides the best explanation I've ever heard for my natural athletic ability or what Doc referred to as my "uncanny hand-eye coordination."

Anyway, by 1911 the population of Mansfield had swelled to just over a thousand, and, since that time, except during the Great Depression, has remained at about that figure. There are two reasons for that: Those that leave never come back, and those that come never leave. Doc was an exception to that rule; he'd left as a young man to get an education somewhere back east and returned some years later after teaching at this university or that. He returned "not because Mansfield is a good place to live," he told me, "but because it's as good a place as any other to die." I gave up trying to make sense out of everything Doc told me ages ago. You probably understand that.

Wandering over to the window, I stuffed my hands in my pockets and stared out on our town. In the luster of the soft morning light it was quite a pretty place. The white steeples of two other churches grappled with the arching green branches of the pecan and stately oak trees for space in a tranquil blue sky. The red roofs of the white frame houses stood out in a crisscross pattern of neatly laid out streets. From up here it all looked so peaceful, but I knew it wasn't *that* peaceful. The town was really like the river, all smooth and quiet, hardly a ripple on the surface, but underneath the current was strong, always pulling down toward the depths, and there were eddies and whirling pools in the undercut banks that could pull you down and hold you until the life drained right out of you in a little stream of bubbles rising to and then disappearing on the river's surface.

What you have to do is stay in the middle of the river and flow with the current, not fight it. Otherwise you'll get yourself in a heap of trouble. Mansfield is like that too; that's the scary part of growing up here—that, and that sometimes what you don't know about a place or yourself is more frightening than what you do. And sex is certainly no exception to that general rule either.

Somehow they all fit together—sex, religion, the town, the river, Roseabeth and Preacher—I just don't know how they fit yet. Even so, Mansfield, for the most part, is a good place, full of good people and good times for a kid growing up. Or trying to.

Just as I started to turn away from the window I caught a glimpse of the car, a black, souped-up '52 Chevy coupe. It turned on to Main from Pleasant Street, and then fishtailed across both lanes in a shower of flying gravel and burning rubber, heading my way. I shook off a sudden chill and felt a distinct tightening way down in the pit of my stomach as the car approached the church and began to slow to a crawl, the twin glass pack mufflers rumbling a low protest. I wanted to turn away, but some kind of strange compulsion held me at the window, forcing me to expose myself as I had done so many times before to the threats and insults from the one person I considered to be the one truly evil thing in Mansfield.

I suppose there's a Jason Clay in everybody's life, somebody that all of a sudden turns the world into an awful place and fills your eyes with tears and your heart with anger or even hate. If I hate anybody, it's Jason, and the reason I hate him is because I hate him. He brings out the very worst in me, things hidden deep down in a dark part of my soul, things that I don't even know are there until they erupt, turning me into a creature with no more sense of reason or justice than a snarling, rabid dog.

Jason peered out the driver's side window as he cruised by; I'm certain he was laughing to himself at my situation and trying to think of how he just might make it worse. I stayed at the window, watching as he circled the church twice. I believe he would have stopped if Preacher hadn't hurried out and started to tidy up the church yard. Jason just sort of nodded to Preacher, and then drove off at a speed that must have been almost legal. For an instant he glanced up at me like he wanted something. I can't help but wonder what.

Thinking, I wandered back to the only chair in the room and plopped down. Not only was I confused and nervous about my situation, now I was scared as well. Jason does that to me. I'm afraid of him and afraid of myself and have been since the conflict began. There are some things you can do something about and some things you can't. And some you've got to try to do something about whether you can or not. My attempt to do the latter, I think, is what started all the trouble with Jason.

It was at the Kiowa County fair in Hobart, a festive time ordinarily. I'd gone there with Doc and Joe Levy for the purpose of seeing Joe display his old red cow in the livestock show; I'd seen that cow do about everything else, so I figured I might just as well see her perform in the show ring. After the show in which the cow did win a third place ribbon in a field of three,

Doc and Joe went to get Joe's pickup while I searched for the bathroom facilities. As I passed one of the empty show rings I noticed a group of men and boys from Mansfield and some of the other towns in the tri-county area; they were all watching something. I was curious, but really more interested in finding the facilities, so I went on. When I was almost past them I heard this kind of "splat," a slapping kind of sound but more forceful and solid; it was an awful kind of thing, savage and unsettling. Until I went back and glanced between some bobbing heads and saw Jason Clay slam his fist into the face of a kid from Alfalfa name Alan Perkins, I didn't even know what it was. There was another sickening "splat!" Then a dull thud as Jason landed a blow to Alan's chest.

Alan fell to his knees and covered his face with his arms, so Jason kicked him in the stomach about as hard as a mule would, doubling him up. Alan looked up at Jason standing over him; his face was a mess, all red and puffy, his lips swollen like crazy and a mixture of blood and snot poured from his nose. His cheek was cut; tears were gushing from his eyes, but you couldn't hear him cry because Jason had kicked the wind right out of him.

Everybody was just standing there, watching, gawking like Romans at the coliseum on a warm Sunday afternoon and I think maybe enjoying it about as much. Maybe not, but nobody was doing anything to stop it either, because it wasn't their business, wasn't their fight. I didn't do anything either because I didn't know what do to. I was afraid of Jason; I did know that. I'd heard he could whip anybody in three counties and that he was a dirty fighter. I had no reason to doubt it. I'd never seen a real fight before, nothing like this, where somebody was dead set on *hurting* somebody else. Not just whipping, but hurting! Sure I'd been in my share of scrapes in grade school and a little beyond; you don't grow up part Indian and part Japanese without having to defend yourself, but those disagreements usually amounted to nothing more than wrestling around on the ground until somebody said "uncle," as often as not, me. The next day it was all forgotten. From what I could tell, Alan would never forget in a million years what Jason was doing to him.

"Git up you piece of shit," Jason taunted. "I ain't done with you!"

Alan was still on his knees, trying to catch a breath. "He's had enough," another kid from Alfalfa said.

"Then you git out here, sumbitch!"

"I ain't got no quarrel with you," the kid said.

"Then shut the hell up or you will!"

It was a pitiful sight, and I just kept standing there, watching like everybody else. The most sickening part of it was that nobody would do anything to stop it. I felt about an inch tall, but if none of the men there would do anything, what was I supposed to do? I was just a kid, and Jason was ready to tear into the lot of us.

"Git up, sumbitch, I want some more of you," Jason yelled.

Alan wiped some blood from his cheek with the back of his hand and managed to say, "Take that ring off; I'll fight you."

Jason held up a bloody fist. "This is my equalizer," he said, displaying a huge square metal ring. "You're bigger than me."

Alan was maybe *taller* than Jason, not bigger where it counted. Jason was a stocky 5'9" with a thick neck and broad shoulders. He was rugged and had gotten pretty strong working for Hebrew Yuckum at the grain elevator in Mansfield. I was bigger than Jason, probably as strong, quicker and undoubtedly in better shape, but I figured he could kill me because I didn't think I could fight like he fought. And against me he'd probably want *two* rings. Anyway, as a result of Doc's influence, I was a pacifist by nature. I couldn't see any sense in fighting, couldn't see that anything was ever accomplished by people beating up on each other.

"Okay, sumbitch, I'm takin' the ring off," Jason said, slipping the ring off and putting it in his pocket. The ring didn't matter by then anyhow; Alan was already badly beaten. But he suddenly lunged ahead, grabbing at Jason's legs but catching only one of them. Jason pounded him a couple of times on the head, and Alan gave up, collapsing in a heap and crying out loud. Jason kicked him in the face and was fixing to kick him again when all of a sudden somebody screamed:

"*Leave him alone!*" In the shattering silence that followed I looked around and noticed the crowd's attention was riveted on ole *Watakushi*; only then did it dawn on me that I'd been the one who yelled. I don't even know what made me do it; I didn't *want* to do it, not on a conscious level anyway, and I was immediately sorry for it. But I'd yelled so loud or so desperately that I'd startled everybody, Jason and myself, included.

Jason found me in the crowd, but at least he didn't kick Alan again. As he moved toward me, the crowd parted kind of like the way the Red Sea had done for Moses way back when, but I'd just as soon it hadn't—parted for me, not Moses.

"Jist what the hell are *you* gonna do 'bout it?" I stood my ground, reluctantly, gulped and searched for my voice. "Huh?" Jason screamed right in my face.

I jumped back a little and said, "Jist leave him alone, Jason. He's whipped." That, I thought, was sufficient reason to stop the violence, but I wasn't dead certain that Jason operated on the same fundamental principles of decency and reason that I'd practically been weaned on. We were standing there, staring at each other, and I recalled how Davy Crockett had been famous for grinning people and animals down; legend has it he even grinned a knot right off a tree once, mistaking it for raccoon. Couldn't do any harm, I reckoned, so I decided to give it a go. I broke into a slight grin, just enough to throw Jason off guard. And for a moment, it did.

"Ezra, I'm gonna knock that stupid grin right the hell off your face," he told me after the effect of the grin had subsided. I noticed Jason had a somewhat limited vocabulary, but didn't figure this was a good time to bring that up. I dropped the grin and decided it was my move, so I looked at Alan, then started over to him. Like I said, Jason was a fighter and about 17, two years my senior at least, so I didn't figure to aggravate him, just to help Alan, but not at the expense of my own self if I could help it. As I approached Alan, Jason slid over to block my path; rather than going through another staring contest I simply stepped around him and knelt down beside Alan. I had a piece of crumpled up tissue in my pocket which I gave to Alan. Then I helped him up to a sitting position; all the while I expected to feel Jason's boot in my back or ribcage.

"You all right?" I asked Alan. Clearly, he wasn't, but he managed a nod. I got him to his feet, and when I glanced at Jason I saw something there—I don't know what—but something told me he'd let us pass, so I started out of the ring with Alan hanging onto my arm.

"You gonna let him git away with that?" one of Jason's cronies yelled.

Damn, I thought to myself. Of course he's not *now*. Before I was sure he would have. If I'd had my choice of fighting anybody, if it came to that, which I most earnestly hoped it wouldn't, I'd have chosen the big mouth, not Jason, even though Jason deserved a good licking from somebody.

"Hell no!" Jason said, "I ain't gonna let him git away. Leave him be, Ezra. This is my fight."

I couldn't rightly explain it, but my mind seemed to be working pretty good just then; I hoped it was working *right*. This time, although I didn't have a notion as to why, I most surely got the message that Jason didn't want to fight me any-more than I wanted to fight him. If he wanted me, he'd have challenged me instead of Alan. So I tried to hammer home my original argument. "He's all done, Jason."

"I wanna hear it from *him*!" Jason demanded.

Alan wiped some blood away from a deep gash on his fore-head and nodded, "Okay, enough." That satisfied Jason be-cause he started to step aside.

Then a man from the crowd said, "I don't think Jason wants any part of that Casey boy." Sometimes I was distinctly disap-pointed by the behavior of the human race. Suddenly Jason was in our path again, his chest blown up like a Christmas turkey.

"Then I guess you'll havta finish it for him." I noticed he'd managed to slip that hunk of iron back on his finger.

"I'd prefer not to," I said, quoting from *Bartleby* and won-dering why Mr. Melville's influence should pop us just then.

"You'd *what?*" Jason demanded.

"He'd *prefer* not to," one of Jason's admirers said. Everybody laughed. Almost everybody; I didn't or Alan.

"Well, I don't care jackshit 'bout what you'd 'prefer.' You're gonna havta finish what he started."

"What *he* started," somebody said.

"You want some too," Jason screamed at the crowd.

Whoever said it didn't; at least he didn't step forward to receive it. "Jason," I said when he turned his attention back to me, "I've got better sense than to fight with you; I don't even believe in fightin'. Now if there's some point of disagreement here I think we ought to be able to sit down and work out the problem through a rational discussion."

With that he slapped me with his open hand and yelled, "How's that for a rational discussion, chicken-shit?"

"It's not what I had in mind," I said woodenly. My cheek stung, but it didn't really hurt. But it shook me up some, and I was brooding on it while Jason assumed a fighting position. According to what Doc told me about Jesus the thing that I ought to have done was to offer up my other cheek, no questions asked. But from what I understood of the Samurai Code of Bushido that Mariko told me about, I hadn't ought to lose face either. I wasn't really too concerned about that, but I was worried about the distinct possibility of losing part of my face and a whole lot of blood, along with an eye, tooth or ear. But that shouldn't have worried me at all according to the Hemingway code I'd read all about. In Papa's code, the most important thing was to be a *man*, and to have "grace under pressure," like Francis Macomber had. Never you mind that a cape buffalo was about to trample him to pieces, or that the guide had entertained the Mrs. for a good portion of the night before, or that his beloved was about two seconds from blowing his brains out. None of that mattered so long as Francis kept up the grace while the buffalo applied the pressure. Nice code. But I didn't want any part of it. Bullshito is what I called the Hemingway code because it was worse than the one for the Samurai. At lease Bushido had a sense of history and culture behind it; Papa's code was nothing more than some crazy notion thought up by a guy who couldn't decide whether he preferred the bulls or the bull fighters for his heroes. Took balls to be either.

Jason was still standing there in front of me, breathing heavily, but I continued to have the idea that he didn't really want to fight me. And if he was scared, I was glad of it. He let a little grin slide across his face and said, "That was jist to git your attention, Ezra, so we can have our discussion." I guess about everybody but me thought that was real funny because they sure laughed. Jason stepped back then, and, sure enough, slipped a huge square steel ring on his left hand to complement the one on his right."

"Matched set," I said with as much humor as I could muster. Nobody thought *that* was funny.

"Don't fight him, Ezra," Alan said. "He'll butcher your face."

Those were my sentiments exactly. "I'm not gonna fight anybody," I said, having decided to follow Jesus and give Doc's notion a try. So I offered up my other cheek and hoped that Jason was as up on his Biblical literature as I was. Evidently he wasn't. Because you know what he did? *He hit me again!* This time with the back of his hand to my other cheek. I couldn't believe it. I stepped back dumbfounded, my cheek smarting like it had been stuck with a thousand needles. I felt something warm trickling down my cheek and finally tasted blood in the corner of my mouth. I still couldn't believe he'd actually hit me. Nobody had ever hit me like that before.

"Come on, sumbitch! Let's finish our discussion," he taunted and stepped back, once again assuming the position

I gulped and tried to blink the tears out of my eyes. He hadn't really hurt me physically, but he managed to anger me. I could feel it building up inside me like pressure beneath a volcanic plug. I wanted to hit him back, and I didn't want to hit him back. I wanted to fight him, win or lose, and yet I knew there was no sense in it. I didn't want to get my face all smashed up, but I had to defend myself. Whereas it might not do any good if I whipped him, I didn't see that it would do any good if he beat the tar out of me either. No fight, I kept telling myself was the best answer, but I didn't know how to reason with a bully who was applying all that pressure in the finest Hemingway tradition. For a moment I got myself under control and said in a low voice, "Don't hit me again, Jason."

"Is that a threat?"

"Jist take the statement at face value," I told him. "Don't hit me again."

"Face value," he laughed. "When I git through with you, your face ain't gonna be of much value." I was afraid that would be his attitude. "Now come on, sumbitch!"

"Don't do it, Ezra," Alan cautioned. I felt his grip tighten on my arm.

"I don't know how else we're gonna git out of here." I had reached the end of my rope.

"What's going on here?" It was Doc's voice, and I was ever go grateful to hear it. Suddenly he broke into the midst of the confusion and saw what was happening. He didn't bother much with me, giving his attention to Alan instead. After a quick examination, he said, "Lord, Boy, we've got to get you to a doctor; those cuts need stitches."

Everyone was still standing around again gawking like they had good sense. Doc took hold of Alan's other side, and we started out of the ring. Jason wasn't really in our path, but Doc made it a point to cross his. When Jason refused to move, Doc said, "Son, one of these days I expect I'll find you in about the same shape as this boy. When I do, I'll do the same for you as I'm doing for him. Stand aside." Jason stared at Doc, gulped, then finally backed away. After we passed, Jason started yelling.

"This ain't over, Ezra. I'll git you, sooner or later, I'll git you. You can't hide behind your family forever. I'll git you; you hear me?" I did, of course, but I didn't say so. "You hear me," he screamed even louder.

I turned around finally and said, "No." Then I moved back under Doc's outstretched arm and continued to plod slowly away with him and Alan. It felt good both to help and to be helped.

Later, at the hospital while we waited for Alan to get stitched up, Doc looked at me with that penetrating gaze of his and asked, "What would you have done if I hadn't come along, Ezra?"

I shrugged and said, "I don't know."

"Fought him?" Doc asked.

"I didn't want to fight him, but . . I'd run outta cheeks to offer him. What else could I do?"

"I don't know," Doc said. " What do *you* think?"

That was the thing about Doc; he always expected me to answer my own questions myself. That kind of thing was hard on a kid. What I wanted was guidance; I wanted him to *tell* me what to do in a tough situation like that. But Doc always left me to figure out things on my own. He said what's right could always be found in the human heart if you look long enough and hard enough. And he told me that people got in trouble when they stopped listening to their hearts and started listening to what some outside authority told them. "What's right," Doc said, "comes from within, not from without."

I thought a lot about everything that Doc told me, things about life and death and problems and human behavior and the way the world works. It was all very confusing to me; I wanted to be decent and grammatical, to be a good person like Doc, but sometimes when I thought about it—his liberal ideas—I didn't know whether to feel bad about feeling good, or to feel good about feeling bad. I mean, I felt bad for Jason because he was the way he was, but then I felt worse for poor Alan. And I felt good that I wasn't like Jason, or Alan either, but I felt sort of bad about feeling good about not feeling bad.

Before I could get it all straight in my own mind they brought Alan out; he was all patched up, and I guess in pretty good shape considering what he'd been through. As we left the hospital, I couldn't help but wonder if Jason would ever have me looking the way Alan looked.

That, to the best of my recollection, is how the trouble with Jason began. You might even call it my original sin as far as he is concerned. Whatever you call it, the feud continues to drag on to this day, even after the awful thing that happened. And I am sorry about that; we both are, but I could hardly be blamed for that either.

Moving back to the window and looking out I was relieved to find the street empty again. No Jason. I didn't know where he had gone, but it bothered me that he kept cruising by the church every now and again, like he had some unfinished business with me. I heard somebody climbing the stairs so I rushed to the door and listened. Maybe Preacher had come to his senses and was going to let me go.

"Ezra," I heard Mariko call through the door.

"Mom?"

"I've got your breakfast here; Preacher's on his way up with the key."

"Good. I'm starvin',"

"Ezra?"

"Yes ma'am."

"We have a few minutes; do you . . . want to talk about it?"

"No," I said evasively, "that will jist make me hungrier."

"I didn't mean breakfast."

"Oh." I knew what she wanted, but I wasn't ready to discuss the catastrophe with anyone, especially my mother.

"Ezra." Her voice was just as soft and as full of concern for me as ever. You'd never have known that I'd just ruined one woman and been unjustly accused of killing another. "Things still aren't—real clear about what happened last night, but Silas says it's clear now that you didn't kill Fanny."

"Of course I didn't kill Fanny, Mom. She was already dead; Preacher knows that. He was there before I was."

"But the truck *did* hit Fanny."

"I don't deny that."

"And you were driving."

"*I* wasn't driving!"

"No?"

"No!"

"Then . . . who was? Roseabeth?"

"No. Nobody was driving; that's how it came to happen. If somebody had been driving the whole thing would have been avoided. Well, maybe not the whole thing, but the worse part of it."

"I don't understand that, Ezra."

"I don't either, and I was there." I was beginning to itch some; I figured I must have run through some poison ivy last night. Mariko was quiet, so I knew she was thinking.

"Ezra?"

"Don't ask," I told her.

I heard her put the tray aside and clear her throat. "I'm curious about something else."

"What?"

"Is—is that—Roseabeth's gown in your room?"

"I can't deny it," I told her.

"That's too bad."

"You're tellin' me!"

"How did it get all torn up like that?"

Unthinking I said, "I must of run through a patch of briars," I explained. That would account for my itch.

"You ran through a batch of briars? In Roseabeth's gown?"

"I'd prefer not to talk 'bout it."

"Ezra, you didn't have on Roseabeth's gown, did you? I mean with that—incident in the locker room . . ."

"Well, I didn't exactly have it *on*."

"Well . . . did Roseabeth?"

"No. Not then, but she did earlier—at the prom. You saw her."

"Yes, I did. And she did look lovely. But I still don't understand how you ended up running through a briar patch with Roseabeth's gown on."

"I didn't have it *on*!"

"You had it, but you didn't have it on—is that right?"

"It's hard to explain."

"You think about it, okay?"

"Mom! All I've been doin' is thinkin' 'bout it! I sure wish somebody would of told me somethin' 'bout sex instead of metaphysics when I was 13."

"I tried to talk with you, Ezra."

"I couldn't talk to *you* 'bout it! You're my mother. Silas or Doc should of told me everythin' I needed to know. And all they'd talk to me 'bout was . . . apples and butterflies for cryin' out loud."

"What do apples and butterflies have to do with sex?" Mariko asked.

"Beats me! I reckon Silas and Doc know something we don't."

"Sometimes I think men don't communicate so well, Mariko said."

"Doesn't make much sense does it?"

Not very much of our world does, Ezra."

I sort of fell against the door and said, "I guess I've fallen some in your estimation?"

I heard her sigh through the door. "Ezra, not a day has gone by since your birth that you have not brought joy into my life. And I know you well enough—probably better than you know yourself—to know that you probably aren't capable of doing anything that you ought to be ashamed of."

"You have more faith in me than I do, Mom," I told her. But it felt good to know that she would stick by me no matter what.

"That's my job. And I spoke briefly with Roseabeth."

"How is she?"

"Still awfully upset, but other than that, she's fine. She said to tell you she's sorry."

"*She's* sorry!"

"Ezra, do you love, Roseabeth?"

"I dunno. I can't tell whether I'm in love or insane. Is there a difference?"

"Yes, there's a big difference, but sometimes it's hard to recognize."

"Roseabeth's 'bout the prettiest thing I ever saw," I said.

That's not love, Ezra."

"And I git all excited and bewildered and everythin' when I'm with her. Sometimes when I'm not."

"That's just hormones."

"Then what is love, Mom?"

She sighed kind of heavily and said, "Ezra, when the war started your father and I realized what a hopeless situation we were in. He was an American naval officer, and I was the daughter of immigrant Japanese who were about to be shut away in what amounted to a prisoner-of-war camp for the duration of the war. My family was as violently opposed to my seeing your father as the Navy and our government were. But nothing that my family or the Navy or the government did kept us apart, kept us from getting married. That's what love is, Ezra. Do you want to marry Roseabeth that badly?"

"No! Why I don't want to *marry* Roseabeth at all. Least not now."

"Today, you mean?"

"I'm mean while I'm so young. I might not mind it by and by, but I need more of a chance to figure out what life—and love—are all about. I *like* Roseabeth; I like her a lot. Oh, sometimes she tends to be a little unreasonable, but I feel somethin' really strong for her."

Something physical?"

"Ah, yeah, I guess you'd call it physical."

"That's not love either," she said, "necessarily."

"I didn't think so, but I mistook it for love and somethin' awful happened so I guess I *havta* marry Roseabeth now—today. That's what Preacher says."

"Do you think Preacher is serious about that?"

"Dead serious. And he's packin' his shotgun."

"He does have a tendency to be dogmatic."

"He a fair shot too," I said. I could hear the plates rattling around on the tray.

"Your breakfast is cold."

"I'm not hungry now."

"I'll get something else."

"Just some juice and toast," I said, "and maybe a couple of eggs and sausage. A few muffins."

"That's *all?*"

"And a short stack of buttermilk pancakes. And a quart of milk."

She started to leave. "Ezra, don't you worry now. We'll talk with Preacher and get this whole mess straightened out. I'm sure what happened was just a . . . misunderstanding."

"A very big one," I moaned.

"But one I'm certain that can be settled by reasonable people," she said, as I listened to her footsteps receding down the stairs.

I agreed with her wholeheartedly; this misunderstanding *could* be settled by reasonable people. Problem was: Preacher wasn't reasonable, and worse than that, he had that shotgun. That being the situation, I walked to the window, looked out on the churchyard and started practicing saying, "I do," although, "I *did*," might have been more appropriate under the circumstances.

5

RESCUE THE PERISHING

Whenever I look up at the ceiling from the old army cot that Preacher threw in the steeple with me last night I see a crack that starts under the light socket and runs toward the door in a line that could have been traced by a drunken cockroach. Halfway to the door the crack splits in two and then those forks separate into two other paths and so on until there are so many paths that it gives me a headache just to look up at them.

Prior to last night, before the catastrophe, my future was like that; there were any number of paths I might have taken out of Mansfield following my high school graduation. But, because of several events over which I exercised very little, if any, control, those many paths have merged into a single superhighway leading straight to the altar—matrimonial or sacrificial—call it what you like. To a kid of seventeen they don't look all that different.

Marriage! Lord it puts me in a sweat just to think about it. Not because I have anything against marriage as a solid institution; I don't. As an institution marriage is fine, but as a way of life, I still have some reservations about it. Just like everything else, there's a proper time and place for it. The problem here is that I'm not nearly as certain as Preacher is that *today* is the proper time for *me* to take such a giant leap into the breach.

I don't know, but Preacher sure makes me nervous. While I don't reckon he'd actually shoot me, I'm pretty certain that he'd shoot *at* me. Certainly he would have last night. I don't understand what a preacher needs a shotgun for anyhow. Jesus never had a shotgun, or Moses, or Abraham, or Jacob, or Isaac, or Amos or Andy. They all did real fine without guns, although I do recollect that some of them carried big sticks and, I assume, walked softly. But that's because they tended sheep, except for Moses whose stick kept turning into a snake and scaring hell out of the sheep.

I was staring at that ceiling again, wondering what path I'd take out of Mansfield if I did have a choice. Then my concentration was broken by some kind of ruckus going on below. Voices. Shouting. Dull thuds.

I jumped up and scurried across the room and put an ear to the door. I heard more yelling and some groans, maybe some furniture being smashed. *Boom*! Now I could have sworn that was Preacher's shotgun. There was more scuffling, more shouting, and finally dead silence. I pressed my ear tight against the door. Suddenly there were footfalls in the stairwell. Then somebody stopped outside the door and gasped for a breath.

"Ezra?"

"Brinton?" I said tentatively.

"Yeah, it's me and Phil."

"What's goin' on?"

"We've come to rescue you," Phil said, "from the grips of unholy matrimony."

"At the risk of our lives," Brinton added.

"Did I hear a shot?"

"Damn sure did! Preacher put a blast through the ceilin' of the vestibule while we wrestled the shotgun away from him."

"Hot damn! Just the two of you?"

"Yeah," Phil said, "along with Ogden, Tilden and Joe. They're still down there tyin' Preacher up."

"I hope they do a good job."

"Don't worry; Tilden made Eagle Scout; he's real good with knots."

"And Preacher's a maniac," I pointed out. "You'd better keep a guard on him, Brinton."

Brinton tried the door, then said, "Hey, Ezra, do you know where Preacher keeps the key to the steeple?"

"Sure, that's the first thing he told me."

"Don't be a smart ass, Ezra, or we'll leave you to your fate."

"Roseabeth's not such a bad fate," Phil said.

"Then *you* marry her, Phil," I said.

"I mean for one night."

"The key, Ezra!" Brinton insisted.

"I dunno. I suppose he keeps it somewhere in his office."

"We already searched the office," Brinton said. "It wasn't there."

"We'll havta break down the door," Phil said.

"That oak monstrosity?" Brinton said. "You've got to be kidding." The door was a monster all right; the church had been built when they built them like they used to. It would take more guile than brute strength to get me out. "We'll git some tools and take it off the hinges," Brinton finally decided.

"The hinges are in here," I told him.

"I know where the hinges are, Ezra. We'll havta drill a hole and pass you the tools so you can take them off."

I heard somebody running off. "I'll tell Tilden to git some tools," Phil said.

"And check Preacher," I suggested, but I don't think he heard me. Opposite me on the other side of the door I heard Brinton slide down the wall to a sitting position.

"Make yourself comfortable, Ez, we're gonna be here a while."

"It looks that way," I said and slid down to a sitting position.

"Ez?"

"What?"

"How're you doin'?"

"Jist fine. How're you?"

"Ezra, I ain't makin' small talk. Now, how are you *really* doin'? Still in one piece and all?"

"Oh, yeah, fine, one piece—jist a few bruises and puncture wounds in my feet, some scratches here and there, my back is sore from Roseabeth smashin' into me, and I can't raise my left arm higher than my shoulder, but otherwise, I'm fine," I told him.

"I'm glad to hear it," Brinton said. "You had us worried." He paused to clear his throat. "I couldn't believe Fanny's place."

"You were out there?"

"Ezra, *everybody* was out there." I was pretty sure I heard him laugh. "Looks like all hell broke loose in Fanny's parlor."

"Fanny's still . . . dead, I guess?"

"As a boot!"

"I figured as much, but I thought maybe I could of been mistakin' about her condition. She *looked* dead all right, but I was kinda in a sweat when I barged in."

"Rufus already embalmed her," Brinton said.

"Didn't waste any time, did he?"

"Nope, when Rufus undertakes an undertaken he don't screw around; can't in this kinda heat, if you know what I mean. The smell and so forth . . . kinda like Vardaman's mother."

"I git the point, Brinton. You don't havta spice it up for me. "

"Sorry."

"It's okay," I said.

"You know what the most amazin' thing 'bout it is?"

"Yeah," I said, "that I'm alive to tell 'bout it."

"Nope. That Si's truck still runs."

"You're kiddin'!"

"No, honest injun, oh, sorry, Ez."

'It's okay."

"Silas climbed in, cranked her up and drove home."

"Don't that beat all?"

"Well, it beats a lot, that's for sure. I dunno 'bout *all*."

"I didn't mean it literally anyway."

"Hey, Ez, what exactly *did* happen last night?"

I thought for a moment; I knew this was coming. "Well, what happened was—was what I'd call a real unfortunate sequence of events. *Real* unfortunate."

"Could you possibly be a little more explicit?"

"It could hardly of been more explicit," I told him.

"Well, what was the first of these unfortunate events?"

"My birth," I said.

"You're goin' back too far, Ezra; I jist wanna know what happened after you left the prom with your beloved."

"Roseabeth?"

"That's who you left the prom with."

That was true, but I'd never heard anyone refer to Roseabeth as my "beloved" before. And it made me nervous. I let out heavy sigh that I suppose carried right through the door. "Well, it actually started before the prom, at the pre-party at Phil's. Roseabeth—"

Suddenly a bunch of people came thundering up the steps. Then I heard Ogden Burgatroid's voice. "Can't find no keys anywhere. Phil sent Tilden home to git some tools; boy, that Preacher is strong as a gorilla."

"Ezra in there?" I heard Joe Levy asked.

"Hi Joe, Ogden," I said.

"Hi, Ezra. How you doin'?"

"He's fine," Brinton told them.

"He asked me," I protested. It really irritates me when other people answer questions that are directed directly to me.

Brinton said, "You jist told me you were fine, Ezra."

"I know, but I've changed my mind. Fact is: I'm awful—sick to death with worry, got a backache, and my feet are killing me. Plus I think I got some poison ivy and I'm face to face with a shotgun wedding."

"Now you jist settle yourself down, Ezra. We ain't gonna let Preacher marry you off without a good cause," Joe said.

"I *can't* settle down!" I said.

"We're all gonna havta settle down," Brinton said, "until Tilden gits here with those tools, so we might jist as well git situated while I git a few of the details figured out."

"What do we havta wait on tools for? Joe asked. Now that Preacher is tied up, Ezra can go right out the window and climb down the tree to freedom."

"What the hell kinda of rescue would that be, Joe," Brinton said, "if Ezra rescues himself?"

"It would be jist that—a self- rescue," Joe said.

"And jist what the hell would we do all mornin'? Did you think of that?"

"No," Joe said.

Then Ogden added, "And this is good practice for the future. What if we're in a war or somethin' and we havta rescue a buddy?"

"I never thought of that," Joe said. "But—"

"No buts," Brinton snapped, "what's begun cannot be unbegun."

"Unbegun? Not exactly Shakespeare," I said to myself. Then I said, "Joe's right, Brinton, I could jist go right out the window."

"Oh sure and screw up the entire rescue," Brinton argued. "Go ahead, after all we done for you."

I could see how important it was to them so I decided to go along with the "rescue" idea. "Okay," I said, "go ahead and rescue me."

"Okay," Brinton said, "down to business. Now, this here rescue is based on the notion that whatever happened last night was of a serious enough nature for Preacher to insist on Ezra exchanging nuptial vows with Roseabeth. Ain't that so, Ezra?"

"Yeah," I agreed, "it was of a serious enough nature for that."

"Can we also assume than that you performed sexual intercourse with Preacher's one and only daughter?" Brinton asked.

"Don't call it that," Phil said, "you'll jist confuse him."
Fact is it *did* confuse me for a moment. I knew what Brinton
was talking about, but to tell you the truth, I'd never heard it
called *that* before.

Brinton cleared his throat and said, "Did you *screw*
Roseabeth, Ezra?"

"I *know* what he's talkin' 'bout, Phil!"

"You do not," Phil said. "You don't know the scientific
name of anything at all, Ezra and you know it."

"Like hell I don't!"

"What 'bout that time I asked you 'bout a vagina?" Phil
said.

"Shut up, Phil!" This wasn't a story I wanted to see circulated too widely.

"A what?" Ogden said.

"When was this?" Brinton asked.

"Years ago," I said, "I was jist a kid."

"Didn't I tell you 'bout that?"

"Hell no!" Ogden said.

"Phil, you—*promised*." Don't do it."

Pipe down in there," Brinton said. "Tell us, Phil."

"It never happened," I moaned and buried my head between my knees.

Phil forged ahead relentlessly. "Wasn't all that long ago—
winter before last it was. I remember 'cause it was the Monday
after the Saturday of my heavy date with Grace Farley. Ezra
was down in the locker room, sittin' on a bench and pickin' at
his toe jam."

"I was examinin' my athlete's foot," I said defensively.

"Don't matter. Anyway, I come in and say somethin'
like: 'Hey, Ez, guess what? I finally saw one.' And Ezra says,

'You did? Yeah,' I tell him. And he says, 'When?' And I say, 'Saturday night.' And Ezra says, 'One what?'"

"He said that?" Ogden asked.

Of course I said it, Ogden; I didn't have the slightest notion of what he was talkin' 'bout."

Phil went on, inexorably. "So I tell him that I saw a vagina. And he says, 'A what?'"

"You didn't know what it was, Ezra, even after he told you?" Ogden said critically.

"Listen, Ogden, I *knew* what it was; I jist didn't know that's what you called it."

"Anyway, Ezra says somethin' real curious like, 'What'd—it—ah—look like?' So I allowed as to how it was kinda dark and all, but from what I could tell, the thing looked more like a gorilla than anythin' else I could think of, a small one."

"A small *gorilla?*" Ogden said.

"Yeah," Phil said, "without the arms or legs. Then Ezra asked me where I saw it and asked him where in the hell he thought I saw it. And he said he didn't know because he'd never seen one around here before."

"One gorilla or one vagina?" Ogden asked.

"Neither," I said.

"No shit!" Joe Levy said. I was pretty certain I heard some muffled laughter.

Phil continued, unremittingly. "So I tell him that it was in my car, and Ezra wants to know how it got in there. That question kinda puzzled me so I asked him flat out if he even knows what I'm talkin' 'bout. And he says, 'Yeah, a—a—va—what'd you call it?' So I say, 'a vagina.' And he says, 'Yeah, that's it. How'd it git in your car?' Well, now I *know* he doesn't know what I'm talkin' 'bout, but I'm curious 'bout where this conversation will go, so I don't let on and jist tell him that the vagina I saw belonged to Grace Farley. And Ezra is real surprised that she would bring it in the car with her. So I tell him that I don't know what else she could of done with it. So Ezra wants to know if she had it *on a leash or anything*!"

Their laughter was muffled no more, but rolling out of them in loud guttural spasms that were accompanied by generous portions of what I took to be foot stomping and wall slapping. After the hubbub died down some, Phil went on, ruthlessly. "So I say, 'Ezra, don't you know that vagina is jist the scientific name for pussy?' And I went on to allow as to how Brinton had come to tell me that vagina was the scientific name for it. And he wants to know again what it looked like."

"Well Brinton never told me," I said.

"Must of slipped my mind, Ezra," Brinton said. "Sorry."

"You're sorry! I'm *ruined*, and you're sorry. And since when did you become so scientific, Phil?"

"Ezra, ain't nobody ever got me mixed up with Madame Curie jist 'cause I know girls don't go around with their pussy on a leash," Phil said.

Boy, they were having themselves a grand old time out there all right. "Ezra," Joe Levy finally said, "how come you were so interested in what it looked like?"

"I was jist curious," I said. "But when he told me it looked like a gorilla I lost all my enthusiasm for seein' one; I mean I'd seen a *gorilla* before—Phil at the zoo in St. Louis—and to tell you the truth, the thing kinda scared me. Even gave me nightmares."

They were at it again, howling and rolling around in the hall. Sounded like a bunch of professional wrestlers pounding on the canvas. "Ezra, that's funnier than the disaster;

Lord a mercy—a gorilla on a leash. Maybe you *would* be better off locked away somewhere. That mind of yours is going to cause you nothing but trouble," Brinton said. I didn't have a real good reason to doubt him. When the laughter finally died away for good, Brinton said, "I didn't mean that, Ez. We've come to rescue you, and that's jist what we're gonna do. So, with all foolishness aside, the question remains: Are you now or have you ever gotten into Roseabeth's panties?"

I thought about it and said, "Being that Roseabeth is most likely sequestered in her room, I quite obviously am not presently gittin' into her panties, nor have I, to my knowledge, in the past entered her private domicile. Although I did once, as you all well know, get into one of her brassieres."

"What the hell are you two talkin' 'bout?" Ogden asked.

"I'll rephrase the question: Ezra, what happened last night between you and Roseabeth?"

"I—I don't remember."

"Ezra, it was jist last night," Brinton said. "Now did you screw Roseabeth or not?"

"Maybe," I said.

"What the hell does that mean?" Phil said.

"That I'm not sure if I did or not."

"If he's not sure, he didn't," Joe Levy said.

"How can I be sure 'bout somethin' I'd never done before," I said defensively. "*Somethin'* happened, but I'm not sure what it was, exactly."

"Ezra, you do know what I'm talkin' 'bout, don't you? "I'm talkin' sexual intercourse; I'm talkin' gittin' laid; I'm talkin' screwin'; I'm talkin' knowin' Roseabeth in the Biblical sense."

"Somebody better check on Preacher," I suggested.

"Don't change the subject," Phil said. "And don't worry about Preacher we tied him up real good. Now did you or didn't you?"

"What difference does it make?" I asked.

"Ezra," Brinton said, "it makes all the difference in the world. "Cause if you didn't screw Roseabeth, Preacher can't force you to marry her."

"He shouldn't havta marry her anyhow," Phil said passionately. "This ain't the dark ages. You shouldn't havta marry a girl jist 'cause you screwed her."

"Unless she's pregnant," Joe Levy said. There seemed to be some general agreement on that fine point.

"Ezra?" Brinton said after a brief interlude of welcome silence.

"I'm still here," I said.

"Did Roseabeth . . . cooperate with you, more or less?"

I thought about it and then said, "Well, yeah, I think that's what she was doin', more or less."

"Which," Brinton asked, "more or less?"

"More," I'd estimate.

"All right," Ogden said. "Now we're gittin' somewhere! So, you screwed her with her permission."

"She didn't gimme a note or anythin'", I said.

"Well, did she *say* anythin'?" Phil asked.

"Before or after?"

"Before?"

"Yeah," I explained, "she said, 'Please—don't—stop.' So I didn't. I wasn't sure how she meant it."

"Jeeze," Brinton said. "What 'bout afterwards? What'd she say then?"

I just couldn't repeat her last words because they weren't true. So I started a little earlier. "Well, she said, 'Oh God!' a number of times."

"How'd she mean that?"

"I dunno, but I don't think she was prayin'," I said.

"Oh God, huh?" Brinton said. "That could be good— could be bad."

"But she was cooperatin' right?" Joe Levy said.

"I think she was," I said, "but then we reached a point where cooperation by either of us was beside the point."

"*The point of no return,*" Ogden said dramatically.

"We're losin' sight of the fact here of whether Roseabeth could be pregnant or not," Brinton interjected. "The screwin' is a side issue. So, what we need to know is what method of birth control you used, Ezra."

I thought about it for a moment and then replied, "Gravity." I was real high on gravity; didn't know of anything else that worked as well.

"Jeeze!"

"Tell me some more, and I'll tell you if I used them."

"Abstinence?" Phil said.

"Nope, didn't use that one."

"Rubbers?" Ogden said.

"Wasn't rainin'."

"Dammit, Ezra, this is serious," Brinton said. "Withdrawal?"

I thought about that one and said, "Maybe."

"How 'bout this," Phil said, "Can you recollect the last time Roseabeth was feelin' poorly?"

"Well, she 'bout caught her death from bein' left out in the rain a year ago July."

"No, no, more recent than that. Like when did she last have a headache or complain 'bout havin' the vapors?"

"The *what*?"

"What 'bout swimmin'?" Ogden said.

"Swimmin'?"

"Or ridin' a bike?"

"What does that have to do with anythin'," I said.

"You guys are jist confusin' the issue," Brinton said. "Ezra, now *think*, when was the last time Roseabeth had a headache?"

"She's probably got one this mornin'."

"Dammit! It don't work unless she has it *before*hand."

"What don't?" I asked.

"The *rhythm method*! Ezra, what I'm tryin' to establish here is when Roseabeth last had her period. 'Cause if we know that we can determine whether or not she was even *capable* of gittin' pregnant, if you *did* screw her."

"Oh," I said and thought about it. "Well, how should *I* know when she last had her period?"

"'Cause you been goin' with her since the beginnin' of time. Think! Is there any particular time of the month when Roseabeth is particularly hard to git along with?"

"Roseabeth is *always* hard to git along with, but I thought it was 'cause she was a Baptist."

"Ezra, think about it!" Phil pleaded.

I got to thinking about it all right. I kind of felt like I was in the concentration booth on the $64,000 Question TV show. I was in a real sweat to come up with something, anything, so I thought it might help to tell them about when Roseabeth felt good. "You know," I said, "sometimes Roseabeth is more pleasant than other times; I mean *easier* to git along with 'cause she gits kinda silly and all. And she's always rushin' off to the bathroom with somebody and gigglin' and everything."

"That's *it*," Phil said.

"When, Ezra? When does she act like that?"

"Oh, 'bout the same time every month."

"When was the last time?" Phil asked.

"What's today?"

"Saturday, May 21st. The prom was last night."

I scratched me head and said, "Well, she was actin' strange all week, giddy and all. I jist figured she was excited 'bout the prom."

"And when did she become her normal domineerin' self?"

"Thursday," I told them because Roseabeth told me that day that she was planning on adding more color to my wardrobe. Evidently I've been wearing too much gray to suit her taste."

"Yahoo," they all screamed in unison and started carrying on like a bunch of fools. Then Brinton said, "Ez, it looks like you're in the clear; we can rescue you with a clear conscience."

"How do you know?"

Brinton explained: "'Cause if Roseabeth jist finished her period on Thursday she couldn't of ovulated by Friday which means she couldn't of gotten pregnant even if you did screw her."

"Don't that beat all?" I put my head to the door and asked, "Brinton, why didn't you tell me any of this before?"

"I figured you knew," he said.

"My dad's not a doctor; how could I possibly know?"

"It's not my fault, Ezra. My dad told me not to go blabbin' everythin' he told me all over the place 'cause if kids know all 'bout it, they might be more likely to try it."

"Brinton that's 'bout the dumbest reason I ever heard for anythin', I countered. "Does the fact that I've taken Driver's Education mean that I'm gonna go out on the highway and wreck my truck?"

"Why no; it means you'd be less likely to," Brinton said.

"Then how could knowin' a little somethin' 'bout sex cause me to wreck myself on the highway of life? It's *not* knowin' anythin' that's got me in the fix I'm in."

Brinton thought a moment and then said, "Ezra, I *did* tell you 'bout Margaret Mead and those kids on that island called Samoa."

"Yeah," I told him. "And that was 'bout as helpful as Silas tellin' me that Moby Dick was a disease! Thanks a lot."

"Sorry, Ezra. I jist thought you knew."

"Brinton," I said, "I want you to tell me somethin', and I want you to tell me the truth."

"What's that?" Brinton said.

"The truth?" I asked.

"No!" Brinton snapped, "I know what the truth is. What is it you want me to tell you?"

I laid it on the line. "I want to know whether or not you've ever really done—it with a girl or not?"

Before he could answer there came this clatter in the stairwell—heavy footfalls, labored breathing and the clanking of steel. "Tilden," Phil said, "where the hell you been?"

"You sent me to git some tools," Tilden said. "How you doin', Ezra?"

"He's not so good," Ogden said.

"Don't worry," Tilden said cheerfully, "we'll have you outta there in a flash."

"Gimme a screwdriver," Brinton said.

"Brinton?" I said. "Answer my question—have you ever done it with a girl?"

"If I've done it, you can sure as hell bet that it was with a girl!" Brinton said.

"Joe? What 'bout you?" I asked.

"I ain't sayin', Joe said. "

"Ogden?"

"Shit, Ezra, why . . . well, maybe I ain't ever actually done it, but I sure as hell know how to. And if I had, I'd know it."

"Okay, Tilden," I said, "you're up. What 'bout you?"

"Ezra, this is the kinda thing I take up with my priest; it's none of your business." Tilden was one of those Roman Catholics; even so, I don't know why anybody would ever want to tell their priest or preacher about having sexual intercourse. I sure as heck would never tell Preacher about it, especially if I've done it with his daughter.

Just then the doorknob fell out onto the floor as Brinton jerked the other knob and shaft through his side of the door. I peeked into the hole and saw him. "Hi, Ezra," he said.

"Hi Brinton."

"So far so good," he said. "If we can git the rest of this junk outta here I think maybe I can pass you some tools to get at those hinges with."

Just then from below there came a mighty roar, sort of a combination of the worst elements of Mighty Joe Young and King Kong. Then I heard some thundering footfalls in the stairwell, eating up three or four steps at a time. "Preacher!" I said.

"Great God Almighty! He broke the ropes," Phil said.

"Ohhhh shit," Ogden said.

I looked through the hole and saw Preacher standing on the top step; broken strands of rope dangled from both his wrists and his shotgun was trained on my pals.

"He broke the ropes," Phil said incredulously, "he *broke* the ropes!"

"You should of cut his hair," I yelled then backing away from the door.

"Don't one of you little sneaks move an inch or Mr. Winchester here is gonna move you 12 feet," Preacher snarled. It sounded as if the boys were remaining pretty much motionless. "Now you, Turkle, git away from that door." I heard Preacher approaching. "Ezra, you'd better hope to hell you're still in there 'cause if you ain't I'll consider you fair game. After what you done to my angel there's no place in this world where I wouldn't find you. And if you'd like to try the next one, I'd be more than happy to give you a fine Christian send off, if you know what I mean."

"I got the general idea," I said.

"So let it be did, so let it be done," Preacher said.

"I'm right here, Preacher, thankin' my lucky stars and stripes forever that I live in a free country," I told him.

"It ain't, evidently, as free as you and these boys here think it is," Preacher said. "That right, boys!"

"Oh, yeah," Brinton said.

"That's right, Preacher," Phil agreed.

"Not free. No sir. That's right," my buddy Joe added.

"Now, Turkle, Son, you jist fix that door there same as you found it 'cause your friend Ezra ain't got no place to go. That right, Boy?"

"Yessir, that's right. I ain't got no place to go," I agreed and held up the knob to the hole while Brinton inserted the shaft. Then I added, "'Till my honeymoon."

"Now ain't that nice? Ezra's thinkin' 'bout his honeymoon and a full life of domestic tranquility."

"Actually, I never got past the honeymoon part," I said.

"But you will," Preacher assured me.

"All done, Preacher," Brinton said. "Good as new."

"Good, good," Preacher said as he twisted the knob. "You do good work, Son. Now if you boys 'ill jist hightail it outta here, I'll let you go *this* time. But if I see jist one of your young asses 'round here again before the weddin', I'll shoot first and you'll find out why later, if my aim's bad. Is that clear?"

"Perfectly," Phil said.

"It crystal clear to me all right," Brinton said.

"Yessir," Joe said.

"Then git out!" Preacher yelled.

A stampede is what happened then. Beneath the thunder of the rushing feet somebody yelled, "All the best, Ezra."

And, "Good luck to you and Roseabeth."

That's what I like: Commitment to a just cause. "Boy?" Preacher said.

"Yessir."

"You jist stay where you are and think 'bout what you done to my angel; you think real hard. And ask yourself if you'd run out on her even if you had the chance, which you ain't gonna git." Preacher never missed the opportunity to deliver a small sermon. "You think 'bout it, you hear?"

"Yessir," I said woodenly and gulped. "I'll think about it." Fact is, I'd been thinking about nothing else for some time. Hearing Preacher leave, I rushed to the window and looked out. There went Brinton and the gang, tearing off towards town in an awful rush. Not a one of them so much as bothered to look back, which is something I still have to do. I'm thinking what happened was as much an accumulation of errors as it was a single night's folly. I mean, I didn't get to where I was last night without having waded through a good bit of mud and murky water along the way. And it was much more than just my misunderstanding of sex that got me where I am; my behavior was a reflection of what I thought everybody else thought about sex and decency and religion and life as well as what I thought, or what I thought I thought.

Anyway, I'm going to tell you about some of the turning points in my own ethical training and about my extensive repertoire of sexual disasters so that you might better understand what I so far haven't been able to figure out. God help us all if nobody can make any sense of it.

6

HARANGUE AND HOLY WATER

I'm not a Baptist, Free Will or otherwise. But, I was often mistaken for one. That *was* my fault. I spent a good deal of my spare time in the company of the daughter of the Baptist preacher, and I occasionally made the mistake of attending regular meetings or even sometimes a revival meeting at the Baptist Church. And once, briefly, I attended the Baptist church camp over in Devil's Canyon; I say briefly because I got thrown out of camp on the third day after my arrival. Not for smoking or cussing or getting "lost" in the woods with a member of the same religion but opposite sex; those things were pretty much expected and even tolerated up to a point. I was thrown out for committing heresy and blasphemy on the same day, the latter being a direct consequence of the former. I remember it like it was just yesterday.

From the moment you got to church camp, preachers and counselors (soon to be preachers, God willing or not) were harping on you about seeing God. About everybody there had seen Him at one time or another, but since I made the error of telling the truth that I'd *never* seen Him before, they were on me about it most all the time. Let me tell you: With Baptist preachers standing on three sides of you it's hard to see *anything.*

One morning they got us all up before dawn, marched us through the thickest part of the forest, had us climb a sheer cliff and then expected us to stay awake through a sunrise sermon—all before breakfast. The one time I did open my eyes the rising sun nearly blinded me, and all I could think of was how hungry I was. One kid had a package of crushed Twinkies, but there weren't enough to go around. I was sort of hoping that maybe Jesus would show up and multiply and divide them for us, but He never showed. I reckon Jesus knew better than to give kids Twinkies, or maybe He was afraid the Hostess Company would come down on Him—them or the health department.

I guess about everybody there but me did see God that morning; I couldn't find him anywhere once I did start looking. One kid said He was a bird, a raven sitting atop a dead oak tree; another said He was the tree itself. One even said He was a rock—the clouds, the sun and sky. They were *all* God. I don't know what to tell you. He must have been all over the place, but you couldn't prove it by me. I *wished* I'd seen him too—to get those preachers off my back—but, like I said, I didn't, and I didn't figure you ought to lie about something like that. He'd know sure enough whether you were faking it or not even if the preachers didn't.

When I didn't see Him that morning at the sunrise service, they took me out again, this time in the heat of the day to a lake deep in the bowels of the canyon. Somebody would say, "Don't you see God out there, Ezra?" about the same time someone in front of me would about take off my head by releasing a tree limb in my face. "No," I'd tell them, "but I'll keep lookin'."

When we got to the lake we got to sit down and eat a snack. I'd brought my own Twinkies this time so I didn't have to miss out, but I wished I hadn't have done it. I ate six Twinkies about as fast as I could stuff them in my mouth; they left me a little dry, and I had worked up a good thirst on the hike, so I emptied my canteen on top of the Twinkies. They ought to put some kind of warning on the Twinkies package about that kind of thing.

Those Twinkies absorbed all that water like dry sponges and started expanding in my stomach. As my stomach expanded the skin over it grew tighter and tighter, and I thought it was going to split, but it didn't because suddenly that mushy dough started working its way back up my throat, causing me to gag some. "God," I moaned.

"What's that?" a preacher said, "Where?"

"I don't feel so good," I mumbled.

"What is it, son, you feel the spirit of the Lord moving inside you?"

"It's the Twinkies," I told him.

"The what?"

"I think he got hold of a bad Twinkie," a kid told the preacher.

The preacher put his hand over my shoulder and pulled me close. "You'll be all right," he said, "jist look out there at that beautiful lake and see if that don't make you feel better."

I swallowed real hard and forced myself to look at the lake. It was right pretty, so blue that couldn't tell where the

lake ended and the sky began, but it didn't make me feel
any better. Fact is: Watching the motion of the waves made
me feel worse, and I threw up in it; after that I don't think
even the preacher thought the lake was such a beautiful
sight. I don't suppose it was, but, to tell you the truth, I sure
felt a lot better than before. Later, I saw a snake and a frog
and two catfish in the lake, but none of them looked like
God to me.

Towards the end of the third day the preachers were getting *real* disappointed, and I was getting *real* tired of traipsing
all over the countryside and kind of desperate to see God because everyone else had. I thought that maybe something was
wrong with my eyes. Then, just when I'd all but given up on
it, it happened.

Evening it was; the sun was just settling below the western
rim of the canyon, and in the shadows there was a kind of ma-
jestic purple haze clinging to the canyon walls like heavy velvet
drapes. I'd forgotten to take my Bible to the evening service,
so they sent me back to get it. I had just stepped in the cabin
when I heard something move in the darkness and make a
sort of grunting noise. I froze right where I was, perked up
my ears and gazed into the gathering gloom. "Who's that?" I
didn't get an answer, but I heard something scurrying around
and then caught a glimpse of something—two beady eyes
shining out at me from the darkness. I knew right off it was
God; it had to be, and looking out from beneath my very own
bunk. And there I'd been traipsing all over tarnation looking
for Him when He was right there under my bunk all the time.
"God," I said, relieved, "am I ever glad to see you. They were
gonna make me sit in the chapel tonight all by my own self 'till
I saw you, even if it took all night." He just sat there, staring

at me and made another grunting noise. "Look, I gotta switch on the light to find my Bible, but I don't reckon you'll mind that." When I pulled the chain to switch on the light, He lit out, scampering across the floor and then disappearing through a hole in the far wall. I just let Him be; nothing else I could do. Then I raced down to the chapel where everybody was and broke into the service yelling, "Preacher, Preacher! I saw Him!"

Reverend Blackwell, the camp director, was conducting the service, and it looked like I busted in on a prayer. Right from the start he was vexed with me. "What is it, Son?"

"I saw Him!" I said again.

"You saw the light, son?" he asked excitedly.

"No," I said a little confused. "He saw the light."

"He?"

"Yessir."

"Who?"

"God," I said.

"You saw the light of God?"

"No," I insisted because I wanted to get it right. "I saw God. We *both* saw the light; that's when he lit out. It's jist this naked bulb hanging down from a wire."

"Son," Blackwell said, "You saw God, you say?"

"Yessir! That's what I'm tryin' to tell you," I insisted.

"Why that's wonderful, Son," he said and tucked me under his arm. "Hear that boys and girls? Ezra here has finally seen God. Share your enlightenment with us, Ezra." I don't know why he kept harping on the light thing; turning on the light is what had screwed the whole thing up. If He hadn't seen the light, He might still be in the cabin. "Tell us about it, son."

"Well," I began hesitantly, "I'd gone back for my Bible; it was on this shelf over my bunk, but I plum forgot it in the excitement and all. I got to the cabin and—"

"There in the blue-black shadows left by the falling sun," Blackwell said softly, "you saw . . . *Him.*"

"No sir."

"Then in the sun-drenched yellow-orange western sky?"

"Huh?"

"Where did you see him, Ezra?" Blackwell asked a little impatiently. I was beginning to feel a little uncomfortable about the whole thing myself to tell you the truth. I mean, I was sure I'd seen Him, but looking back on it then, it seemed a little— weird, I guess. "Where did you see Him, Son?"

"Well," I said and cleared my throat; I kind of felt like one of those Twinkies was after me again. "He was in my cabin, number seven, down by the showers."

"I *know* where your cabin is, Son."

"Good. 'Cause that's where he was—in my cabin, number seven . . . under—under my bunk." This revelation pretty much managed to disrupt the evening vespers. Reverend Blackwell was gazing at me somewhat sternly, I'd say. "He was jist peekin' out from beneath my bunk, watchin' me."

"Watchin' over you," Blackwell said tenderly.

"Actually, I was watchin' over Him," I said, "Him bein'under my bunk and all."

Blackwell intensified his gaze and said, "Son, are you sure you didn't see Him out there in the woods somewhere?"

"No sir, I mean, yessir, I'm sure I didn't. He was in my cabin all right—number seven, but He's probably in the woods *now.* Like I said, He ran off when He saw the light."

"When *He* saw the light?"

"Yessir."

"Now settle down out there," Blackwell told the gathering. Then to me he said, "Ran off you say?"

"Yessir. Went right through a hole in the wall!" That pretty much brought the house down, and I was sure by then that I'd made a *very* big mistake, not seeing God, but telling anyone about it. But then people didn't believe Moses either, at first. Then I was no Moses either.

"Ezra," Blackwell said earnestly, "in what manifestation did God appear to you?"

"Huh?"

"What did God look like?"

"Oh," I said nervously, "I jist got a glimpse of Him."

"Yes. And?"

"A woodchuck," I mumbled under my breath.

"Speak up, Son."

I decided to go for broke. Hell, Charlton Heston thought God was a burning bush. "A woodchuck," I said, "he looked like a good size woodchuck." That was the heresy, and I'll admit that such a revelation shot the evening vespers all to hell.

Blackwell stood there glaring at me; his nostrils were kind of expanding and contracting with every breath he took. His eyes were ablaze with righteous anger. He finally said, "Ezra, are tellin' me that God revealed himself to you in the form . . . of a—*woodchuck?*"

"Yessir," I assured him, "but it was no *ordinary* woodchuck. He was *good* size, a woodchuck to behold. A woodchuck of Divine proportions, I can tell you. There's no tellin' how much good this woodchuck could chuck if this woodchuck could chuck—

"Get out," Blackwell screamed.

"What for? It's the god-awful truth," I argued. "If He can be a bird or the sky or a tree or a burning bush for crying out loud, why can't He be a woodchuck? Goddamn!" That was the blasphemy. And within thirty minutes I was on my way home—just because the God I saw was different from the one that everyone else saw. I thought the important thing was to see Him regardless of what He looked like.

You can never be sure of what people want, especially preachers.

The autumn following that very summer when I got tossed out of church camp, I made the mistake of allowing Roseabeth to talk me into attending a revival meeting in a tent the Baptists had set up in the church yard. I didn't even pretend to know why they went to such trouble when it would have been a far sight easier just to have the revival in the church instead of the tent right next to it. But Preacher said not to worry because God was in the tent same as He was in the church. That *did* worry me, but it was too late to get out of going because I'd already promised Roseabeth. And Roseabeth never forgot a promise, least of all one that someone else made to her.

So there I was one evening, sitting between Roseabeth and Ogden Burgatroid, singing *The Old Rugged Cross* at the top of my lungs. I didn't much cotton to all the words, but I sure got a kick out of singing those old hymns. Since Hilda wasn't on key it didn't matter much if anyone else was on or not, so I just belted those words right out like I meant it. Sometimes my singing got on Roseabeth's nerves because she had such a beautiful voice, but she was fairly patient about it. She wouldn't deny anybody the pleasure of singing, or trying to. Now and again she'd smile at me and shake her head or just squeeze my hand when Hilda and I got too far apart. The singing was okay, but the sermons sure got on my nerves, that and the saving of the lost souls.

The hymn died a horrible death as Hilda went into one of her coughing spasms and started hammering randomly on the organ keys like a kid beating on the old upright piano in the church basement. Rufus got to her in a hurry, whacked her a good one between the shoulder blades, and something yellow came flying out of her mouth. It was not a pretty sight. This time of year the air was full of cotton dust from the gins, and lots of people were wheezing when all they wanted to do was breathe. Hilda was okay, but *The Old Rugged Cross* was left hanging on a C note.

Preacher got up and said a little prayer—the third one of the evening. Then he read from the Book of Genesis, the first chapter, where it tells all about creation and everything. I already knew the story by heart so I couldn't keep my mind on it. What drew my attention was Preacher his own self.

I was comparing myself to him, more specifically, my hair to his because I knew he was a mature man, grown up, full maturated and all. Looking at him up there I decided if hair really did have anything to do with it—maturity—Preacher was about the maturest man to ever walk God's little acre, except for maybe Samson. Curly dark hair grew on him wherever there was a vacant spot, like weeds shooting up in a vacant lot. You know how grass and weeds sprout between cracks in the sidewalk? That's how Preacher's hair was; in addition to where he was supposed to have it, he had it everywhere else— sprouting out his nostrils, in his ears, and even on the palms of his hands. I took a quick glance at Roseabeth and found no family resemblance whatsoever. I reckon she took after her mother's side of the family, and I was glad of it.

Preacher's eyebrows ran in a straight uninterrupted line across the bridge of his nose and intersected on either side of his head with his thick sideburns. The hair on the sides of his head was slicked back behind his ear in a ducktail; I'm sure he had no idea how much he resembled Elvis in the hair department. And he was mature all right. And strong! I guess he'd given Samson a pretty good run for his money, even before Delilah got hold of him. Big men were just naturally strong, and Preacher was big, big enough to fill most any doorway. He towered over my six-foot plus frame and had shoulders half again as wide to go with a chest as big around as a rain barrel.

As you'd expect of a man of God, Preacher ordinarily carried a Bible with him but not your average-size Gideon edition. He carried something that resembled an unabridged dictionary, and from what I understood, had used it to hammer home particular points of doctrine into the heads of more than a few non-believers. That made me nervous, that and his shotgun.

More often than not he toted a shotgun; Preacher being president of the local chapter of the NRA could account for that, and the rumor was that on more than a single occasion Preacher had used what he termed, "a blast of the Lord's fiery breath," to convince skeptics of God's will. It was an attention-getter in any case, just like Roseabeth's elbow was in my side. After removing her elbow from my ribcage, she nodded to her dad and said, "Listen." I did. Just long enough to hear him say something about original sin and the nature of good and evil. It got me to thinking about good and evil, mostly evil because I found it to be the far more interesting of the two. And good seemed to get me in more trouble than evil did.

Take the tampons incident, for example: If I'd gone down to Yeager's to steal those tampons for the heck of it, I'd probably have gotten away with it. But, *noooo*! I had to go down there to do a good deed, and I got humiliated for it. Sometimes it made me wonder about the nature of good and evil. I thought about them and read a lot about them too. It puzzled me that "evil" spelled backwards was "live." Don't that beat all?

I glanced over at Ogden because Preacher had just said that he, Ogden, was evil, along with the rest of us sinners. I don't know, but Ogden didn't look all that bad to me. He may not have been a mental giant, but his heart was good as gold. And he'd do about anything for you. But that wasn't enough according to Preacher. He said we all had to be saved from our sins by Jesus, who, by then, had been dead for nearly 2000 years. I was like Huck Finn in the respect that I didn't put much stock in dead people. That being the case, I didn't see how Jesus could save anybody from anything, but Preacher just kept insisting He was the only one who *could* save you. And the first thing Jesus saved you from was original sin.

True, I was only a kid, but I'd done my share of sinning—some cussing, thinking bad stuff, blasphemy and heresy, knocking guys around under the backboards, a little fibbing now and again, but nothing that I consider to be particularly "original." They had all been done before. Then I recalled as Preacher continued preaching that *I* didn't commit the original sin at all; *Adam* did. And he'd been dead longer than Jesus! Adam didn't get the full blame for it anyhow because whoever wrote the story put most of the blame for it on poor

Eve, Adam's wife; at least I think she was his wife. I don't think they had a license, but they lived together there in the Garden of Eden, and he evidently knew her in what's referred to as the "Biblical sense." That is to say Adam had carnal knowledge of Eve. I knew what that was because I'd looked it up; but I just wasn't sure of how you went about getting it.

According to Preacher, Adam's original sin was that he ate from the Tree of Knowledge; I think maybe it was the tree of *carnal* knowledge, but Preacher didn't carry it that far. Now I'd learned from Doc that we need to get as much knowledge as humanly possible to better understand the world and our place in it. But God must have agreed with Mr. Pope's contention that "A little learning is a dang'rous thing." Otherwise, I don't see why getting knowledge of *any* kind would be such a sin. Preacher never made that clear, but he did establish a direct link between sex and religion in my own mind. Here's how: God created Adam and Eve and in the process, He created sex, but they weren't supposed to use sex or even know about it, or else He'd of told them about it in the first place.

So, instead of hearing about it from God, they found out about it secondhand from a snake that talked them into eating an apple from the Tree of Knowledge. Well that irritated God to high heaven, so He threw Adam and Eve out of the Garden and the snake along with them. Now God did mention to Adam that he wasn't supposed to eat from that tree, but if He *really* didn't want him to, telling him about it in the first place was the worst possible thing He could have done. You know how kids are, and it says right in the Bible that Adam and Eve were God's children. If God hadn't said anything about the tree in the first place, Adam probably never would have even noticed it was even there. If God knows *everything*, you'd have thought He'd have known *that!*

When Preacher finally finished preaching, we all stood up and started singing *Just As I Am*, and Preacher started yelling for all the sinners to come up front and get saved from their sins, the ones they'd done recently and the one Adam took care of years before. I had a powerful urge to leave, but Roseabeth had a firm grip on my arm.

Fanny Boltwood, God bless her, was up front before you could say, "Billy Graham." That's because she was a religious pluralist and a living example of a link between sex and religion. She attended every church for miles around and fully endorsed the teachings of everyone from Socrates to Sartre. She was the only Christian existentialist I'd ever met and a whole lot more. After living what Fanny described to Doc as a "life of disgusting pleasure" in Dallas for years on end, she reasoned that the only rational thing to do was to keep herself covered on the religious front. So she seldom missed the opportunity to be saved, blessed, healed, prayed for, or even Baptized. She was a Holy whore if ever there was one.

Before we finished the first verse of the hymn, Roseabeth had jumped up and joined Fanny at the makeshift altar—two orange crates covered with a yellowish-white tablecloth. I don't know if Roseabeth had been sinning or not—she sure hadn't been with me—or if she just had a natural inclination to jump to the front of *any* line. Some folks were like that. I figured Preacher made her go up there to encourage other people to come up too. If so, it worked, because when we started the second verse, Ogden poked me in the ribs and said, "Let's go."

"What?" I said.

"Let's go," Ogden insisted.

"Up there?" Ogden nodded. "What for?"

"To be saved from our sins," Ogden said.

"I ain't done nothin' that serious," I told him.

"Then you gotta be saved from original sin."

"Jesus already paid our dues for that one," I argued.

He looked at me and said, "Well, Roseabeth is up there."

"That's *her* business," I told him. "Besides, if I go up there too, Preacher's gonna wonder what we been doin' that we need to git saved from."

"He won't think that, Ezra. Now come on. Even if you ain't done nothin' yet, you need to git saved in case you do."

"You mean you can git saved ahead to time?"

Ogden blinked and nodded. "You sure can. It's like money in the bank—a savings account."

By that time the sinners were pretty well filling up the front of the tent, crowding around the altar and the edge of the freshly dug Baptismal pool. The singing was getting kind of out of hand, and people were crying some and every now and again somebody would all of sudden shout, "Amen," and it would about scare the pants right off you. I never thought so many people would be so willing to own up to their sins right out in public and all. There was something downright indecent about it, like airing your dirty laundry on Main Street. I was feeling real uncomfortable because people kept looking back over their shoulders at me. I couldn't help but wonder about all the awful things they'd been up to and why they kept staring at me when I'd hardly done anything at all. It made me itch all over and put me in a pretty good sweat, so I decided to light out before things got any worse. Just humming the hymn a little, I started to sidle out of the makeshift pew towards the center aisle. I made it and had just started to turn when a hand clamped down on my forearm like a steel trap.

Rufus Ruffin had hold of me, and before I could protest I was swept forward in a sea of pitiful sinners seeking salvation. Suddenly the singing stopped, although Hilda played on, lost in a self-induced reverie, and Preacher kind of lost control. "Lord! Lord," he shouted, "Glory be on high. Look what the Lord hath done delivered unto us this night."

"Rufus Ruffin done it," I said.

"Glory be!" Preacher raved on like Buddy Holly. "From the house of heartless heathens and sinners doth this boy come. Come—"

"Wait a minute," I protested, "heartless heathens!"

"Come to the altar of the Lord to confess his manifold sins and be saved by the precious blood of Jesus Christ."

"I don't want any blood shed on my account," I assured him.

Preacher grabbed me and spoke right in my face. "Have you been Baptized, Son?"

"No," I said, "but I been circumcised."

"That don't count for nothin' here," Preacher said. "Do you know," he went on, "that if you was to die at this moment you'd go straight to hell?"

"Without passin' go," I said.

"This is no jokin' matter, son. I'm talkin' hell-fire and eternal sufferin'. I'm talking damnation for ever and ever; I'm talkin' unendurable and unending pain."

"I ain't done nothin' to deserve that," I said.

Preacher pressed a little closer. "You don't have to do nothin', Boy. You can go to hell for what you don't do jist the same as for what you do do."

"Do do," I said, hoping to inject a little levity into the situation.

"Dammit, Boy, I aim to save you, but you're makin' it right difficult."

"Then lemme go. I'll go do somethin' I need to be saved for and come back another time. And if I don't git saved in time, 'least I won't be goin' to hell for nothin'."

"Ezra, you don't havta go to hell," Roseabeth said.

"I think I might prefer it!" I countered.

"No, no!" Preacher yelled. "You must be born again!"

"Again? Why I'm still tryin' to figure out what happened the first time. Now lemme go!" I struggled to free myself from the vise grip of salvation. Then I saw Fanny moving at me with outstretched arms.

"You don't have to drink and smoke to have a good time, Ezra," she said in her quiet sweet voice.

"I don't drink or smoke, Fanny," I insisted.

Then Roseabeth yelled, "Ezra, we're gonna save you whether you like it or not!"

"Like hell," I said just as I managed to break free. I hurdled a pew and ran broken-field fashion through a maze of domestic missionaries and sinners. If they were going to save me, they were going to have to catch me first.

"Do you accept Jesus Christ as your personal savior?" I heard Preacher yell as I hit the rear flap of the tent and took in a breath of fresh air. "Think of your soul, boy. You'll roast in everlastin' hell if you don't follow Jesus. It's evil not to follow the path of the Lord." I just kept running, following the path the city fathers had laid out parallel to Main Street years before.

About three blocks from the church I slowed to a walk, caught my breath and glanced up at the twinkling stars through the half-barren branches of the trees. And I brooded on the idea of being evil. Maybe I was; I didn't know for sure. I might not have minded following Jesus if I'd seen him in the tent, but from what I could tell He was nowhere in sight. And a lot of people had gotten on the wrong track entirely because they *thought* they were following Jesus when they were following a misguided disciple instead. I knew that was so because I had studied all about the Crusades of the eleventh and twelfth centuries with Doc. *That's* where the root of all evil was, not in the Tree of Knowledge or Adam's original sin.

This is what happened: The *Christians* in Rome sent out so called "armed pilgrimages" or Holy armies to recover the lost Holy Land from the Moslems. And they did a slam bang job of it too, but at the expense of thousands and thousands of innocent people—burning their homes, killing women and children, plundering entire cities, and slaughtering folks just because they had a different point of view on matters of a theological nature. It was pretty awful, and a perfect example of what Doc told me was the worst kind of evil—evil done in the name of good.

During the fourth crusade, the "pilgrims" got carried away with their progress and ransacked Constantinople which was a Christian city, and all the while they waved the cross of Christ above the burned out ruins. Frankly, I don't think Jesus would have had anything to do with the crusades, his being the Prince of Peace and all. Jesus never would have said, "Go ye therefore and loot and kill and burn and plunder in the name of the Holy Father." No sir, not Jesus. He was dead set against violence; made him sick to his stomach and gave him an ache in his heart.

Having brooded on it for a while the conclusion I came to was this: If *Christians* were doing all those awful things to people, why Lucifer had to think up all kinds of *new* horrors just to stay ahead of the Christians. That's why I thought the crusades were the root of all evil. Once the devil realized what he was up against he had to work overtime to outdo the Christians. Doc loved my theory; he told me that although it may not have been empirically verifiable, it was real creative and a sure sign that I was an original thinker. And if I could come up with a theory like that when I was only a teenager, it was almost frightening what I might do by and by. I think he meant it as a compliment.

It's hard to believe after what happened, but I went back to the Baptist revival the next night, not so much at Roseabeth's insistence as to satisfy my own curiosity. Preacher was scheduled to talk about the origin of the universe and of life; both were topics that I had a keen interest in, so I went, and regretted it.

Ogden, Roseabeth and I sat in the back row of pews near an exit, and we didn't even go in until the service had started. They were half-way through singing, *Washed In The Blood Of The Lamb*, when we slipped in, pretty much unnoticed. After that hymn Preacher made a few remarks, said a short prayer, and then we sang, *This Is My Father's World.* Then Preacher prayed some more, this time for all the sinners in town, which, from what I could gather, included about everybody who wasn't present. After passing the collection plate, another hymn and one more prayer, Preacher finally got down to preaching in earnest.

The real meat of the message was lifted from the Book of Genesis, chapter one of the King James Version of the Holy Bible. There are a number of other versions or translations of the Bible he could have read from because the thing kept changing, not as fast as the Sears catalog, but just fast enough to keep up with the times. I watched Preacher closely as he scratched at some itch under his arm and read passionately if not eloquently.

> "And God made the beast of the earth after his kind and cattle after their kind, and everything that creepeth up the earth after his kind: and God saw that it was good.
>
> And God said, Let us make man in our image, after our likeness; and let them have dominion over the fish of the sea, and over the fowl of the air, and over the cattle, and over all the earth, and every creeping thing that creepeth upon the earth.
>
> So God created man in his own image, in the image of God created he him; male and female created he them.
>
> And God saw everything that he had made, and, behold it was very good. And the evening and the morning were the sixth day."

After he finished reading he waited until people started to get kind of jittery in the silence, then with one of his huge hands he slammed the Bible shut. "So let it be did, so let it be done. May the Lord add His blessin' to the reading of His Holy word." Preacher looked out over this congregation then, eyeing us inch by inch, row by row and scratched at that itch under his arm again. "Brethren, I wish to speak to you this night, in God's Holy name, about His highest creation, that of *Man* his own self."

Roseabeth poked me and said, "He means women too."

"He said, 'Man'," I told her.

"Well, you're supposed to understand that women are included," she argued.

"Then what'd you tell me for?"

"'Cause men don't understand *anything*."

"Well I understand that!"

"Shhh," she cautioned because Preacher was looking at us.

"According to God's Holy word, from whence I jist read the preceding passage verbatim, God created man on the sixth day of creation," Preacher said thoughtfully. "The sixth *day*." And we know from our earlier reading that God created light and darkness, this is to say day and night, on the first day."

Ogden leaned over to me and asked, "How'd He know how long to make them?"

"Good boy, Ogden," I said.

Then Roseabeth said, "He jist *knew*, Ogden, 'cause He was God."

"How'd He know *that?*" Ogden asked.

"Adam told him," I said.

"Oh, Ezra, will you jist shut-up before Daddy makes us move up front!"

Preacher went on as if he had the final say. "We can ascertain from these indisputable facts that by the sixth day, the solar system, indeed the entire universe as we know it, was in *full* existence. Now what does that mean, Brethren?" Nobody ventured a guess. "It means simply that when God created man on the sixth *day*, He created him on the sixth day, one twenty-four hour period, one revolution of the earth on its axis, a day jist like yesterday, today and tomorrow. It does not suggest a period of time of any longer duration than 24 hours. So let it be did, so let it be done."

Preacher paused because he was preaching hard, working up a good lather that made rings around the armpits of his black coat and trickled across his brow into his dark eyes. He pulled out a yellow handkerchief and mopped his brow. "The days of God, then, were *not* periods of time, some of them covering *millions* of years as some so-called scientists would have us believe. And, more importantly, it means that man, being that he was created in God's own likeness, came out lookin' like a man, *not* like a monkey, as so eminent a atheist as Mr. Charles Darwin would have us believe."

"Darwin wasn't an atheist," I told Roseabeth.

"Well, we might jist as well of been."

"Shhh," somebody cautioned so I didn't debate the point even though I could prove that Darwin was closer to a preacher than an atheist.

Preacher paused and emptied the contents of a pitcher of water down his throat. Then he wiped his mouth on his sleeve and went on but not before scratching his underarm for the third time. "Let me remind you at this point that I am a theist, a believer not a atheist, a non-believer." There seemed to be some confusion on that point, but Preacher forged ahead bravely, gripping the pulpit with his huge hands and leaning so far forward that he was practically dangling over the unfortunate few in the front pew. "Now I know that you are all fully aware that there is a certain 'scientific' faction that exists, even in this enlightened community, that would have the audacity to suggest that man was derived from monkeys through that hog-wash of a theory called evolution. Brethren, nowhere, *nowhere*, in the Holy Scriptures will you find the word or any reference to the word or process of evolution. Evolution does not exist in God's vocabulary. The whole thing was *made up*, came right out of a man's head without a shred of Biblical evidence to support it. Let me tell you brothers and sisters, you righteous believers who comprise the Holy Many, that there are present in our society, yes, even in our own precious community, a decadent few who fully endorse Mr. Darwin's rubbish and *want to teach it in our schools!* I say never. *Never!* And let me assure you that they will pay the *full* price for their folly; they will burn in hell and see God make *monkeys* of *them* in His own good time. There is no room for the teaching of *'eviloution'* in our schools."

"Amen," Rufus Ruffin shouted, "let them burn!"

"Thank you for that, Brother Ruffin." Before he continued, Preacher reached under his coat and started scratching his chest like maybe the itch was spreading now. "It isn't enough that this *foreigner* said we came from monkeys, but he also said that the monkeys came from the tiniest creatures in the ocean, tiny animals you can't even see, and that *they* came from the slime and muck from the swamps of a prehistoric wasteland. Now isn't that the most ridiculous thing you've ever heard?"

"Amen!" a true believer shouted.

"Thank you for that Brother." Preacher wiped his brow. "The esteemed Mr. Darwin also maintains that it took not one day for God to create man, as *God* says in His Holy Scripture, but millions of years. *Millions!* Now Mr. Darwin could have saved himself considerable trouble and a lifetime of fruitless labor if he had simply picked up his Bible, read it and accepted God's word like the Holy Many instead of wasting his life lookin' for a scientific explanation for creation that would do nothin' but satisfy the minds of a decadent few and confuse might near everybody else! I contend, Brethren, that we have too many scientists in the modern world and not enough good old fashion faith!"

"Amen," Rufus shouted again. "Amen brother!"

"I appreciate that Brother Ruffin," Preacher said a little impatiently. Then, "I contend that we have too many thinkers and not enough believers, too many doubts and not enough blind faith! Mind you brothers and sisters, I'm talkin' faith in God, not faith in science. Faith in the Word, not in technology. There isn't a thing in this world that science can do for you that God can't, and do a better job of it—from washing your clothes to healing what ails you. Let me assure you brothers and sisters . . . "

What he said got me to thinking; I knew I wasn't supposed to, but I couldn't help it. Maybe God *could* do the wash and heal your ills, but whether He *would* or not was a different matter entirely as far as I could tell. I waited all day once tryin' to get Him to dig some post holes for me, but He never did. And *I* got the blame for it.

And as for healing your ills? Why Nellie Bostock was killed while trying to get God, with the help of the Reverend Willie Nation, to heal her arthritis. Here's what happened: Nellie was trying to do something about her corns her own self by soaking her feet in a washtub of Epsom salts; at the same time she was trying to get the Lord and Reverend Nation to do something about her arthritis by watching the latter on television. Well, when Willie Nation started praying and everything and having people reach out and touch their televisions—that came right after he had them reach for their wallets—Nellie must have plum forgotten herself and grabbed hold of the rabbit ears without taking her feet out of the tub of Epsom salts. Pow! Burnt to a crisp on the spot! That put an end to her suffering all right, and some people said it lifted a terrible burden from the family. But when it came to life and death, I'd pick life every time, even with all the suffering thrown in.

The very next week Silas shot Willie Nation right in our own living room. Shot him with Hebrew Yuckum's shotgun. Sunday morning it was, right after Doc's irregular service, and I'd switched on the television to see if Willie Nation, who led many of the Holy by the same name, had anything to say about Nellie's misfortune. I figured he knew about it because he said he talked to God every day, and I knew God knew about it because He knew everything. But if Willie Nation did know about it, he didn't let on; instead he told about this dream he'd had, a wonderful dream he said it was. In the dream he was wandering around in the wilderness, the desert I think it was, trying to raise funds so he could spread the word of God to people in the world who never heard of him (I don't know if he met God or himself). Anyway, there were no people in the wilderness, so he wasn't having much luck raising money, and he was kind of down in the mouth and all. After wandering about in the desert for 40 days, he looked up in the sky and saw this cloud, and you know how you can make out shapes and images from clouds? Well, this cloud looked like a giant hand, and I don't reckon I have to tell you whose hand it looked like.

As Willie Nation stood there in the wilderness the hand came down to earth and started scribbling something in the sand, and it took a long time to trace something out and whatever it was went on for miles and miles. Willie Nation couldn't make out what it was the hand had traced because it was way too big for him to see. So he had to follow the outline of the thing by walking all the way around it, and then he had to go inside the border and see what was inside. It took him another 40 days and 40 nights to walk around the thing, and when he finished he was sore as hell, but he finally got it figured out. And he was mighty happy he'd gone to the trouble. What it was the hand of God had done was to draw a giant bank draft in the sand and write Willie Nation a check for ten million dollars. Like I said, Willie was *real* happy, at first; then he realized he didn't know how in the world he would ever get the check to the bank or how the banker would be able to make out that God His Own self had signed the thing. Then all of a sudden the check began to shake and all like there was an earthquake. The check began to fall apart, but what was actually happening, according to Willie, was that each grain of sand that made up the check was turning into the individual hand of a true believer and every one of them was writing a check to Reverend Willie Nation so he could do God's work more efficiently—not to mention a lot more comfortably. Willie Nation was so happy that he could hardly see straight because that little bit of God that was in every Christian soul was responding to his plea for funds to help save the sinners in the world. And since there were so many of them—sinners—it would take the whole ten million to save them from Lucifer's grasp.

About then Doc and Silas came in and wanted to know what in heaven's name I was doing watching television on such a lovely morning when I ought to have been out getting some exercise or at least improving my mind if I was staying in. I told them I wasn't exactly sure why I was watching the thing because I was half bored with it, but I couldn't seem to muster up the initiative to get up and walk away from it either. They huddled in the corner for a minute, then Silas hurried off in a sweat. Before long he was back with Hebrew's shotgun. Then before Willie Nation could collect another penny from one of the Holy Many, Silas Willie Nation have it right between the eyes.

That was the end of Willie as far as I was concerned, and the end of my television viewing for good because Silas never replaced the thing. Silas and Doc carried it out back; it was still smoking and some sparks were flying out of it now and again, but by the time they got it to the trash barrel it was dead. That was the only act of violence I ever saw Doc involved in. When the thing hit the bottom of the trash barrel, I heard Doc say: "Amen."

Roseabeth and Ogden getting up on either side of me shook me out of my ruminations. When they started singing *Just As I Am* I decided to do everybody a favor and leave. The singing stopped after the first verse so Preacher could do some praying, and when everybody was supposed to have their eyes closed I made my move. As I slid through the canvas flap I heard Preacher raise his voice and say, "You can't run from God, Son." But I kept going anyhow because I wasn't running from God. God was okay, a little reckless now and then, true, but otherwise okay. It was His *servants* that made me nervous because you could never be sure of what they were up to; all too often, it was no good.

That's why I decided that I wouldn't mind too much going to hell for not being saved; there couldn't be much more suffering going on there than right here in the territories. And in hell I'd know what I was up against: evil people doing evil things all the time. In the territories you had evil people doing good things some of the time and good people doing evil things some of the time. But you seldom had good people doing good things all of the time. That's why growing up in the territories was so confusing most of the time.

Doc was a good example. Preacher said that Doc was an evil man, but as far as I could tell, Doc did nothing but good most of the time. And Nathan Burton, a deacon at the Free Will Baptist Church, shot Gil Hilbert dead over an argument in a card game. And poor Alice Darling drowned her baby in a creek because she thought God could take better care of him that she could. That was awful. And there was a separate church on the edge of town for Indians because nobody but Doc wanted them in the churches in town. And from what I could tell the few Negroes in the county weren't welcome in *any* organized church. Doc's services were far from organized, but anybody was welcome so long as you brought an open mind and open heart. But other churches weren't like that. Mansfield even had a town ordinance that made it illegal for Negroes to be in town after dark. Now what kind of law was that? Not one of God's! Civilization sure did funny things to folks, that and religion.

That's one thing I liked about the Catholics, *Roman* Catholics they were called and came from the same place as Roman candles, I suppose. They'd take about anybody into their fold; it didn't matter how bad off you were or what color skin you had or how far you may have "strayed from the flock" as Preacher would put it. Their door was always open, and I admired them for that, although I didn't much cotton to everything else they stood for. But then I'd had just an elementary introduction into the faith.

Tilden Warner and his family were the only Roman Catholics in Mansfield that I knew of; even so, the twelve of them had the religious liberals outnumbered three to one. Tilden Jr. was a classmate of mine, and we hung around together some because of a mutual interest in athletics and a natural curiosity about one another's metaphysics. Tilden, upon my advice, had struggled through *The Great Chain of Being*, and hadn't understood it any better than I had. I did feel good about that.

One thing Tilden told me about Catholics was that they didn't believe in birth control; I didn't know what that had to do with religion, but it was a sure sign that sex and religion were somehow directly linked to one another. Anyway, from what I could tell from my frequent visits to the Warner's home north of town, Catholics didn't, evidently, believe much in controlling kids *after* their birth either. The idea was that the older kids, say from Tilden Jr. on down to Tammy, who was ten, were supposed to exert some kind of favorable influence and control over their younger siblings while poor Mrs. Warner hammered out her eleventh child in seventeen years of marriage. I don't know, and it was none of my business, but it looked to me like they already had more kids than they could ever possibly use. What they needed was more land; what God gave them instead was another mouth to feed.

Tilden's father was a terrific farmer, one of the best in the county, but you could only do so much with a quarter section of land, even irrigated bottom land. Food they always managed to have enough of because Mrs. Warner was as good a gardener as her husband was a farmer, and they had enough livestock to keep all their bellies full through even the cruelest winter. But I never saw one member of that family with anything new—clothes, toys, furniture, farm machinery, nothing—not even at Christmas time.

You could be sure of three things about everything the Warner's owned: It was come by honestly; it had had a previous owner, and it would be used until it literally fell apart. Like my mom, they never wasted anything and, according to Doc, "refused to make the country great by supporting planned obsolescence."

I only attended church—what they called "Mass"—once with Tilden, but once was more than enough. The church was in the next town over from Mansfield, and the preacher was from Poland. Poland! I never had the chance to find out how he ended up in Yellville, but I figured it had something to do with the war, most everything did, including my own existence. Anyway, one day in the early spring when I was in my middle teens, I piled into the back of the Warner family pickup with the rest of the brood and off we rambled towards Yellville and the only Catholic Church for miles around. Saint Michael's it was called, and I wondered why.

"Tilden?"

"What?" he shouted over the rushing wind and chatter of seven siblings.

"Why do they call your church Saint Michael's?"

"What?"

"Your church! Why is it called Saint Michael's?"

"Oh, 'cause—Jeremy, sit down! Hush up, Katie! What'd you say, Ezra?"

"The church?"

"Oh, yeah," he yelled, nodding. "'Cause—'cause that's its name. I dunno, Ezra."

"Well, *who* was Saint Michael?"

"I don't remember, jist some Saint. We got a lot of them. Father Joe could tell you."

"Who?"

"Don't hit him, Jan!" He looked back to me. "Father Joe, the priest."

"The minister," I said, "like Preacher Bascom?"

"Yeah, sorta, but without the shotgun."

"Is he a saint?"

"No, no. Saints are different—Jan, put that book down!"

"How do you git to be a saint?" I asked and took the book away from Jan. She looked at me and started crying so I gave it back to her. "Now don't hit your brother. Promise."

"I promise," she said. Then she whacked him a good one.

"Gimme that thing," Tilden said and grabbed the book. Jan immediately started crying again; Tilden sighed and gave it back to her. "Books are for readin', sister."

"Okay," Jan whimpered and opened the book.

"What have you got to do to be a saint, Tilden?"

He thought for a moment and then said, "Well, you gotta do somethin' *real* good."

"Is your mom one?"

"Naw, she's jist my mom. To be a saint you gotta do something *special*, like—like havin' a vision or starvin' or holdin' up in a monastery for about a thousand years."

"What good is that?"

"Holdin' up in a monastery?" I nodded. "Well, I reckon it does a whole world of good."

"Tilden," Jan cried, "I gotta go."

"You're gonna havta wait, honey." He banged on the window and pointed to Jan; Mrs. Warner glanced back, said something to Tilden's dad, then I felt the truck surge forward.

"I can't wait," Jan said again.

"You're gonna havta. Daddy's hurryin'; now hang on," Tilden told her and looked back at me.

"What good does holdin' up in a monastery do, Tilden?" I asked again.

"Well, it does a lot of good because the food the saint ought to be eatin' while he's up there starvin' in the monastery can be given to the poor," Tilden said.

"Yeah, but if he's holed up there in the monastery havin' visions and starvin', how's he to know that some fat rich oil man doesn't git the food?" I thought it was a logical question.

"'Cause he knows God will look out after the poor. I mean if he's up there starvin' so he can be a saint, the least you can expect God to do is watch after the food for the poor." He glanced around and then added: "Besides, a fat rich oil man wouldn't touch the kinda food the poor havta eat."

"Oh," I said and swayed with the truck as we rounded a curve. Then I brooded on this saint business. I couldn't see much sense in becoming one, not that I had a shot at it anyhow. Seemed to me like they ought to do something more useful than to starve and have visions. Seemed like maybe one of them ought to come up with a scheme where the rich weren't so rich and the poor weren't so poor, where everybody on both sides had enough and where nobody got all fat and out of shape and nobody went hungry either. Maybe that's what Saint Michael was working on when he died of starvation; I didn't know. I did know one thing though: if he was going to have a vision it was a good thing he went up in the hills to have it because if you have them in public, they lock you up, saint or sinner.

Saint Michael's was located on a small rise south of Yellville among a grove of scrub oaks and stunted pines. A small red brick structure it was, made from a typical blend of Oklahoma red mud and wheat straw. The people had designed and built it themselves in the finest Cherokee Gothic tradition, and they were awfully proud of it you could tell. The parishioners as they were called were a small but growing band of Polish farmers with large families, elderly women, former Protestants, folks from back east that started west and didn't get any further than the territories, Fanny Boltwood and a smattering of Kiowas who weren't well received in the churches of Preacher's Holy Many.

Inside, the place was as fascinating as it was bewildering. I thought it was a little heavy in the use of stained glass, and, it was on the whole, more decorative than your average Baptist meeting house. Other than on Doc's 79th birthday I'd never seen so many candles in one place before. Little kids were scurrying about lighting them, and every now and again someone would chime a tiny bell; up front there was this huge cross with Jesus nailed right on it, looking down at you ever so sorrowfully. It was so real it made you want to cry. You could see where the spikes had been driven into his hands and feet, and he had this open wound on his side where they'd speared him in the liver. He looked ever so sad and hurt, but still full of compassion.

"Who's that?" I whispered to Tilden and pointed to a statue not far from the one of Jesus.

"The Holy Mother," he told me.

"The *what?*"

"It's *Mary,* the mother of Jesus. Who'd you think it was?"

"I didn't have any idea," I told him. "I never saw a picture of her or anythin'."

"Well, nobody has!"

"Then how do you know that's who it is?"

"Ezra, *everybody* knows who it is; you can tell by the way she's lookin'. You ever seen anybody else look like that?"

I studied the statue for a while. She was mighty comely, and she did have this look of peace and love about her, but I'd seen pretty much the same look on the face of Minabell Perkins when she rocked her baby to sleep, humming a lullaby. But I didn't argue because I could see that Tilden had it set in his head that the statue was of Mary.

I looked around some more, taking it all in because we'd arrived early and people were still coming in and aside from the candle lighting and bell ringing not a whole lot was happening of an official nature. I noticed all the women in the place had hats on or else they had a little doily on their head. I thought that was curious because Doc had told me that in Jewish meeting places the *men* kept their heads covered. It had *something* to do with maturity, I figured. I guess there must have been some freelance praying going on because I heard some whispering here and there. Over to the side of the pews were a couple of little cubicles about the size of a telephone booth that looked kind of interesting. There was a little bench in each one so you could sit down, and a curtain could be drawn across the front so nobody could see who was in there. Of course everybody could see you *going* in there. I turned to inquire about them, but Tilden was way ahead of me.

"Those are confession booths, Ezra."

"What?"

"Confession boots," he repeated, a little impatiently.

"That's what I thought you said, 'confession booths'."

"That's what I did say." I looked at him and he explained it to me: "That's where we confess all our sins."

"Oh," I said and nodded. It sure beat the devil out of getting up front of everybody and doing like the Baptists. But I wasn't entirely sold on the idea. "Tilden?"

"What now?"

"Why don't you confess your sins right here in the pew?"

"'Cause the priest couldn't hear you."

"*Couldn't* hear you! You mean you *want* him to?" This was getting more ridiculous all the time.

"Ezra, he *has* to hear you," Tilden insisted.

"How come?"

"So he can tell God so he can forgive you."

"So *who* can forgive you?" I asked.

"God!"

"Then why don't you jist tell God in the first place?"

"This way you don't havta tell God; the priest tells God for you," he explained.

"Wait a minute!" He looked at me and shook his head. "Doesn't God know 'bout your sins anyhow? Doesn't God know everythin'?"

"Well, yeah, I reckon He does, His bein' omniscient and all."

"Then He doesn't need the priest to tell him, now does He?"

"Ezra, you are so bull-headed that you can't understand anything. The priest still has to know your sins so he can tell you how much penitence to do."

I just stared at him and said, "I'm not even gonna ask you 'bout that?"

"It's real simple; it's what you do to be forgiven for your sins. Like how many Hail Marys or Rosaries you havta say. Say you take God's name in vain: you tell the priest in confession that you done it, and he tells you to say—maybe 10 Hail Marys. Then you say them and you're forgiven. That's all there is to it."

"Then everythin' is okay?" I asked.

"Yeah, but you're not supposed to do it again."

"And if you do?"

"You go back to confession."

"And say more Hail Marys?"

"Now you got it," Tilden said seeming somewhat relieved. But not for long.

"Well if you know one blasphemy is worth 10 Hail Marys," I said, "why don't you jist say them yourself and not bother the priest?"

Tilden looked at me and shook his head. Then he plodded ahead: "'Cause *that* would be a sin, and you'd end up havin' to say a Hail Mary for sayin' unauthorized Hail Marys. And you wouldn't be able to take communion either."

"Why not?"

"'Cause you havta be in a state of grace to take communion: All your sins havta be confessed, forgiven and penitence done," Tilden said emphatically.

"Whew! I don't see how you keep it all straight." I shifted around in my seat to get more comfortable and asked, "Tilden ain't it . . . embarrassin'?"

"Naw, he can't see who it is."

"Tilden?"

"*What*, Ezra?"

"Do you—tell him *everythin'*?" He knew what I was talking about.

He hesitated then said, "*Almost* everythin'. Just as I suspected. "Now be quiet, the service is startin'."

I sat there in this strange place and started taking it all in. Things began happening awfully fast and I grew more and more fascinated. One of Tilden's younger brothers, Jeremy, had somehow got hold of this fancy white smock and was coming down the aisle with a torch of some kind. At the altar in front of the crucified Jesus he lit the remaining unlighted candles then went out through a side door. Father Joe came out of nowhere wearing about the fanciest outfit I'd ever seen in the territories; white it was for the most part, silk, with some gold and purple ribbing. On his head was a tall crown or something that sort of squashed his neck down, but that didn't keep him from tinkling a little bell just when you'd least expect it.

People were standing, then sitting, then kneeling, then standing again and crossing themselves, maybe double-crossing themselves. I don't know. I tried to keep up but was always about one position behind everybody else. Tilden finally told me just to sit still, and I was glad of it. All of a sudden the priest started sort of singing, but there was no piano or organ; that didn't much matter though because what he was singing didn't have much of a tune, and, to tell you the truth, I couldn't understand a word of it. I decided he was talking in Polish because that was where he came from and because lots of the farmers there were Polish and still talked it sometimes. You could hear them in the street, but you'd never know what they were talking about.

Father Joe went on, sometimes talking, sometimes singing and sometimes sort of moaning; it was as interesting as
it was confusing. Pretty soon Jeremy showed up again with a
pretty silver cup that you'd have thought belonged to a king
or something, and I thought we were going to have some
refreshments. But we didn't. The priest took the cup and
poured something in it, but it wasn't enough to go around;
then he started singing and talking again, sometimes to
the cup and sometimes just off into space. He finally took
a sip from the cup and decided to share it with the parishioners. He also took a box of tiny wafers that Jeremy had
under his smock and started talking to them. They looked
like fish food to me, but he ate one anyhow. Then he held
out his arms, inviting people to come up and share some
with him. Then I knew this was just the Catholic version of
communion. The Baptist did it too, but the ceremony there
was a lot less elaborate and considerably more emotional.
And Baptist, I think had more money, because everybody
got their own little cup. The Catholics all used the same
one, and I was sure they were all going to come down with
something even though Father Joe wiped the cup with a rag
every now and again. Everybody that went up there looked
a lot happier when the whole thing was over with. Tilden
came back to our pew and said, "Ez, my boy, my slate is
clean."

I figured my slate would remain forever tainted because I
didn't much cotton to the idea of eating flesh and drinking
blood either there with the Catholics or in Mansfield with the
Baptists. I found the whole idea of it disgusting, pagan even.
Mr. Melville, I knew, had consumed some prime rib of ques-
tionable origin when he was holed up with those cannibals

in the South Seas, but that wasn't his fault. Those people didn't know any better. Since we were supposed to be *civilized*, I didn't see any point in letting on you were eating flesh and drinking blood, I don't care who it came from. Besides, Mrs. Warner had also fed us a huge breakfast.

After the Mass we were filing out past the priest when Tilden asked, "How'd you like it, Ezra?"

"I couldn't understand a word of it," I told him.

"Well, of course you couldn't."

I scratched my head and said, "Do *you* understand Polish, Tilden?"

"That wasn't Polish he was talkin', Ezra. It was Latin."

"Oh, Latin," I said and nodded. "Do you understand Latin then?"

"No, I don't understand Latin either," Tilden said. "Father Joe is probably the only one in the entire church who knows Latin. It's one of them dead languages."

I looked back over my shoulder at Father Joe. I don't know why he conducted the service in Latin. If he'd spoken in Polish about half the people there would have understood him. If he'd have spoken English, *everybody* would have understood him, but he chose to speak in a dead language that *nobody* understood. Religion was a strange thing all right, just like sex. Before we got to the truck I grabbed Tilden by the arm. "Tilden," I said, "if you don't know what the priest is saying, how do you know whether you agree with him or not?"

"Ezra, I agree with him 'cause he's the priest."

"Even though you don't know what he's sayin'?"

"He wouldn't say anythin' I wouldn't agree with. And what he says is what I'm supposed to believe, so I do. Don't you agree with everythin' Preacher Bascom tells you?"

"I most certain *don't!* Stuff he says is downright impossible."

"I guess that's the difference between a preacher and a priest. A priest knows better than to try to get people to believe the impossible."

I saw it wasn't any use arguing. Tilden had it all set in his mind the way things were, and I couldn't see how debating the point would do any more good than to argue with a Baptist. The thing that bothered me was this: I didn't understand how the Catholics and the Baptists could *both* be right.

7

AMAZING GRACE

The disaster was the second most embarrassing thing that ever happened to me. At least it's the second most embarrassing thing that I remember happening to me. It's entirely possible that any number of other things have happened that would fall somewhere between the incident and the catastrophe and that I quite naturally have allowed to slip from my mind. Of course I tried to forget the disaster too, but that was impossible.

If you ever want to remember something just try to forget it, and if you want to forget something just try to remember what it is you're trying to forget. I forget who told me to remember that. No matter. Because the disaster was something I couldn't forget even when I tried to remember it. And other people, of course, were always kind enough and more than willing to remind me of it. People are like that; they refuse to let you forget what you're trying not to remember, especially when it's something as humiliating as the disaster.

The disaster wasn't my fault, really; you have to understand that. It was an accident or maybe a Divine Providence. It was the fault of everybody who was involved in it because it was in the final analysis a misunderstanding, a misunderstanding of some magnitude. And I had the extreme misfortune of being who it was who was being misunderstood.

It happened in the gymnasium, the gymnasium that we built at Mansfield High School in my sophomore year and which was the showcase of the county with its padded bleachers and glass backboards. Officials and groups of people from other towns and schools were forever coming by to tour the facility. You never knew who was going to show up. Or when. Those were contributing factors to the disaster, that and the well-meaning exuberance and reckless abandon of a 16-year-old man-child.

The facility included new locker rooms and showers, and naturally—to save money on plumbing—the boys and girls dressing rooms were right next to one another. Well, I probably don't have to tell you that an arrangement such as that gave many a bored adolescent male a whole new purpose in life. A hole simply *had* to be drilled through that wall so we could have a clean shot at what went on or, more specifically, what came off in the room to which we were soon to have a view. You'd have thought the school was a prison by the way guys were smuggling in files, hammers, chisels and drills to burrow through the concrete blocks separating us from the girls next door. I had a good notion of what was going on, but didn't pay it much mind until it was too late. Much too late.

After regular basketball practice one winter afternoon I was still on the floor by my own self working on my shooting when the ball took a strange bounce off the rim and careened towards the entrance to the girls locker room situated beneath the seats on the north side of the gym. I took out after it, but before I could grab it, the ball tumbled down the steps, hit the wall and bounced right into the dressing room proper. Was this a stroke of luck or what, I thought? It was. But not the kind you hanker for under ordinary circumstances. Or any other circumstances I was to learn later. I didn't reckon anybody was in there, but I quite naturally hesitated before I—how shall I put it?—leaped into the breach.

"Hey, hello, anybody in there? If you're in there throw me my balls—*ball*. Hello." Satisfied that the room was unoccupied by any member of the fairer sex, I went in after my ball. Easing down the steps gingerly, I finally reached the door, looked in, then dared to step boldly where no man had dared to step before. I saw the ball immediately, resting against the far wall; it was kind of hard to miss actually, but to tell you the truth I was in no hurry to leave. I was kind of taken with the place, having never been in a girls' locker room before. Physically, it wasn't all that much different from the boys— benches along the wall, hooks screwed into two-by-fours over the benches, a couple of little shower stalls instead of one big open shower and so on—but what had me fascinated was that I wasn't supposed to be in there at all, and that I'd come by the situation honestly rather than by design. It was like eating the forbidden fruit, but by *accident.* Without having to feel guilty about it you could enjoy it all the more. Like Adam was having a grand old time eating that apple Eve gave him until he got the bad news about where the apple had come from.

There were some shorts—red, size 10—dangling from a hook; some bobby pins were scattered across the floor, a wet towel hung here and there, some kind of a contraption I couldn't make heads or tails out of was suspended from a nail, and against the rear wall, just above where my ball was, there was a—a brassiere I guess you'd call it. First one I'd ever seen close up, except for Mariko's, but you can't count your mom's stuff like that. Pink it was, and on the frilly side with little satin bows and a thin fishnet kind of stuff around the top edge. It was just about the most fascinating thing I'd ever laid eyes or anything else on. I had a powerful urge to reach out and touch it, just for a second, and I could almost feel my hands involuntarily reaching out for it. But my ethical training got the best of me, and I decided I couldn't do it. I didn't want to answer to Plato or Jesus for anything else. So, I reached for my ball instead of the brassiere, and as I did I became aware of a sound. I heard something, a funny grinding sort of noise, something scraping against stone or cement. A cold hard sound it was. I surveyed the place, trying to pinpoint the sound and finally did, just as a little chunk of the wall below one of the 2x4s holding the hangers began to disintegrate. I watched until a drill bit ate its way through the wall. When the bit was withdrawn I put my eye to the hole and saw another eye peering back at me.

"What'd you see?" I heard somebody asked. Phil Vandaver I think it was.

"Looks like an eyeball," Ogden's unmistakable voice answered.

"A what! Lemme see." The first eye disappeared, then another appeared —brown instead of blue. I just kept my eye to the hole. "Oh, shit," Phil said.

"Phil?" I said.

"Ezra?" Phil said, relieved. "Is that you?"

"In the flesh," I said.

"What the hell you doin' in there? You scared the livin' daylights outta us."

"Didn't mean to. I'm jist gittin' my ball," I told him. "What are *you* doin'?"

"Well, what's it look like? You got eyes, Ezra; I can see one of them," Phil said.

"Looks like you're drillin' a hole into the girls dressin' room," I said.

Phil said, "You got that right, Ezra. Good for you,"

"What are you doin' that for?" I asked without thinking.

"What for? Ezra, you dumb shit! What do you think for?"

"Oh, that," I said. I guess I did know, but it kind of took me by surprise, being right there when they finished the job. Even so, Phil didn't have to call me a "dumb shit." "I know what for," I told him

"All right. Now, back outta the way there so we can see what kinda shot we're gonna have to work with here." I took my eye away from the hole and took a step backwards, stumbling over the ball I'd come to retrieve. That irritated me some. "Move over to the left some, Ezra," Phil commanded.

"Mine or yours?"

"Yours," Phil said. I moved, but my heart wasn't in it. "Now back to the right." I sighed and followed his instructions. "Okay, good, hold it right there."

I was getting more and more vexed all the time with them ordering me around like some kind of servant or something. Finally, I lost my patience and said, "You guys are crazy! What's the big deal? Think you're gonna git a cheap thrill or somethin' by gawkin' in here at all the pretty girls?" Then, I don't know what made me do it, maybe it was because I secretly wanted to touch it anyway and this was the perfect excuse, but I grabbed the brassiere off the hook and started slinging it around, holding it up to the peep hole and all. "This what you're lookin' for, boys?" I said breathlessly.

"We wanna see it *on* somebody," Phil said.

Then Ogden said, "I thought we wanted to see it *off* somebody?"

"That too," Phil explained. "But first on somebody."

"Okay," I yelled. "Big deal!" Then, and only God and Plato know why, but I snapped the thing together, slipped it over my head like a T-shirt, then started dancing around the dressing room, accentuating my movements with a few hip gyrations and shoulder shimmies. I heard them just howling behind the wall. What a show! Not what they expected to see, but entertaining nonetheless. Then all the laughter stopped abruptly, and I noticed they had slipped a plug of some kind in the hole. I stopped my dance and turned my attention to the brassiere.

The thing had sure gone on easy enough, but when I tried to get it unhooked I seemed to be all thumbs. I felt a little like Harry Houdini trying to get himself out of a strait jacket. As I struggled to free myself, I finally noticed what all the silence was about. Standing there in the doorway was Hilda Fartok and what looked like the local chapter of the Daughters of the American Revolution. Not a good omen by any stretch of the imagination.

Evidently, she was more surprised to see me than I was to see her because she had gone speechless in the middle of whatever spiel she was delivering and fallen back against the wall. I was pretty sure I detected some muffled laughter coming from the far side of the wall, and quite naturally found myself at a loss for words. Even bad ones. I sort of raised my hands in a grand gesture of futility and forced what I hoped would be interpreted as an innocent half smile. I felt like a has-been or worse than that, a never was, on the Great Chain of Being. Before I could offer up some kind of an explanation some of the women starting running out screaming and carrying on like they were sore afraid. I suppose they were. I know I was. I didn't know exactly what to do, but I figured I'd better help Hilda before she fainted or something and cracked her skull on the concrete floor. Her eyes widened with terror as I approached, then she passed out and fell into my outstretched arms. I couldn't even *try* to get the brassiere off then so I picked up Hilda like a bride and carried her up the stairs, across the threshold and in to the gymnasium proper. Well, you'd have thought I was the creature from the black lagoon from the way those women were carrying on, zipping helter-skelter all over the place, screaming their heads off, taking swipes at me with their handbags and carrying on something awful. When I'd get one cornered to give me a hand with Hilda, she'd faint. Before you could say smelling salts there were three or four of them laid out on the floor like dust mops. I decided the best thing I could do for any of them was to get the hell out of the place.

So, I found Hilda a good seat in the bleachers and put her down so as not to do her anymore harm. Then I stood up, let out a mighty roar and ripped the brassiere off, letting it fall to the bleaches in pink, frilly pieces. Then I lit out. Wearing nothing but shorts, jock and my P.F. Flyers, I flew into the January afternoon and headed for home, figuring it would be a good long while before I got any kind of favorable endorsement from the DAR.

I was about halfway home when I heard a car coming up on me from the rear. I turned and saw Jason Clay's black monster bearing down on me like a dive bomber on a carrier deck.

I jumped a good two feet off the road and kept on running, trying to ignore my old pal Jason. He zoomed by then slid to a stop a half block away. Inside the car I saw him lean over to the passenger side and roll down the window. "Need a lift, Ezra," he asked as I came up on the car. I was in no position to be picky about who I rode with; my house was still six blocks away and the January air was frigid on my bare back and shoulders.

"You bet," I answered. This was a most opportune moment to bury the hatchet between us as far as I was concerned. I stepped into the street and reached for the door. As I did Jason stomped on the accelerator. His rear tires dug into the gravel, throwing up a blast of tiny rocks and sand that tore into my shins and kneecaps. He left me there, standing in the road with nothing but the smell of exhaust, burning rubber and my faded hoped of reconciliation for companions. I shook my head, fought back some angry tears and ran the rest to the way home.

Doc, Silas, and Mariko were all seated in the living room when I came rushing through. "Don't ask," I said as I hurried by. Once in the safety of my room I caught my breath and barricaded the door. Then I dealt with the philosophical question of why I had been born. As close as I could figure it, I was born to lose.

I was fully aware that an explanation such as that, while it might serve as some sort of balm to me as an individual, would do very little to explain or justify my behavior in the dressing room to anybody else. I had to come up with something better to tell the good people of Mansfield who undoubtedly would need some kind of a rational explanation for my behavior. The problem was this: I didn't have any idea of what possessed me to put that brassiere on.

True I'd meant to entertain my cronies, but I couldn't tell anybody else the truth because then they'd know about the peep hole, and my friends would hold my ratting on them against me from that day forward. Nor could I think of any plausible way in which I could have accidentally put the brassiere on, like when I reached for ball the thing fell off the hook, over my shoulders and snapped itself. They'd never buy that. So, when they grilled me I simply told them that they wouldn't believe me if I told them how it had happened so I wasn't going to bother. Everybody seemed satisfied with them, and relieved. Of course I told Mariko the truth. She tried not to laugh, but she just couldn't help it. And Mariko told Silas. He laughed too, but didn't want to talk about it. He didn't want to talk with me about *anything* that had to do with sex. And the disaster did, even if indirectly.

At school they didn't want know what to do either. There was nothing in the dress code about boys wearing brassieres, so all that happened was that I got kind of an oblique chewing out from the coach, my homeroom teacher, the principal, the superintendent, the janitor and a 7th grader named Molina Memphis. And I had to pay the girl who owned the brassiere I had ripped to shreds. That, naturally, was Roseabeth. I handed her four dollars just before English class started and said, "This is for your brassiere. And I don't want to talk 'bout it."

"Ezra Casey," Roseabeth said, " I am so embarrassed I could jist die."

"It's *over*," I said. "I don't want to talk 'bout it!"

"What in the world were you doin'' wearin' my bra anyway?"

"It wasn't his fault," Phil told her.

"It wasn't my fault," I said.

"Well, I would sure like to know jist whose fault it was then." The bell rang and Mrs. Schroder cleared her throat, a sure sign she was planning on teaching us something. "This isn't over," Roseabeth told me.

"Okay, I'll tell you 'bout it someday," I whispered, "but not today! Okay?"

"Well, you'd better," Roseabeth said, "that was my prettiest bra. And you jist *ruined* it."

"Roseabeth, *please*," I pleaded, "not now!"

"Ezra," Mrs. Schroder said, "do you recall what we were discussing yesterday when class was dismissed?"

"No, ma'am, I'm sorry, but I don't recall."

"You think about it real hard for me will you?" Mrs. Schroder said.

I tried not to remember it, and sure enough, it popped right into my head. "We're were ah—doin' somethin' to verbs."

"Conjugating," she said.

"That's it," I said, "conjugating." If she knew I don't know what she asked me for.

Ogden poked Phil and whispered, "I'll like to conjugate *her.*"

"You're thinkin' of *conjugal*," Phil told him.

"Ogden scratched at his crotch and said, "I didn't know you could even do it to a verb."

"You can't do *that* to a verb, Ogden, but you *can* conjugate them!" Phil said.

"Oh," Ogden said and nodded. I don't know whether I told you or not, but Ogden was probably not ever going to be a candidate for a Nobel Prize. He sat there nodding his head, mulling it over. Not a good sign for any of us. Mrs. Schroder, wondering what the ruckus was all about intervened on her own behalf.

"Ogden, would you like to conjugate a verb for us?" she asked.

Ogden looked up at her surprised. "Huh?" Metaphorically speaking, she'd caught him with his pants down. She was a fine teacher, patient and understanding and all. And so pretty I'd have jumped off a cliff for her, but she did tend to get vexed when we didn't recall something from one day to the next.

"Ogden, I asked if you'd like to conjugate a verb for the class?"

Ogden nodded; he had a very sincere nod. "Shoot yeah, I don't know why not."

"Go ahead."

"Right." He sat there just staring at her.

"Start at your own convenience. We're waiting."

"Can I ask a question first?"

"Yes," Mrs. Schroder said, forcing a slight smile, "you *may*."

Ogden screwed up his face a little and said, "What's a verb?"

Mrs. Schroder threw her head back and closed her eyes; then she squeezed the bridge of her nose and took a couple of real deep breaths before answering. "Oh, Ogden, we've been reviewing verbs and verb tenses for a week. Where have you been?"

"Right here in my seat," Ogden said.

"I thought so," she said. "Roseabeth, tell Ogden what a verb is."

"Verbs," Roseabeth said, "are a category of words that express action or being and sometimes happenings. Like *throw* the ball or *shoot* the basket."

"Oh, yeah, I remember now," Ogden said, "throw, shoot, hit, catch—anything you can do with a ball is a verb."

Mrs. Schroder nodded. "But let's not limit it to just that."

"Now, what'd you want me to do again?" Ogden asked.

"Conjugate a verb," she said patiently. "I want you to conjugate the verb of your choice."

Ogden poked Phil and with a new-found confidence whispered. "I can conjugate the shit outta verbs. Watch this. How 'bout shoot, ma'am?"

"Fine," Mrs. Schroder said, "you *can* shoot a ball."

"Yeah," Ogden agreed, "especially Ezra."

"Leave me out of it," I said.

Ogden cleared his throat and said, "Okay, here goes. First person singular—*I shoot*." Mrs. Schroder nodded.

"Way to go, Ogden," I whispered, but he didn't hear me.

Ogden swallowed and went on. "Second person singular—*you shot*." There were some muffled cheers and minor catcalling, but Ogden forged ahead undaunted. He nodded, smiled, and continued. "Third person, singular—" He paused and I heard him whisper to himself, "shoot, shot—shit." Then he looked up boldly. "He shit! Shoot, shot, shit."

Well, we just went all to pieces on hearing that. Ogden sure had a way with words; you couldn't deny that. Mrs. Schroder just stood there staring at him, trying to keep a straight face. She probably didn't want to make Ogden feel bad; but I doubted that she wanted him to feel good either. And he did. We were all cheering him and slapping him on the back and carrying on like he'd just won the heavyweight boxing championship of the world. He loved the attention. When the laughter finally died away under Mrs. Schroder's stern gaze she said, "Ogden, that was incorrect. I want you to find the correct conjugation and write it down enough times to learn it properly. Is that clear?"

"Yes ma'am," Ogden said.

"Now, does anyone recall how to use the infinitive form of a verb?" If they did, nobody owned up to it. "Phil?"

"Yes ma'am. In the infinitive, the verb is preceded by the word 'to'."

"Can you give us an example, Phil?"

Phil nodded and then broke in a slight grin that widened as he spoke. "Yes ma'am. I am goin' *to shoot* . . . the shit with Ogden!"

"Class dismissed!" Mrs. Schroder said.

You can't blame her for dismissing the class and you'd have thought that would have ended it, but it didn't. That incident and the disaster and a related but independent event haunted me during a basketball game that very night in Chickasha. It was a close game, very tight, tied going into the end of the first half, and it was getting a little nasty under the boards, even for a humanist. Some guy ran under me while I tried to stuff in one of Ogden's miscues, and if Ogden hadn't caught me in midair I'd probably would have broken my neck. It was clearly an intentional foul so I got two shots. Small consolation as far as I was concerned.

I stepped up to the free throw line and adjusted my shorts and waited for the ref to hand me the ball. Ogden caught my eye because he was just staring at me. I looked at him hard and said, "What the hell, Ogden?"

"Ezra," Ogden said, "are you goin' *to shoot* the ball?"

I glanced around a little uneasily and said, "Ogden, don't start." About then the ref slammed the ball into my belly.

"First one's dead," the ref said. "Two shots."

I stood there holding the ball and tried not to look at Ogden.

"*Shoot* the ball, Ezra," Ogden said.

Some guy from Chickasha looked up and said, "What the hell is this? English class or somethin'?"

"Jist a little review," I said. "Ogden . . ."

"Hey, Casey," another guy said, "when you goin' *to wear* a brassiere again?" Nothing spreads faster than bad news.

"That ain't funny," I said.

"Not funny? Hell, I heard it was hilarious. You chasin' a bunch of old ladies 'round in your girlfriend's panties."

"Panties! That's a lie. I only had on her brassiere!"

"No panties? Hear that fellas; he *only* had on her brassiere." Boy, they thought they were real hilarious.

"You need to shoot the ball, son," the ref said.

"*Shoot* the ball, Ezra," Ogden insisted.

"Dammit, Ogden, lay off!"

I tell you there was some malicious snickering going on up and down that foul lane. Under ordinary circumstances I was better than a ninety percent shooter from the foul line, but these circumstances were far from ordinary. I took a huge breath and tried to shut out all the distractions. I bounced the ball, looked at the rim, then just as I dipped to shoot I saw a sight that just about undid me for good.

Grace Farley, "Amazing Grace" she was called for reasons I don't care to elaborate on, the daughter of the Presbyterian minister in Chickasha, was seated up in the bleachers directly behind the glass backboard supporting the goal. Her skirt was hiked up over her knees, and as I dipped my knees to shoot, she opened her thighs up wide enough to admit a company of the U.S. Marine Corps finest. My knees buckled right under me, and I collapsed in a heap right there on the foul line.

Coach Hayes, "Hawk" we called him, raced out to me with the trainer and scorekeeper to see what had happened. I just sat there trying to catch my breath and get another look up Grace's skirt, but she had snapped her legs shut by then and was sitting there just as pretty and innocent as the day she was born.

"Goddammit, boy!" Hawk yelled. "What happened?"

I was faced with a tough decision. If I told the truth I knew Grace would just deny it, ethics not being her strong suit from what I understood, but what was worse was that, if I told the truth I ran the risk of her not doing it again. "I—I don't know, Coach. My knees jist buckled right under me."

"Well, shit," Hawk said in that sympathetic way of his, trying, no doubt, to console me. Then he grabbed my legs and bent the knees back and forth one at a time like he knew what he was doing. "Looks okay to me," he said.

"Oh, yeah, yeah," I said climbing to my feet. "It was jist a—a recurrin' relapse of a previous condition."

"Son, you're shakin' like a leaf. You seen a ghost or somethin'?"

"Or somethin'," I admitted cryptically.

Ogden looked at me curiously and said, "When you goin' *to shoot* the ball, Ezra?"

"Right now, Ogden," I said, grabbing the ball from the ref. Then, I waited until the floor was cleared of all who had rushed out there on my behalf. I didn't know what to expect from Grace, other than the worst, and that's what I got. Again, as I dipped for the shot, her legs swung open as if there was an invisible wire strung between my knees and her thighs. I let the ball go anyway, looking at Grace, not the goal. And I heard Ogden.

"Ezra *shot* the ball." And I did, but not well. Air ball. Missed everything. Under the circumstances I felt fortunate that the thing even stayed in the gym. Then Ogden cried, "Shit!, he missed. He looked at me then and said, "Shoot, shot, shit! I was right all along."

"Don't talk to me 'bout grammar, Ogden," I snapped. "I gotta shoot another one."

"From where you standin' you're gittin' a pretty fair shot, aren't you Casey?" one of the Neanderthals from Chickasha said. All his teammates chuckled and elbowed each other, for a change.

"Did you put her up to that?"

"Grace you talkin' 'bout?" I nodded. "She's amazin' ain't she?"

"If you say so."

"You ain't seen nothin' yet," the guy who fouled me said.

That was quite true. Because she was so far away and the lighting was so poor, all I could really see was a kind of dark passage up her skirt. I couldn't make out anything in particular, not that I'd have known what I was seeing if I did see anything else. Hawk was on the bench giving me his usual encouragement. "What the hell's wrong with you, boy? You blind? The ball goes *in* the hole!"

"I know where the ball goes, Coach," I yelled back him, not hiding my vexation.

"Well, you sure as hell could of fooled me." Hawk had a real knack for providing constructive criticism. It was just his way.

"*Shoot* the ball, Ezra," Ogden said. He was sure focused; you could say that for him.

"Ogden, dammit, lay off!" I grabbed the ball from the ref and zeroed in on the basket, or tried to. Grace smiled and I think even winked at me. Too much! I didn't know what I was going to do, but it was clear to me that Grace was again going to give me *her* best shot. So I decided to shoot left handed. I didn't have a chance of making the shot otherwise. By shooting left handed I'd have to concentrate so hard that I thought maybe I could shut the thought and image of Grace right out of my mind altogether. Wrong! Her gate swung open again, and I put up another air ball. Chickasha got the ball out of bounds and raced down court for a score. Hawk was not a happy man. "You shot that *left* handed, son! What the hell are you doin'?"

As I raced by him, I said, "You told me to work on my left hand, Coach."

"Not during' a goddamn game, you idiot!" Hawk retorted.

We lost the game by 12 points, and I ended up missing 12 free throws. Fact is I never hit a free throw in Chickasha from that night on. I was far too mesmerized by Grace to concentrate on something so trivial as basketball. I hate to admit it, but I kept staring up that dark tunnel of her skirt, hoping for just the slightest glimpse of what I'd heard so much about and yet knew so little. She was a long way off, but from what I could tell, Phil was right: the thing did look sort of like a gorilla, a small one.

Hawk never understood and never forgave me for what he thought was my incompetence, but which was, in fact, my fancy. But then compassion was not a trait with which Hawk was heavily endowed. To Hawk, compassion meant shooting someone instead of hanging them. Violence is what Hawk believed in, and that's what he preached, so called "controlled" and "justifiable" violence like in a war and on the football field. He participated in plenty of the former in the South Pacific where he served with the US Marines during the war. Had he been given the option, which he hadn't been, he would have remained one of the Corps' finest, but since they turned him away he became a coach and high school history teacher in the territories. It aggravated him to no end that a Japanese-Irish-Native American could be his best basketball player, but I was, except in Chickasha.

I don't know if Hawk was a good coach or not because he was the only coach I'd ever had, but I did know that his view of history, consisting primarily of a rambling narrative of his heroic exploits in the Pacific, was fairly narrow. Sure as a fairy tale starts out, "Once upon a time," Hawk's war stories started out with, "Now this is no shit." And he subjected us unmercifully to his version of history, to say nothing of his philosophy of winning which was a direct consequence of our victory in the Pacific.

I differed with Hawk philosophically on a number of major and minor points. Hawk, you see, was dead set on winning at any cost; winning was the ultimate and only goal of competitive sports. Now I'd been brought up to believe that the goal of sports was twofold: to keep your mind and body healthy and to have a good time. But Hawk insisted that there was an important lesson about *life* to be learned on the athletic field. Maybe there was, but from where I sat, it looked like we all ultimately ended up losers in the game of life, so I didn't see why winning a game here or there along the way was so all-fire important. I figured a dead winner didn't look any different than a dead loser when either was pushing daisies in the wrong direction. And if I followed Hawk's philosophy on the gridiron, I'd be likely to meet that end a lot sooner than if I followed my own.

I didn't see any point at all in risking life and limb over a ball that you couldn't even count on to take a predictable bounce. Footballs were like cats: highly independent and you never knew what they were going to do next. Just as soon as you thought you had one figured out, it'd do something altogether different. You should never count on a cat!

Now a basketball was more like a dog, good old Shep or Lassie. It would come back to you every time, unless you bounced it off the side of your foot or something. That's why I preferred dogs to cats and basketball to football. Also, there's a lot less of a chance of getting your brains kicked out in basketball. But in the beginning Hawk made me play football because he had so few players, Mansfield being such a small town. To keep from getting killed on the gridiron I developed the pigskin philosophy of "go with the flow." To tell you the truth, Hawk wasn't all that high on it, and as a result I didn't see a whole lot of action. No, that's not true. I *saw* a great deal of it; I just didn't participate in all that much of it. I didn't care though because the action I was most interested in wasn't taking place on the field of battle anyhow, but on the sidelines where Roseabeth and the rest of the cheerleaders were prancing and dancing around in their skimpy little skirts, tight sweaters and ruffled red panties. Lord, I never knew whether we won or lost a game from one week to the next. And didn't care!

I was hanging off the end of the bench watching Roseabeth one night while the farm boys from Lone Wolf were teaching us that the best offense was for your opponent to have a porous defense when somebody cold cocked Tilden Warner, and I was pressed into service.

"Casey!" Hawk bellowed. I heard him, faintly, but I couldn't quite tear my eyes away from Roseabeth's rosy cheeks—all four of them. Then somebody poked me, and I heard Hawk screaming, "Casey, git over here!"

"Yessir," I said and scrambled off the bench I'd been warming for the better part of the season.

"Git in there for Warner."

"For Warner. Right, Warner." I turned and started trotting onto the field. "Oh my God," I gasped as two trainers moved towards me with Tilden draped over their shoulders. Tilden looked kind of . . . happy, except that he was bleeding from the nose and mouth.

"Casey!" I heard Hawk yell.

"Yessir?"

"Git a helmet. You'll need it."

We didn't have enough good "game" helmets to go around, so Phil and I shared one, our heads being about the same size. But Phil was still playing so I had to borrow Tilden's which was about four sizes too big for me. I slipped it on and asked a trainer what had happened to Tilden.

"Got wiped out on an end-around," he told me.

Tilden smiled a crooked smile, spit out a tooth and added, "Sumbitch cold-cocked me."

"Excellent!" It was time for me to turn my pigskin philosophy into concrete action. For me, survival was the key, not winning or having your guts spread out there all over the turf just to prove you had some. I hurried onto the field, thinking everybody would be real glad to see me, but they weren't. My teammates all started screaming and growling and hitting me and slapping the side of my helmet. Then Ogden came over and slammed both fists down on my shoulders, driving me about six inches into the ground. I was anxious to start the game again; I didn't figure it would be any rougher.

When play resumed I moved up to the line of scrimmage and assumed my position at defensive end. Lone Wolf's offensive tackle, and believe me he was offensive, glared at me and snorted, digging at the turf with his cleats. "New meat," he snarled.

"Works both ways, Pal," I said in good humor and kind of forced a laugh. I'd seen smaller barns than this guy.

"I'm gonna break your lousy neck, funny boy," he said.

I saw right off that the guy had no sense of humor at all, and decided that I wouldn't even play this game for money. I swallowed hard and said, "You don't even know me."

"If I knew you I'd probably wanna break your face *and* your neck!"

Perfect. The "Thing" on steroids. "Well, you're gonna have to catch me first," I said.

Just before the snap I saw Lone Wolf's running back leaning towards the end opposite me and I took that as a sure sign the play was going in that direction. And it did. So I took out at a high rate of speed away from the neck-breaker but evidently right into the path of a leg-breaker. Whoop! Down I crashed amongst all manner of grunts and groans in a tangled mass of misguided humanity. The blast of the ref's whistle finally stopped the carnage, and we began to untangle ourselves. As I climbed off the pile somebody let me have it in the side of the head. Wham! My head bounced back and forth in that cavernous helmet like the gong of a bell. I looked up to see their tackle, old number nine, snickering as he jogged back to the huddle. I knew then what had happened to poor Tilden. When it came to being a good sport that tackle wasn't exactly what you'd call a Gatsby type, if you know what I mean, which you probably don't.

"You okay, Ez?" Phil asked and herded me off in the general direction of our defensive huddle.

"Great," I said, "jist a little . . . I dunno . . . groggy, I guess."

"Let's high-low that sumbitch," Phil said.

"Okay," I said.

"Great! I'll hit him high, you low? Okay?"

"Excellent plan," I agreed, nodding. "You high, me low." To tell you the truth I wasn't all that crazy about the idea, but I couldn't let Phil down at this point. The ape would kill him. So, when the ball was snapped I dived to the ground and grabbed the monster around the ankles. I caught him off guard because he stood straight up and just stared down at me. About that time Phil hit him a real good shot to the rib cage and over he tumbled backwards like a giant Redwood. We lay on top of him, holding him down until the play was blown dead; only then did we realize what a mistake we'd made. He got up in the state of a gut-shot grizzly, and I sensed we were in some *very* deep shit.

We should of killed him," Phil said.

It was an awful thing even to think, but Phil was right: we should of. "What now?" I asked a little desperately.

"Protect yourself as best you can, Ezra. I think my jock jist snapped a strap. Gotta go check it out." He started for the sidelines

"What? Wait a minute! Phil."

Phil's replacement was Nathan Dumas, a kid with a lot of heart but not much common sense. A bad combination on a football field. Being that Nathan was about half my size and a blind advocate of Hawk's "winning is everything" philosophy,

I figured he was going to throw himself in harm's way every chance he got. "Nathan," I said, "keep away from number nine; he killed a kid in Hobart last week."

"No shit."

"Knocked his head right off," I said. I hated to lie to the kid, but it was for his own good, not mine.

"Did they stop the game?" Nathan asked.

"What, are you crazy? Stop a game of football jist 'cause somebody gits killed? Hell, they didn't even call time out! Jist rolled his head off the field and kept playin'."

"I'll watch it then, Ezra. Thanks." He shook his head, letting it all soak in and I heard him mumble to himself, "Sumbitch, *killed* a kid!"

When Lone Wolf lined up this time number nine looked like a raging bull; he snorted and dug at the turf like Francis Macomber's Cape buffalo. This time I noticed the running back was leaning in my direction and figured the end was near. Tilden, being Catholic and all, could have said a quick Rosary or something, but we religious liberals didn't have any place to hide. The ball was snapped, and it was the old end-around all right. I started drifting to my left to turn the play inside which, theoretically, is the proper thing to do. The ape had a different blocking assignment and went after our middle linebacker, leaving me at the mercy of a blocking back, a pulling guard, the end, and the quarterback, after pitching the ball. Half the Lone Wolf team was bearing down on me like hard rain. In that moment of extremis my philosophy of football crystallized into overt action. Before the gang arrived I turned and started to run *with* them, going with the flow so to speak; some called it chicken. I called it smart.

It was a move that pretty much confounded everybody on both sides on and off the field. Nobody could block me without clipping, so I managed to stay just ahead of the pack until the ball carrier got impatient and tried to pass me. Then I just drifted a step to my right, grabbed him from behind and threw him on the ground. Didn't even get my pants dirty. The first half ended with that play.

"Casey," I heard Hawk screaming, "What the goddamn hell kinda play was that?"

"Smart," I said.

"Whose side are you on anyhow?"

"Our side, Coach."

"Damned if you're on mine," Hawk said. "You was runnin' *with* the enemy!"

"But if I'd gone against the flow," I argued, "they'd of killed me at the line of scrimmage."

"That's your job."

"To git killed?"

"You bet your ass," Hawk said, "if that's what it takes."

"To what?"

"Win!" Hawk said. "That's what this game is all about, Son! Winning is everything."

"Well, if I'd gotten killed they would of scored because everybody else got knocked down." I had him there.

He stopped, scratched his head and stared at me. "I don't give a shit; it ain't never right to run *with* the enemy. Now git in that locker room and see if you can find some guts to go along with that brain of yours. And you leave the thinkin' out here to me!"

As I moved away I heard the Lone Wolf coach complaining to the ref that we ought to be penalized for my play. But

Hawk would have none of that; he jumped right in there and said, "Nowhere in the rules does it say a man can't go with the flow." I was real happy that Hawk had stood up for me.

Even though I'd managed to stop their last drive, we were in the somewhat unenviable position of being on the wrong end of a 37 to 0 score when the half ended. It was as bleak a picture as you'd ever hope to see, possibly bleaker, and we all knew we were in for a real dressing down. Hawk's "pep" talks were infamous, bombastic harangues full of piss and vinegar. We were waiting for him, sitting there on rows of low benches with our heads hanging down low like willow branches.

Our new locker room already smelled exactly like the old one, a heady blend of sweat, antiseptic, Vitalis, and some kind of a sweet moldy fragrance that I'd just as soon not identify. I don't have any idea of what kinds of bacteria ran pell-mell in there, but it was something to think about while Hawk chewed us out. Bearing the unbearable built character, Doc told me once. But I didn't plan on listening to Hawk anyway.

Just as everybody got more or less comfortable, Hawk came storming in, slamming the door after him and kicking a dirty jockstrap across the floor. He stood silently then in the middle of the room and shook his head for a long time, staring down. Then he said, "She—it! Shit, shit, shit, shit, shit!" He suddenly looked up at me and barked, "You hear me, Ezra?"

"Yessir!"

"What'd I say?"

"Ah ... shit."

"How many times did I say it?"

"Ah ... five?"

"Six, son, I said it *six* times, not five. You didn't count the first time before the other five now did you?"

"I think I got the first one," I said. "It's the last one I missed or maybe one in the middle."

"Why is that?"

"I . . . dunno."

"'Cause you didn't hear me, that's why. And why didn't you hear me?"

"I dunno."

"'Cause you weren't listenin', that's why. And why weren't you listenin'? 'Cause you were thinkin' 'bout them cheerleaders out there dancing' 'round with their tight little asses shakin' in them red frilly panties. Weren't you?"

"Well, I was thinkin' 'bout thinkin' 'bout it," I admitted.

"Now goddammit I want you—-all of yous— to listen up now and listen good. You hear me?"

"Yessir," I said.

"What?" Hawk yelled.

We roared in unison like a company of U.S. Marines. "Yes sir!"

"That's more like it," Hawk said as he started pacing the floor; at the end of the room just in front of the showers he stepped in the container where we treated our feet with anti-fungus powder for athletes foot. After that he laid out a neat white path as he paced. "Well, I never thought I'd see the day when I'd be ashamed to look you boys in the eye, ashamed to call myself an American. But the way you boys is gittin' your asses kicked all over the field tonight almost makes me wish I was a goddamned Chinaman. No offense Ezra."

"I'm part Japanese," I said woodenly.

"Whatever," he said and went on. "Lemme tell yous some-thin' right now, and this is no shit: If the Marines hadn't dis-played any more guts on Guadalcanal than you boys is showin' me out there tonight, them Japs—no offense Ezra—would of kicked our asses to hell and back again. You boys have got no backbone." We had them all right; we just wanted to keep them. Hawk stopped in the center of the room and stared at each one of us, trying to make eye contact as if that was the key to getting kids to sacrifice themselves for an inflated pig bladder. "Now I want you boys to git back out there and do to them Wolverines what Custer did to the Indians—no offense Ezra—at the Battle of the Washita. What'd he do? Kicked their asses, that's what! And that's exactly what I want you boys to do out there this next half—kick ass. No more lollygagging' around, turnin' tale and runnin' with the enemy. You hear me, Ezra?"

"Huh! Oh, yeah, no more of that," I said. My mind had begun to wander on me. Sometimes it had a mind of its own.

"No more collaboratin' with the enemy, right?"

"Right, no more of that," I agreed. Then repeated to myself, "collaboratin' with the enemy?"

"Now I want you boys to git out there and kick ass! Kick ass like we did on Guadalcanal, on Saipan, on Okinawa and Iwo Jima. I want you to kick their asses up the field, down the field and across the goddamned field. Do you understand me?"

"Yessir!" I didn't join in this time. I was thinking about something else entirely by then. Hawk was still ranting and raving, but I was tuning him out.

"Kick ass! Kick ass . . . " I heard him keep saying.

All this talk about asses had got me to thinking about Roseabeth; her image kept dancing in my head like sugar-plum fairies. Her rear end was so sweet and firm and it sort of vibrated under those red frilly panties as she jumped around and kicked up her legs. I guess *kicking* that fanny of hers was about the furthest thing from my mind. Tilden was back among the living, and since I hadn't exactly distinguished myself in Hawk's eyes, I figured to be back on the bench where I belonged and was thinking where to best situate myself for an optimum view of Roseabeth's rosy cheeks.

Suddenly Hark had me by the shoulders, and he was about to shake my head off and everyone was screaming and yelling. Then Hawk put his face right in mine and yelled, "Goddammit now, Ezra, what are you gonna do when you git back out there?"

"Kiss ass!" I screamed in a panic before I had a total grasp of the situation.

Hawk blinked and stared at me with an incredulous expression. Then he looked around the room and asked, "Did he say, 'kiss ass'?"

"That's what he said," Ogden assured Hawk.

Hawk just raised a finger and pointed to the door. "Git out! Git the hell out, and—and don't come back . . . 'til—'til basketball season."

That was the last year I had to play football in order to play basketball too. The only part about it that I regretted was that I had a better view of the cheerleaders from the bench than from my position up in the stadium. But I didn't mind it all that much. I got a good front view of the cheerleaders from the stadium, and there was a whole lot of shaking happening on their front sides too.

8

MY FAIR LADY

In football they call it a double reverse; in baseball they call it a squeeze play; in basketball, it's the old give and go. In the game of love, however, I don't rightly know what to call it. Probably unfair. That's what they *should* call it, because that's what it was: Unfair. Unfair to me. Unfair to Fonda. And I suppose even unfair to Roseabeth because she didn't understand it any better than I did. I doubt that Fonda did either although she was aware of the unfairness of *one* aspect of it. Roseabeth wasn't even that. That's why it was maybe more unfair to Roseabeth than to Fonda.

It all started pretty much as you'd expect it to: Roseabeth asked me a question that I couldn't possibly answer in a way that would satisfy her. High summer it was, evening, ever so warm and sultry. We were swaying back and forth in the old swing on Roseabeth's front porch, sipping lemonade, and I suppose resembling more a Norman Rockwell painting than real live folks. We were watching the heat-lightning illuminate the far horizon with quick flashes of frightening light. When I wasn't drinking my lemonade or wiping the sweat off the back of my neck, I was holding hands with Roseabeth.

Sometimes you could hear the low growl of thunder way off there in the distant sky, like God had indigestion or something. The swing was kind of creaky; the ropes holding it were straining against our combined weight and humming like taut banjo strings, and a kind of sheer blue light filled the sky after a flash of lightning. It sort of made you feel lost sometimes because of the vastness of it all. I was going to ask Roseabeth if she ever did, feel lost, but she beat me to the punch.

"Ezra, Hun," she said, resting her cheek against my shoulder and smiling up at me with her perfect white teeth, "do you think I'm pretty?"

"That's a silly question," I said.

"I don't see anythin' so silly 'bout it, Ezra. Either you think I'm pretty or you don't."

"Roseabeth, you're 'bout the prettiest girl in Mansfield," I said and watched her lovely smile fade to distinct pout. Doc always told me before you ever answer a question to be dead certain that you know what the person is asking. I hadn't done that this time. A *very* big mistake.

Roseabeth raised up her head and asked, "What do you mean, 'bout the prettiest,' Ezra?"

"Is that what I said: 'Bout the prettiest'?"

"You sure did. I heard you plain as day."

"Well, what I meant was that you're *one of* the prettiest girls in *all* Mansfield."

"Oh," she said curtly, "I see what you mean—*one of.*" I was still in some hot water. "Well, who do you think is prettier?"

I took a sip of my lemonade and stretched my neck some. "I didn't mean to say that I thought *anyone* was prettier than you, Roseabeth," I told her, hoping for the best.

"What *did* you mean?"

"Jist that there are a number of girls in Mansfield that are all 'bout the same—all *real* pretty."

"For instance?"

"Well, you, like I said, and Norma and Kathy and Heather and Patricia and Elizabeth and Fonda—"

"That's enough, Ezra! I get the point."

"Okay, Jeeze. I'm sorry," I said, but it was too late.

She threw her head back causing her hair to fall back softly over her shoulders. "What I don't understand is how you can say we're all 'bout the same when some of us are tall and some short, some with blond hair and some brunette, some with freckles and some without."

I thought about it and said, "I should have said *equivalent* instead of the same, Roseabeth. There are a number of girls in Mansfield that I consider to be of equivalent, but not necessarily, identical beauty. It a matter of personal preference."

"And your personal preference doesn't lie with brunettes, obviously!"

"Of course it lies with brunettes, Roseabeth. Otherwise, why would I be *your* steady?"

"I don't know, but if Fonda was a brunette and I was a blond, you might jist as well be *her* steady."

"But you *are* a brunette, Roseabeth," I pointed out.

"That is exactly the point I'm tryin' to make—that you would go out with *any* brunette without any regard whatsoever 'bout a girl's other characteristics. And of all people, Ezra

Casey, I'd expect you to look beyond the mere physical aspects of a girl's beauty." I was beginning to see her point. "I mean, do you think it matters to me that you're part Chinese?"

"Japanese," I said.

"Whatever. And part Indian?"

"It's actually the Irish part that causes me most of the trouble," I told her.

"You see, Ezra, I look beyond what you look like to what you really are."

"And jist what is that, Roseabeth," I asked curiously. I sure didn't know.

"Well," she said, "you're on the honor roll in school, class president, All-State in basketball, and you git along with jist 'bout everybody—'cept for Jason Clay and Daddy."

I poured us both some more lemonade. "You really think that's what I am?"

"It's a fact, Ezra," she said, fluffing up her hair. "Why, what do you think you are?"

"Jist a kid tryin' to make some sense out of growin' up. And half afraid to 'cause I don't much like what I see in the adult world," I told her and gulped down my lemonade.

"What don't you like, Ezra?"

"The poverty, the misery, the intolerance and prejudice—all the bad things."

"Well, all you gotta do is shut your eyes and you won't see them. That's what I do."

"I tried that once, Roseabeth," I explained, "but when I opened my eyes all the bad things were still there, and some of them had gotten worse."

"Daddy says that when bad things happen to people they're bein' punished for their sins."

"Well, what 'bout those people in India that got washed out to sea in that typhoon. They weren't sinning! Why'd they all get drowned?"

"'Cause they weren't Christians, Ezra. Anybody ought to know that."

"In Italy a bunch more were buried in a earthquake—jist poor people that didn't have the energy or money to be bad," I countered.

"That's 'cause they weren't Protestants."

"What 'bout those people in Kaw City who got hit by that tornado?"

"They was Presbyterians!"

"And those *Baptists* in Holdenville? What were *they* doin'?"

She just stared at me and calmly asked, "Don't you know?"

"No, and I don't wanna hear it."

"The preacher's wife was runnin' 'round all over the county with the Choir Director and they're the exact one who was killed in the fire. Now if *that's* not bein' punished for your sins, I don't know what is," Roseabeth said.

I just shook my head and said, "But what 'bout everybody else, Roseabeth? You think God would do things like that to people He don't even know?"

"Well, I don't reckon He'd do it to somebody He's real chummy with. It's all in the Gospel, Ezra. Daddy can show you."

"But Roseabeth, it doesn't make sense!"

"Not to you 'cause you question *every little thing*," she said. "Some of us accept what the Lord says in the Gospel; that makes things a lot easier. But you gotta go 'round frettin' all the time 'cause you don't think the world works right. You'd be a lot happier, and I might add, a lot better company if you'd stop frettin' so much and jist start believin'. God knows what He's doin'." She finished her lemonade, handed me her empty glass to set on the railing. "Speakin' of things of a theological nature, you do know that I'll be goin' to church camp next week, don't you?"

"I know that, Roseabeth; you must of told me seven times already."

"That's 'cause you're so forgetful."

"I don't recall bein' particularly forgetful," I said.

"That's jist what I mean. Remember that time you left me standin' out in the rain in front of Yeager's?"

"No, I do not," I said,

"See there."

"No, I don't see there. I don't recall it 'cause it never happened."

"Well then how in the world did I git soaked? And chilled to the bone, I guess!"

"I don't know!"

"You jist don't remember."

"Roseabeth—when? When did this happen?"

"Last July. In front of Yeager's."

"It was somebody else. I was on wheat harvest last July, probably somewhere in Kansas."

"Well, that's why you don't remember," she said.

I glanced at her and then stared off into the vast reaches of space. She was dead serious, considered her position to be completely rational. Her mind was funny like that, and once she got something set in her head you could forget about changing her mind. Ran in the family I guess. I finally leaned back in the swing and said, "You don't have to remind me anymore 'bout church camp; I know you're goin'."

She looked hard at me and said, "Is that *all?*"

"Is that all *what?*" I said carefully.

"Is that all you're gonna say?"

I cleared my throat and decided to have some more lemonade. I poured it, took a drink and said, "Mantle hit two homers last night; had seven RBIs."

"Oh, Ezra," she cried.

"What?"

"I don't care beans 'bout the New York Dodgers—"

"Yankees."

"I don't care nothin' for them either," Roseabeth cried. "You could at least say you're gonna miss me."

"Well, *of course*, I'm gonna miss you, Roseabeth. That's goes without sayin', which is why I didn't say it, but I can't miss you until you leave. How can I miss you when you're sittin' right here next to me lookin' pretty as—"

"Fonda or Norma or Kathy," she snapped.

"You're puttin' words in my mouth," I protested, but I didn't mention the ideas she was putting in my head.

"Oh, Ezra, you don't havta actually miss me now, but you could at least start worrin' 'bout it."

"Why should I worry 'bout it beforehand?"

"Well, *I* am."

"Then don't go," I suggested. "You've been 'bout a hundred times already, and it's the same old thing year after year."

"I want to go, Ezra."

"How come?"

"'Cause I think—the separation will be good for us."

"You do?"

"Yes, I do," she said firmly which puzzled me some.

"But you jist said you were already worried 'bout missin' me?"

"I am. And I'll miss you whether you miss me or not."

"I'll miss you, Roseabeth, you know that."

"Then why don't you come too?"

"Oh no! Not after what happened last time."

"Ezra, that wasn't your fault. How could you of known God was gonna reveal himself to you in the form of a woodchuck?"

"I couldn't of, but nobody believed me either. And I'm not goin' back under any conditions. I've got stuff to do here. Besides . . . I think the separation will be good for us."

"*What* on earth do you mean by that?"

"Jist that—I dunno, maybe—maybe we're seein' too much of each other."

"Well! I had no idea you felt like that," she cried. "Maybe I'll stay a month!"

"Roseabeth," I said, trying to take her hand, "all I'm doin' is repeatin' the exact words you said one minute ago."

She jerked her hand away. "And what I'm sayin' is that I didn't know *you* felt that way!"

"Roseabeth, I don't know how to feel or how you want me to feel. This is all very confusin' to me, and I'm jist kinda feelin' my way along."

"Well," she said obliviously, "if I'm away a while maybe you'll appreciate me a little more when I git home."

"Roseabeth, I appreciate you now, I jist don't . . ."

"Don't what?"

"Understand you," I said.

"That's 'cause you spend so little time with me when I am here." I was curious about what Aristotle would have done with the likes of Roseabeth; she might have set Greek thought back a thousand years. I'd narrowed the problem down to one of two possibilities: I was either seeing too much of her or not enough. I didn't know which. While I brooded on it she snuggled against my shoulder and said, "What you gonna do while I'm gone?"

"Miss you," I said.

"What else?"

"Oh, jist sit around lookin' at your picture, and think 'bout how easy you are to git along with."

"Ezra, what are you *really* gonna do?"

"Help around the house, play some ball, ride my bike, read, talk with Doc and maybe take in a movie or two."

"Oh," she said in that special way of hers that meant trouble—for me. "Who will you be goin' to the movies with?"

"Doc, I reckon, Silas and my mom. Maybe I'll be goin' by my own self."

"And that's *all*?"

"What are you gittin' at, Roseabeth?"

"Oh, jist that ordinarily people don't go to the movies by themselves."

"Well, then maybe I'll be goin' with some of my adolescent chums."

"But not with any members of the fairer sex?"

"Girls?"

"Yes, *girls!*"

"No, 'cause I'm goin' steady with you."

"And if you weren't?"

I rubbed my eyelids real hard with my palms and said, "Roseabeth, please don't start. My mind jist can't deal with another one of your hypothetical situations."

She sat up and said, "I'm not startin' anythin', Ezra that you didn't already start when you implied by your silence that you'd take somebody else to the movies if I wasn't your steady."

"Now how did I imply somethin' by my silence?"

"Oh, you do it all the time, Ezra Casey."

"But, Roseabeth, I am goin' steady with you!"

"What difference does *that* make?"

"It makes all the difference in the world 'cause long as I'm goin' steady with you, I won't be goin' to the movies with anybody else even if I have a notion to."

"Which you so obviously do!" I allowed as to the fact that I did sometimes *wonder* what it would be like to go out with somebody else. And she said, "Well, then what if I said you could jist go ahead and go out with anyone you darned well pleased while I'm gone?" I glanced at her suspiciously because I couldn't tell what she was getting at. Fact is: I was pretty well satisfied. True, I did have a notion to go out with some other girls, but actually doing it would be a frightful lot of trouble. I was used to Roseabeth or as used to her as I figured I'd ever get. And with somebody new I'd have to think about what to say and all. Then I'd have to decide on stuff like when to hold hands, when to put my arm around her, when to try a kiss and if I should take her out again. I'd been through all that before with Roseabeth, and a gut-wrenching experience it was too. Besides, with Roseabeth I never had to worry much about conversation because she did enough talking for both of us.

"Well," I heard her say, "what would you do, Ezra?"

"Well, I reckon I'd pass, Roseabeth. For two weeks I figure it'd be less troublesome to do without female companionship than to go to all the trouble of gittin' used to someone new."

She looked real hard and said, "Exactly, what do you mean by 'trouble,' Ezra Casey?"

"Trouble was a poor choice of words," I said, backtracking. "What I meant was . . ." I almost said agony, then bother, and then worry. When I saw that I had more time than vocabulary I gave up on it.

"Don't you go tryin' to think of some highfalutin' word that Doc taught you, Ezra. 'Trouble' is what you said and I reckon trouble is jist what you meant. Now, if I'm so much *trouble*, I don't know why you bother to go out with me anyway!" Roseabeth had a slightly hysterical side to her that wasn't a pretty thing to see.

I thought maybe I could calm her down when I said, "You're not any trouble *now*, Roseabeth."

"But I was?"

Didn't work. "No, Roseabeth, you don't understand. The trouble wasn't with you; it was with me."

"I'll bet!"

"Roseabeth, what I meant was that it would be a lot of trouble for me to git used to somebody new."

"Oh, I see: You're already *used* to me."

"No, no, no—"

"And *bored*! Which is why you want so desperately to go out with some other girl."

"That's not it at all."

"Well, if that's the way you feel, you jist go right ahead—maybe you're right—maybe we are seein' too much of each other. Besides, there's a good chance I'll be selected as queen of the camp, and if I am, that means I'll havta go to the coronation dinner with the king, whoever he might be."

"Roseabeth, if that's what this is all about, all you had to do was say so. I don't give a hang 'bout who you go to any ole coronation dinner with."

"You don't?"

"No! Why I'd be pleased as pie for you to be queen of the camp."

"And what if—what if the king, whoever he might be, had to kiss me?"

"He could do a whole lot worse," I said.

"That's not what I mean, Ezra."

"Then I don't reckon one kiss would do him any harm."

"Him!" Roseabeth shrieked.

"You?" I ventured.

"*Us*, Ezra," she finally said, correcting my mistakes. I was kind of lost in space of the adolescent female psyche. Roseabeth looked at me, narrowing her eyes, eyes that were glowing with a mischievous twinkle. "Oh—oh, I see what you're doin' plain as day now, Ezra Casey. What's good for the goose is good for the gander, huh?"

"Jeeze!"

"Don't you swear at me, Ezra Casey!"

"Roseabeth, you jist do whatever you wanna do and leave me out of it. Please!"

"Ezra, I can't leave you out of it 'cause you're my steady. All I want to do is what's right, what's *fair*. So if I havta go out with this king, whoever he may be, then I thought you ought to know that I'd have no objection to you goin' out with some-body else while I'm gone. Isn't that fair?"

I thought about it. It *sounded* fair, but I was still reluctant to endorse the idea wholeheartedly. "Okay," I finally said, "that's fair."

"But that don't mean you *havta* go out with someone," she added.

"I know," I said. "But, I wanna be *fair*."

"That's the important thing—to be fair."

"I know," I agreed, "'cause you are the fairer sex. That's what I want too—to be fair."

"Then you *will* go out with someone?" she asked.

"If you insist, Roseabeth." What I saw here was a golden opportunity to wrap her circular logic around her pretty neck.

"I'm not *insistin*'; I'm doin' nothin' of the kind!"

"But to be fair I have to, Roseabeth. 'Cause if I didn't and you did, you'd probably feel real bad, now wouldn't you?"

"Well, of course I would, Ezra, but—"

"And I couldn't stand the thought of you feelin' down and out on my behalf. So, to be fair and to keep you from feelin' guilty, I reckon I'll havta go with someone—jist to be fair." I was sure I had her then; I was just starting to tighten the noose.

She looked at me innocently and said, "But what if I'm *not* selected queen?"

"Huh?"

"That would mean that you'd be home jist havin' yourself a grand ole time, hobnobbin' with all the pretty girls while I'm at camp doin' nothin' but prayin' and singin' all day and night with a bunch of born again—whatevers. That wouldn't be fair."

"No," I conceded, and noticed a slight unraveling of the noose, "it wouldn't be."

"Then what shall we do, Ezra?"

"Well," I said, "maybe you ought to go out with somebody at camp even if you aren't selected as queen, jist in case."

She caught her breath and said, "Why, Ezra, that's a *good* idea; I never would of thought of that in a million years. Now if you insist."

"I don't recall insistin'," I said woodenly.

"But that's the only fair thing; you said so yourself. Okay?"

"Okay," I said and shrugged.

"Okay" Roseabeth said, "I won't say another word 'bout it. Okay?"

"Okay!" I snapped. I was suddenly irritated because I didn't know how it had happened. I was supposed to be the logical one. And I'd given her the go-ahead for I didn't know what, other than that it was exactly what she wanted all along.

Logic was a great thing when it got you where you wanted to go, but with Roseabeth, you'd wind up somewhere else and never quite know how you got derailed along the way. I seldom accepted things on faith, unless it was my faith instead of somebody else's. But this time Roseabeth hadn't even asked me to do that; she's turned my only weapon against me and had come out on top.

I looked at Roseabeth and forced a smile, knowing full well that that wouldn't be the last time she buffaloed me. She returned my smile, nestled her head on my shoulder and sighed ever so contented. The low growl of thunder rumbled off somewhere in the distant night sky.

I don't recall actually asking Fonda out; I do recall picking up the phone, dialing a number—evidently Fonda's, because she answered, but I don't recall what either of us said— probably not a whole lot on my part. But an agreement was struck whereby I was to escort her to the movies in Yellville on Monday night, that being the Monday immediately following Roseabeth's Sunday departure for the Baptist Church

Camp at Devil's Canyon. I called Fonda Sunday night with the sweet fragrance of Roseabeth's dusting powder, and God's only know what else, still fresh on my mind and in my nostrils. Forbidden fruit I guess had a powerful attraction to me; like Mr. Mark Twain, I learned the value of such fruit early in my occasional visits to Sunday school.

There are a number of reasons why I acted so hastily on Roseabeth's wishes, if not on her behalf: 1) I needed to get it over with in a hurry; 2) If Fonda accepted my offer, I'd have time to ask her out again; 3) If she didn't accept my offer, I'd have time to ask somebody else out, and 4) if the stories about Fonda I'd heard were true, I'd have the opportunity to learn something about sex and have a good time while doing it—or so I thought.

My plan was to catch the early show in Yellville, grab a burger and fries at the Dairy Queen and then maybe take Fonda parking out on Huckleberry Hill. With Fonda I didn't figure I'd have to worry too much about what to do or when. From what I understood, with Fonda, you did about everything in one night. Sounded pretty efficient to me. With no trouble at all I could get her home by 11:30 or so and have the rest of the night to brood on what had happened, or hadn't. And why. After finishing my chores around the house I showered, let on that I shaved, splashed on a double shot of after shave and put on my best Levis and a madras shirt that looked like maybe it had been bled maybe once too often, but remained one of my favorites nonetheless. Then I went down to the kitchen real casual like so as not to alert anybody of what I was up to.

Mariko and Silas were cutting up chicken and vegetables, dipping them in a soy sauce and ginger marinade and then stringing them on long skewers to be broiled over charcoal.

Silas looked up when I came in and sniffed the air. "Hot damn! What's that?"

"What's what?" I said defensively.

"Why, I dunno; smells something like a mobile perfumed garden."

"It's Old Spice," I said and saw Mariko poke him in the ribcage.

"Oh," Silas said, "I guess I caught the scent comin' up from the feedlot."

"Silas, that's enough," Mariko said. She was most always on my side; I don't mean to imply that Silas wasn't, but whereas he didn't exercise much authority over me, he did exercise his sense of humor at my expense.

"That yakatori you're makin'?" I asked.

"Your favorite," Mariko said.

"I know," I said woodenly.

"Don't git too excited, son," Silas said. "What are you all spruced up for?"

I gulped and said, "I—ah—sort of—a—have a—date. I was hopin' I could use your pickup."

"Sure, son, but ..."

They glanced at one another and then Mariko cocked her head and said, "Didn't Roseabeth leave for camp yesterday, Ezra?"

"Ah—yes, that's right. I believe she did," I told them.

"You'd better hope she did," Silas said.

"I-ah—saw her off; I'm sure. And this is all set. We—discussed it at some length."

Silas smiled and said, "I'd like to have heard that conversation."

"No you wouldn't of," I assured him.

You mean that Roseabeth agreed that you should be dating someone else while she's gone?" Mariko said.

"Right," I said, nodding. "I think that's pretty much where it ended up. She's gonna be a queen or something', or maybe not; I'm not sure. To tell you the truth, I'd prefer not to talk about it."

"All right," Mariko said, "so long as Roseabeth knows."

They looked at me, at each other, then back to me. "Well," Silas said, "You gonna tell us who the lucky girl is?"

"Oh," I said, "yeah."

"Who?" Silas was real persistent.

"Fonda Peters," I said. Reverend Peters' eldest daughter, Fonda."

Silas started chuckling and shaking his head. "What's this affinity you have for the daughters of preachers?" Fonda's dad was the Methodist minister in Mansfield.

"I reckon it's an inherent interest in theology," I told him.

"Theology, yeah," Silas said doubtfully.

"Silas don't you start in on him," Mariko said. "That's none of your concern anyway. Now, Ezra, what about Roseabeth?"

I sighed heavily. "It's okay, Mom. This was all her idea."

"*Her* idea?" they said in unison.

"I think so. We were seein' too much of each other, or maybe it was not enough, I'm not sure. Anyway, Roseabeth thought it would be a good idea for me to take somebody else out while she was at camp."

"You didn't waste much time," Silas said.

"No, I didn't," I agreed. Then I added, "Roseabeth's gonna go out with a king or somethin'."

"A king?"

"Don't ask me to explain it. You'd have to of been there to understand it. I mean, I was there, and I don't fully understand it."

"All right, Ezra," Mariko said, "just so long as you're being fair to Roseabeth."

"That's the whole point!" I said passionately.

"What is?" Silas asked.

"To be fair! You see, in order to keep Roseabeth from feelin' guilty 'bout goin' out with this king or whatever, I have to go out with somebody my own self too. But in case she's not the queen and somebody else goes out with the king, I won't feel guilty for goin' out with someone else 'cause she can go ahead and go out with somebody other than the king, you see."

"Sit down, son," Silas said.

"Can't. Gotta pick up Fonda."

"Where you takin' her?" Silas asked.

"*A Streetcar Named Desire* is playin' in Yellville."

"You saw that with Doc," Silas said.

"I know, with Roseabeth too," I said. "This way I'll have something intelligent to say 'bout it."

"Why don't you bring Fonda over here for dinner and then catch the late show," Mariko suggested.

I glanced at the skewers of yakatori; Silas went out to stir the charcoal under the grill. "That's a terrific idea," I said. "I'll be right back."

It didn't take me five minutes to get to Fonda's place; the parsonage was on Main right next to the Methodist Church. Fonda came bounding across the lawn when she saw me turn into their drive. She waved to her mom as I hurried around the truck to get the door. She climbed in with a casual smile and said, "Good evenin', Ezra."

I let out a heavy sigh and managed to say, "Hi." I guess I'd never really noticed just how lovely Fonda was until then. A pale yellow sundress against her deeply tanned shoulders and back looked ever so pretty, and her hair sparkled like liquid gold, dangling in soft folds over her shoulders and then turning up on the ends. She had deep dreamy blue eyes that were moist, glistening like maybe she was about to cry, but she wasn't. I'd never been all that much attracted to blondes as a group, but with Fonda sitting there as fresh and soft as a morning dew, I was suddenly a convert, as much as if I heard the bidding of the Lord, which I had heard but had not yet heeded. "You sure do look pretty," I said and backed into a tree at the far end of Fonda's drive.

"Ezra!"

"Boy, they just plant that thing there?"

"Ezra, that ole oak is at least a hundred years old," Fonda told me.

"You okay?"

"Jist fine, but you keep your eyes where they belong."

"You sure do look pretty." I said, thinking I was coming on too strong or maybe not strong enough.

"You already told me that, but thanks. I appreciate the compliment. Now watch where you're going before you wrap us around a utility pole," she cautioned.

"I will," I said, "watch where I'm goin'." At the intersection of Main and First I ground the truck into low gear and turned east toward my house instead of west toward Yellville.

"I thought we were goin' to the movies in Yellville?"

"We are," I said.

"Well, I was under the distinct impression that Yellville was in the other direction."

"We're jist goin' over to my house for dinner before the movie," I told her.

She looked surprised. "We are," she said, "with your folks?"

"And Doc," I said. "If you don't mind."

"Why no, of course not, but . . ."

"What?"

"Oh, nothin' really. It's jist that—nobody ever had me over for dinner before."

"Well," I allowed as I ground into third gear, "I don't recall ever havin' anybody over before, a girl I mean."

"Not even Roseabeth?"

"Especially not Roseabeth. Preacher won't let her come near our place; thinks Doc would be a bad influence, says there's evil in our house."

"Evil? That's silly. My daddy says Doc is a good man, maybe good for the wrong reasons, but good."

"What difference does it make *why* someone's good, jist so long as they're good?"

"Doesn't make any difference to me," Fonda said, fluffing up her hair.

"Me either, but I'd like to find out why it does to some people. That's somethin' I'm interested in," I explained, "good and evil. And why evil seems to pay so much better."

"You know, I think a lot 'bout that. Like—why are some things good if boys do them, but bad if girls do?"

I shrugged and said, "I dunno. Like what?"

She smiled at me and said, "Ezra, you're such a sweet kid; you probably don't even know what I'm talkin' 'bout."

I thought about what she said as I pulled into our driveway. It's true I was a year younger than she was because I'd skipped third grade, but I was a little hurt at being called a kid, especially a sweet one. I'd been around, some. But later, after we'd talked with my folks and Doc for a while, I noticed how easily Fonda mixed with my family, how at ease she was and how well-mannered. I'd spilled my lemonade, put my hand down on the hot grill and tripped over the garden hose all before dinner. Maybe to her I was still a kid. Ordinarily she went out with guys that were ahead of us in school, sometimes guys that had already graduated, so I may have seemed immature to her. That made me want to prove to her all the more that I wasn't.

After Doc directed a blessing for the food—To Whom It May Concern—we sat down around the picnic table on the patio to eat. There was the yakatori, rice, fresh tomatoes and cucumbers, lemonade and angel food cake for dessert. It was a feast fit for nothing less than kings and queens. After dinner we sat out in the cool of the evening and listened to Doc spin tales about his years in Boston and New York as a young man at a time when the country was growing, the frontier disappearing, and the East filling with immigrants, every one of them hoping to fulfill a promise that would prove to be well-nigh impossible for all but a few to achieve. He recalled like it was just yesterday what he had been doing when Orville and Wilbur Wright gave up fixing bicycles and took wing over Kitty Hawk and when the Titanic sunk into the icy depths of the North Atlantic. He told us that night of working people fighting for some sense of decency as the country became more and more industrialized, of continuous outrages against my grandmother's people. He told us about how he'd met, courted and finally married my grandmother before Oklahoma was even a state and about the Sac Nation when it still had a remnant of identity and pride, and he promised to one day take us out to the site of the Battle of the Washita.

Mariko talked to us then; she told us how she'd been born and brought up in a settlement of Japanese immigrants in San Francisco; how she'd been educated in both American and Japanese fashion, and how she recalled visiting Osaka and Kyoto as a little girl. And she told us how happy she was that our government hadn't had a third atomic bomb to play with because there probably wouldn't be a Kyoto anymore. She remembered what had happened to her parents after Pearl Harbor and how awful she had been treated even after marrying my dad. She cried about it because it was so painful to remember, and Fonda cried too. I didn't actually cry because I knew I wasn't supposed to, but I did get this huge lump in my throat and had to blink a lot to keep from crying.

It was fascinating, listening to them, a history book open wide with the stories marching right off the pages in front of your eyes, everything alive and real in an immediate sense. And the way Doc told it, everything was connected in some way with everything else—time and place and people and events. There was no way to escape it; we were all part of it, all a living part of history every day.

Fonda showed a keen interest in everything Doc and Mariko told her. Not all of it was a pretty story, most of it wasn't, I guess, but it was history happening to people you knew, and, in my case loved, and sometimes it hurt an awful lot to hear about it because so much of history was the story of people doing awful things to other people, usually for some noble cause. And it made you think that you were part of history too, and that if you weren't careful you might end up doing awful things yourself whether you meant to or not. When they were all done, Doc closed by saying: "Remember, history depends on who lives to do the telling."

As we drove out of town Fonda sighed heavily and said, "Well, I've never heard history told like that before. Imagine, Ezra, when Doc was born we didn't even have cars or airplanes."

"I know," I said.

"Do you think we'll see changes like that?"

"Doc says we will, says we'll see people on the moon and Mars. Says we're entering a new age of science and technology—Mr. Huxley's, Brave New World."

"What's that?"

"A book, 'bout the future, kinda."

"Good?"

"No, it's awful."

"What'd you read it for?"

"It's the future that's awful, not the book," I explained.

"Oh," she said and brushed some long strands hair back from her beautiful eyes. "I think it's excitin', everythin' that's gonna happen, all we gotta learn. Kinda scary too, sometimes."

"Yeah," I agreed, "sometimes real scary."

She slid over close to me and said, "Ezra, you know in some ways you're really very mature."

"I know," I said confidently. "That's 'cause of biology."

"I was thinkin' more in terms of your intellectual maturity, things you git from books and from talkin' to Doc and all that broodin' you do."

"Oh," I said, and then added, "but I'm also pretty hairy."

She just laughed. Then she looked out the window, and I thought I saw her bite her lower lip, like maybe she was trying to keep from laughing again. When she finally turned back to me she said, "But I suppose, too, that there are a number of things you don't know much 'bout."

"Girls, you mean?" She didn't say anything else; she just stared out the window, watching the countryside roll by in the moonlit night until we got to Yellville.

The movie was terrific; I enjoyed seeing it for the third time and was anxious to see how Fonda would respond to Mr. Williams' adaptation of *Streetcar* to the big screen. It took me a while to get settled in because I couldn't decide whether to hold hands with Fonda or not. I wanted to, but I had no idea of what she was thinking because she'd gotten so quiet all of a sudden. Finally, I sort of let my hand brush against hers, and she settled the issue by saying, "Ezra, do you wanna hold hands or somethin'?"

"Ah, yeah," I whispered, "I guess I do." So she took my hand, and I wasn't about to let go after that, not even when my hand got all cramped up and started sweating and all. Then it went to sleep, and I couldn't have turned loose of her hand if I'd wanted to. After the movie I couldn't move it all until she pried her hand loose from mine.

"What's wrong, Ezra?"

"I think my hand is paralyzed."

"Oh, Ezra," she laughed, "why didn't you jist turn loose?"

"Then I'd of had to git my nerve up to take your hand again."

"You don't have to git up your nerve; girls don't mind holdin' hands with their dates. Here," she said, "take my hand." I did. "Okay. Now let go." I did. "Take it again." I took her hand again. "See how easy that is? Why there's nothing to it. If you want somethin' from a girl, Ezra, you have to let her know it. Well, it's late; I'd better git home."

Parking somewhere I knew was out of the question then, but I still thought I might have a chance for, at the very least, some light necking in front of her house. On the ride home I switched on the radio, and there was Hank Williams singing *Your Cheating Heart*. Fonda asked: "How come you go out with Roseabeth, Ezra? You got 'bout as much in common with her as a rattlesnake."

"She's my girl," I said, "but I'm tryin' to broaden my horizons."

"I can see that you are," she said cryptically. When I pulled into Fonda's drive and killed the engine, she turned to me, smiled and said, "Ezra, I had such a good time." In the darkness there I slipped my arm around her real quick like and tried to nudge her towards me. "Ezra, what on earth are you doin'?"

"Well," I said, "I—I wanted to show you my intentions, jist like you said I ought to do. I—I—wanted to—to kiss you."

"On the first date?"

"In case there wasn't a second," I said.

"What kinda girl do you think I am?"

"Well, I thought . . ."

"Thought what?" she said icily. I gulped and looked away, starting to feel real bad. I'd had a swell time and had enjoyed Fonda's company without doing anything else. I didn't know what to tell her. "Oh, I guess you've heard plenty of stories 'bout me," she spat out bitterly. "Haven't you, Ezra Casey?" I hated it when girls called me that. "Is that why you asked me out? Is it?"

Staring out through the windshield into the darkness, I managed to say, "I guess so." Then I looked at her. "But I don't feel that way now, Fonda. I had a swell time."

"But not as swell as you'd like to have had?"

"Different," I said, "probably a lot better time."

Suddenly she slipped over real close to me, closed her eyes and threw her head back. "All right," she cried, "go ahead, kiss me and feel me up all you want." I couldn't move; my mind had my body paralyzed. Usually it was the other way around. "Go on," she said, "it's jist like holdin' hands." I gulped and felt some sweat trickling down my temples. "What's wrong?"

"I don't want to," I said.

"Why not? That's what you're here for!"

"I feel kinda rotten 'bout the whole thing. I didn't know we'd have such a good time, didn't know I'd—I'd like you so much." I just sat there then, fiddling with the steering wheel.

After what seemed like about an eon or two of silence, she finally touched my arm and said, "All right, we'll forget all 'bout this, pretend it never happened. I'm sorry I got so upset with you, Ezra, but don't you see? It jist isn't fair! Good night." She kissed me quickly on the cheek and was gone.

I drove home and tried to figure it out; it didn't make much sense to me. The reason I didn't go ahead and kiss her and get some feels when she offered herself to me was because I liked her so much. And yet I was pretty certain that the reason people did touch each other like that was because they liked each other. Then I reasoned that if I hadn't of liked Fonda so much I probably would have gone ahead and accepted her of-fer. But if I had, I just knew that she would have hated me for it. Hot damn! What's a kid supposed to do when everything is exactly backwards from what it's supposed to be? I tell you, all of my book learning hadn't taught me anything about what I really wanted to know about.

The next time I saw Fonda we made a day out of it. We loaded up Doc's old Pontiac sedan with a picnic lunch, a cooler of drinks, all the fishing gear we could carry, and set out for Sunset Lake in the Wichita Mountain Wildlife Refuge. Midsummer it was; ordinarily such days in the territories have a lot in common with a blast furnace, but this day was something right out of a romantic novel. You couldn't find a cloud in that sky with a looking glass, and everything around the lake was still green and bursting with life, soft and fragrant. The sun was ever so warm, beaming down from that cloudless sky and carrying the chill of the spring-fed lake way off into the atmosphere somewhere.

Fonda was a marvelous swimmer, strong and fluid, propelling herself through the water like she'd been born there. I was an okay swimmer, but not comfortable or powerful in the water like she was. In the lake, I was pretty much at her mercy; on land too I guess. We swam, played, dunked each other and wrestled around and raced from one shore to another. She beat me every time and about drowned me once. After wearing ourselves out, we climbed out of the lake; Fonda had on a kind of skimpy two piece suit that about drove me crazy because of the way she bounced around in it. It seemed like I didn't have any control over what my mind was up to, and I knew that I should have been missing Roseabeth, but I wasn't, not with Fonda right there in the flesh and not much else. I'm sure Roseabeth would have been lovely in a swim suit too, but I'd never seen her in one. Baptists thought it was a sin for kids of the opposite sex to swim together, and to tell you the truth, I sort of understood why, under the circumstances.

I reached out and took Fonda's hand sort of natural like, and we moved down the shoreline to where Doc and Silas were trying to fool a bass and where Mariko had laid out a feast—fried chicken with a light golden crust, potato salad, Japanese rice balls, freshly sliced tomatoes and cucumbers from our garden, home-made wheat bread, watermelon, peaches, plums, red and green grapes, and slices of chilled honeydew melon. And if Doc or Silas had any luck we would have sashimi—fresh raw fish dipped in soy sauce.

We got all comfortable under the cool shade of a big weeping willow and fished and ate and listened to Doc and Mariko tell us more stories about the lot that life had cast them and about what they'd done about it. Silas didn't say much; he was more of a brooder, always had been, but promised one day to put all his brooding down in book so we'd all know what he'd been brooding about all these years. I don't think he thought the world worked right either.

When I took Fonda home, evening had turned into the full bloom of a summer night with the shrill cry of cicadas competing with the light of fireflies for our attention. A lazy half-moon was illuminating the sky with a hazy kind of light that diminished the twinkle of the stars and made everything look kind of fuzzy. And that's just the way I felt—fuzzy. Fuzzy with a strong attraction to Fonda, and guilty because of my ties to Roseabeth. Then there were all those stories about Fonda. Why, I didn't believe any of them now! She was as decent a girl as I'd ever hope to see, and I decided I wouldn't like her any less even if they were true. I really felt like I'd like to kiss and hold her, but I didn't know if I dared even try after what happened last time. The fact is, I didn't know what to do.

On the drive home Fonda had taken hold of my arm and nestled her cheek against my shoulder and kind of let out a sigh every now and again. Those sighs always confused me; I couldn't tell if she was just tired or what. I was pretty sure I could kiss her without offending her, but I wasn't sure I wanted to take the chance because I still didn't know exactly what to do with the other powerful impulses I was feeling. So when we stopped in front of her house I just sat still, listening to the sounds of the night. A dog howled off somewhere down the street, and I finally said, "Fonda, would you be offended if I tried to kiss you?"

"No," she said, so I slipped my arm around her. "I'd be offended if you didn't, but that doesn't mean I'll let you."

I started slipping my arm back to my side. "Why wouldn't you?" I asked.

"'Cause I'm fond of you, Ezra."

"I'm fond of you too, Fonda," I said and started the arm back around her. "That's why I want to kiss you."

"And that's jist why I can't let you," she said.

I started another strategic withdrawal; my arm was getting kind of tired. "I guess I'm supposed to understand that," I told her.

"But you don't?"

"It's not crystal clear to me, no," I admitted.

"That's because you're still pretty *immature*, Ezra." There it was! "I know how boys are, and I know how I am and how one thing leads to another even if you don't particularly like each other. That's why I can't kiss you, Ezra."

"But you would if you didn't like me?"

"I'd probably be a lot more likely to. That way I wouldn't mind hating you and maybe even myself later if things got off in the wrong direction."

"I don't care anythin' 'bout direction," I said.

"But I do! Besides you don't even know where it might lead. Ezra, I don't want to git involved with you 'cause you're so nice."

"What'd you mean by that? I asked.

"I mean—*innocent*. And I don't want to be the one that changes you."

"It's okay," I assured her, "really! I don't mind at all."

"But I do. You have an unblemished reputation."

"That's not my fault!" I protested.

"Besides, you're still attached to Roseabeth; 'till that changes, I figure I'd better not see you again. It'll be easier for both of us. I do like you, Ezra, and I know I'm doin' the right thing by rejectin' you. Now you jist run along now; stay as sweet as you are, and thanks for a wonderful time. I love your family." And she was gone again.

Sitting there in the dark with the sweet fragrance of her skin and hair lingering in the air like a misty cloud, I came to one inescapable conclusion: it was as hard to live down a good reputation as a bad one.

You'd think that would have ended it, but not for me. Word spread like a prairie fire that I'd been seeing Fonda, and I knew that would elevate me in the eyes of my cronies and at the same time just add that much more dirt to Fonda's reputation. Only then was it that I began to understand some of Fonda's general disgust with how the system worked differently for boys than for girls.

Not long after the picnic I saw my pal Phil Vandaver in front of Yeager's. "Hey, Ezra," he called and crossed the street to catch me. "I hear you been seein' Fonda."

"A couple of times," I admitted reluctantly.

He smiled, winked and asked, "How'd you make out? Huh? Huh?"

"I didn't do anythin'," I said. "She's a very nice girl."

He stared at me and then broke into a wide grin. "You sly devil. You got some, didn't ya? "Huh? Huh?" He kept poking me in the ribs and saying, "Huh?"

"Phil, I'm tellin' you the truth," I said earnestly, "she's not like that at all. Fonda is a nice girl. All we did was . . . where you goin'? Phil!" He hustled across the street and disappeared into the barber shop so I lit out. I didn't want to face that gang.

Later that afternoon I had the misfortune of crossing paths with Ogden Burgatroid at the post office. He poked me in the ribs and said, "Hey, Ez, I hear congratulations are in order."

"Huh?"

"Come on. Don't give me the innocent act. You took Fonda out. Tell me, how was it? Huh? Huh?"

"Quit poking me in the ribs, Ogden!" Now I'd already witnessed what happened if I told the truth, so in an effort to protect Fonda I said, "Oh, you know, Ogden. You've been around."

He stared at me a moment, thinking, then said, "You lyin' dog. You didn't do anythin'; you wouldn't of had the nerve."

I left it at that, satisfied that perhaps I'd prevented Fonda the humiliation of being shunned further by her classmates of the same sex. I also figured that that would be the end of it. But it wasn't. The whole episode had caused me considerable pain by then, and I didn't want it to go any further. But the next day I saw Fonda.

"Hi, Fonda," I said cheerfully.

Without saying as much as a single word she rushed over and slapped my face and then cried, "Ezra Casey! How could you?" Then she ran off down the street crying.

"Fonda! How could I what?" I called after her, but she kept on running. And I felt just awful. I stood there a minute or so then touched my cheek. It sort of stung, but as I thought about it I began to enjoy the sensation—not because I liked getting hit, but because it occurred to me that maybe I deserved it, that maybe while we had been wrestling around in the lake on the picnic I'd got some feels and just hadn't realized it at the time. I couldn't figure what else would have set her off like that.

Anyway, I felt for sure that *that* was the end of it. But it wasn't. When Roseabeth returned from church camp, the first thing she did was walk up to me, slap my face and scream, "Ezra Casey! How could you?"

"How could I what, Roseabeth?"

"You know very well what," she cried, "go out with—*that* girl!"

After that I about gave up trying to figure either of them out. I went home and had Doc tell me about Mr. Einstein's General Theory of Relativity; that was something I could get a handle, if not a hand, on.

9

MR. MELVILLE'S BOY, BILLY

Spring in the territories is a violent time. Warm sultry air pouring in from the Gulf of Mexico forces itself upon the stubborn remnants of cold air masses from the north, and the confrontation between the two sets off Mother Nature in one indifferent rampage after another. Many an afternoon from early April to late June you can count on Lucifer's hammer striking indiscriminate blows at man and beast alike—good and bad, believer and non-believer.

By midday you can see thunderheads building way off in the distance, maybe as far away as the Texas panhandle, towering cumulus ominous clouds piling up on one another higher and higher until it seems like they'll push through the roof of the sky. The clouds on bottom get madder and madder with all that weight piled on them so they turn all black and the deepest kind of purple and finally start stampeding across the prairie like raging bulls. Deafening claps of thunder crack like whips and jagged shafts of lightning rip through the sky, tearing it apart like a piece of worn calico.

From the shredded sky rain pours out in broad sheets that blow across the flatlands like discarded candy wrappers. High up in the clouds the moisture starts freezing, turning rain to hail the size of baseballs, and down it comes with enough force to kill cattle where they stand and take out a wheat crop in less time than it takes to say a Hail Mary. It might stop then, suddenly; the sun might even peak through a crack in the clouds before it turns dark again, as dark at midday as late evening. The entire sky is bathed in a luminous and haunting kind of green light. Before you know it you hear this roar, maybe way off, maybe right next to you, and you know what it is because you don't grow up in the territories not knowing what it is and knowing instinctively to fear it like a soldier hearing the deadly whine of a falling artillery shell. *Tornado!*

The warning sirens wail against its roar, but if you've waited until then to find shelter you're probably too late. From whatever shelter you find you can hear it overhead, rumbling through town like a berserk Sherman tank, scratching, clawing and tearing at the earth, devastating and wanton. Debris flies every which way; roofs come apart; cars get tossed around like laundry, and whole ponds are sucked dry in an instant. Houses collapse in on themselves as the funnel sucks the air from the inside and squeezes on the outside. Animals tear around fields in a panic not knowing what to do or where to go. Trees that have stood for decades are uprooted in a second and flung across the countryside in a flying avalanche. Then, for reasons all its own, the funnel slips back up into the belly of the beast and moves on, gathering strength, readying itself to take on the next farm or trailer park or struggling small town.

People climb out of their shelters and sometimes find their town half gone, their homes maybe gone completely, their friends buried in shallow, debris-covered graves. They stand there, devastated, not knowing what to do, what to think, what to believe. Then after the storm passes the sky clears in a rush and the warm sun comes beaming down on you like it has good sense. And always there's a rainbow—that reminder of God's promise not to destroy the world ever again, *with water.* Rainbows, I know, are supposed to be a soothing sight, and to most folks I reckon they are, but to tell you the truth, they make me a little nervous. There's a lot worst way to go than by water.

Boy, I wish I'd thought of that bit of writing before the essay contest last year; the judges are invariably impressed with that sort of over-written descriptive prose, and I could of had myself a scholarship to the teachers college in Weatherford. No matter. I just wrote it to illustrate a point: tornadoes are just one kind of violence. What happened between Jason and me was another kind, just as savage and almost as deadly, and even worse in one sense, not because it was premeditated—not on my part anyhow—but because it happened at all, because it happened between two human beings who should have known better. Mother Nature just tears the hell out of things because she doesn't know any better, because she doesn't know *anything.* People do. That's why people destroying other people is so much worse than people dying in a natural catastrophe, a so-called act of God. When people kill each other I guess that's an unnatural catastrophe, an act of Man. Unless, of course, you think it's human nature for people to go around killing each other, which I don't. I know there's piles of evidence to the contrary, but I believe Doc was right when he told me that, "Humans weren't made perfect, but they were made perfectly capable of seeking perfection." That time I knew what Doc was talking about, and I still believe it, even after the terrible thing that happened.

I'd been on a bike ride to Fort Cobb and back—thirty some miles round trip with plenty of hills. When I started having any kind of trouble with my legs—shin splints or whatever—I'd stop running and ride my bike to keep my legs and heart and lungs in peak condition. Also I just loved getting out on my bike and watching the countryside sweep by in this ever changing panorama of light and color and texture. I was approaching the east edge of town when Jason and a few of his cronies came racing past me, much too close, forcing me off the road.

I was already irritated because Caleb Joshua's Doberman Pincher had, to hear him tell it, "loped alongside" of me for four miles. I'd just managed to get the dog off my tail when Jason raced by with all his buddies yelling their heads off. As they flew by somebody threw out a cup of ice water which hit me in the chest and soaked my shirt and shorts. Terrific! Already I was dog-tired, something Jason must have known, hungry, thirsty, and all I wanted was to be left alone, to go home and be with my family. I was looking forward to Mariko bringing me a big pitcher of iced tea and for Doc to come in and tell me something that I didn't know but probably should have while I soaked in a warm bath.

Ahead I saw Jason slowing to a crawl, so I turned down a side street that would take me across town to our house.

I pedaled along slowly then, listening, and I could hear the engine of Jason's souped-up Chevy, his pride and joy, running about even with me a block over. Whenever I came to an intersection I saw him waiting and watching a block away, and then saw him ease through the crossing the same time I did. Since we both knew I'd have to turn back west to get home, it looked to me like he was dead-set on a confrontation.

It had been a couple of years since the trouble all started, and I'd successfully avoided him for all that time, but only because he didn't seem all that intent on settling things with me either. Unless *he* forced the issue he knew I'd never show up for a showdown. Of course he could have forced himself on me at any time and yet he never had. I couldn't help but wonder why. I couldn't figure it out.

In the years since the beginning of the trouble we had both grown, but in different ways. Jason had just thickened up through the middle and maybe some in the head while I'd added several inches to my height and about twenty-five pounds of mostly muscle, not in my head. He'd since taken up smoking cigarettes, taken to drinking, and from what I could tell, kept pretty awful hours. By contrast I'd never been stronger or in better physical condition; in a fair fight I knew Jason was no match for me, but I doubted too whether Jason knew what a fair fight was. He was as mean as ever, maybe meaner, and the last thing I wanted was to tangle with him in a street fight. But I didn't know if I could keep from it.

Lately he'd grown more aggressive, taunting me when before he'd leave me be, trying to humiliate me whenever he had the chance, especially around my friends. That didn't bother me too much because I hadn't really been humiliated or embarrassed since the disaster. But something was bothering Jason; that was clear. He was particularly bold when I was with Roseabeth. She was so nice she'd take up for him about half the time, arguing that Jason wasn't mean at all—jist misunderstood, and that all he needed was to be saved from his sins.

I pedaled through another intersection and saw Jason shadowing my movements a block away. I decided he'd finally picked his time to settle our long-running dispute. And I knew he probably realized he couldn't have picked a better time— for him—with me being bone-weary from my long ride. Not just physically either, but also lacking the mental stamina to withstand his threats and verbal abuse. That vexed me some; it lit some spark way down deep inside me that *this* was the precise moment he would pick to lock horns with me.

A couple of blocks from my home on Pleasant Street he turned toward me and gunned that slick coup he drove. I lacked the energy to ride another foot so I stopped, straddled my bike and stood my ground, more or less. He stomped down on the gas even further, and his car leaped forward like a panther, its loud mufflers just bellowing. Right off I knew I'd made a big mistake. I couldn't move, not with my crotch pasted against the top tube of my bike frame, so I just stood there gulping until Jason hit his brakes and started sliding at me through the gravel street. Clearly, I was in the frying pan again. Finally his car stopped with his front bumper just nudging my front tire ever so slightly. If I hadn't have been so glad just to be alive, I would have thought of something clever to say. As it was I just swallowed and watched as Jason and a few more of Mansfield's finest crawled out of his Chevy coup like a bunch of circus clowns. Jason pulled about a two-foot long piece of chain from beneath his front seat and began swinging it aggressively in front of him. That chain, I figured, pretty much made up for his drinking and smoking.

"Fantastic," I whispered to myself. Out of the corner of my eye I saw Freda Yeager dash into her house and noticed someone at her window peering out from behind the curtains. I hope most sincerely that somebody would have sense enough to call home for me. I tried to clear my throat as Jason sauntered toward me dangling the chain; he stopped at my front wheel and yelled, "Git your stupid tricycle away from my car!"

"It's a bicycle," I said, "Tricycles have *three* wheels." I then twisted around on my *bicycle* with every intention of riding off into the horizon and living happily ever after, but Jason's cronies blocked my exit. That vexed me some more. So I climbed off my bike, laid it down carefully on the edge of the street and turned back to my nemesis. "All right, Jason," I said, "what do you want?"

"You!" he said.

I was afraid he'd say that. "Me?"

"Your ass," he said. "I wanna whip your ass!"

Yeah, sure he did, him with his stupid chain. I actually had to force myself not to leap on him right then and there. I could feel my muscles tightening up, something deep down in my gut was squeezing ever so hard. I gulped again and managed to say, "Then why don't you come down to school tomorrow. We'll put on the boxin' gloves and you can have all of me you can git in a fair fight." This I took to be a reasonable request.

"I want you *now*," Jason snarled and gave the chain a little shake. "And I sure as *hell* don't want a fair fight."

"Sure, you want me now," I said, "you and your buddies."

"Jist me," Jason said, "and *this* buddy."

He meant the length of chain. Well, there it was. His buddies started laughing and making some not altogether flattering remarks about my reluctance to fight. By then I was starting to shake some, and I felt my hands tighten into fists all by themselves. Inside my head I was feeling some kind of pressure, and I had this pain behind my eyes so my eyes were watering so it looked like I was crying. I bit down on my lip to keep it from quivering, but it didn't do any good. When I wiped at my eyes they laughed all the more and called me a baby. And I was getting *really* vexed because I just knew I could have that chain wrapped around Jason's neck in about two seconds if I had a mind to. And I *wanted* to do it; I wanted to do it so bad, but I knew I shouldn't, knew it wouldn't do any good even if I did. If he'd just *leave me alone* things would be okay. "I'm not gonna fight you, Jason," I said tight-lipped. Then I picked up by bike and tried to move away.

Tommy Roberts blocked my path, forcing me back toward the car. "Git outta my way!" I screamed. They just laughed and taunted me all the more. I grabbed my bike by the stem and seat post and shoved it will all my strength at Tommy, catching him in the crotch. He fell down, and I turned just as Johnny Parker jumped on my back piggyback style. I just bent over forward, grabbed his shirt and pulled him off over my head. He landed flat on top of my bike and started grasping for breath. I shoved him away and picked up my bike again about the time Bruno Franklin and Joe Rizzo started for me.

"Leave him alone," Jason yelled, "he's mine!"

I was madder than I'd ever been in my whole life. My breath was coming in great huge gasps, and this throbbing pain was hammering away inside my head. I thought I was going to crush my bike with my bare hands. I was shaking all over and things seemed to be spinning around me like in a nightmare. "I don't wanna fight you!" I screamed, and felt the top tube of my bike collapse under my hand.

"Well, you gonna," Jason countered. "Or are ya yellow? Yeah, that's it, ain't it? You're yellow 'cause your mother's some Jap whore, a yellow good-for-nothin'—"

His chain got tangled in the spokes of my bike when he took a swing with the chain. I threw the bike aside and grabbed Jason by the collar and front of his shirt. I swung him around just once, spinning him into the fender of his car where he crashed with a terrific force, bending the fender in on the tire. There was a sickening sound of splitting flesh and crushing bone when he hit. Then everything was quiet; I watched in awe as Jason slid down the side of his car, blood streaming from his mouth and one ear and his left shoulder hammered back in a grotesque position. His eyes rolled back in his head and then closed; the car rocked up and down slowly, its springs squeaking a slight protest.

Jason was lying there in a heap with his blood pouring onto the dark street; I was crying and shaking; my bike was a mess, and everybody was staring at me like I was some kind of a monster. I thought maybe that Jason was dying, and I wanted to cry for him but I was already crying for myself. I felt like I ought to help Jason, but it seemed stupid to help him when I was the one that broke him all up in the first place. And he'd said those awful things about my mom.

Suddenly Doc was there, kneeling beside Jason, same as he done for Alan years before. And Freda and her husband and some people from other houses on the street had gathered. I swallowed hard when Doc looked at me and I said, "I'm sorry, Doc. I—I dunno what happened. I—I—"

"Wasn't his fault," Freda said. "These boys—they started it. Ezra tried to go, and they jist wouldn't leave him be."

"Jason had a chain," somebody else said. "Weren't his fault; he forced Ezra to fight."

I didn't see that fault mattered that much by then. Even so, Doc looked at me and held out his arms. I rushed to him. Feeling the comfort of even his frail arms around me, I cried, "I'm sorry, Doc. I tried not to; I tried . . . "

Doc nodded and held me tight. "I know, Son. I know." Then he looked at Freda and said, "You'd better call Doc Turkle right away."

Doctor Turkle arrived soon and started putting Jason back together as best he could until they reached the county hospital in Hobart. Turned out he had a fractured skull, a serious concussion, and a dislocated shoulder. But he was going to be all right, by whose standards, I didn't rightly know. I was happy and very relieved that I hadn't killed him. And, to tell you the truth, I guess I was just about as happy that we'd finally gotten the thing over with. I somehow knew that neither Jason nor his friends would ever bother me again.

Of course Roseabeth heard about the fight; she was very upset, wondering how in the world I could have done such an awful thing. I told her that I didn't know how I could have done it because that was the truth. I didn't. I truly didn't know any more about why it happened than Billy Budd knew about his killing Claggart. And that scared me more than Jason ever had. That was the funny thing about it: I ended up more afraid of myself than I'd ever been of Jason because I had no idea I was even capable of such violence. But I was, and that was a frightening thing.

10

CATCH HER IN THE RYE

S weat is trickling down my temples and across the side of my face; my hands are still trembling, and I've got this tight knot in my throat that I can't seem to swallow. If I wasn't in such good shape I'd think I was dying. I'm not though; I'm just reacting to a recurring dream—one I've had for many years—that has finally ended, but in real life instead of my dream world. And it's a nightmare!

What happens is that I'm in this huge field of ripening grain—wheat I think it is—with Roseabeth. Suddenly she kisses me playfully on the cheek and lights out, running through the wheat into an adjoining field of rye. I take out after her, but I can barely move because in a dream you know how you can't run for anything. But I see by cutting across the field of wheat, I can catch her in the rye. And I do. But the problem is: I don't know what to do with her once I do catch her any more that Holden Caulfield knew what to do with the rest of his life. Well, now I know, and that's why I woke up in such a sweat and all.

At one point in my life I'd intended to become an interpreter of dreams because Joseph in the Old Testament had gotten such a good situation down there in Egypt. So I tried to find out all I could about it, but without much luck. Seemed a foreigner, a fellow called Dr. Sigmund Freud, had done the lion's share of the work in that area. He'd written a book about how to do it, but Doc didn't have it in his library so I had to use the next best thing—a book about Dr. Freud and some of his thinking that was written by another foreigner.

But instead of being about dreams, that book was about Dr. Freud's theory of what he called psycho-sexual development, and I found it to be fairly fascinating even without a clear understanding of it. The book was called *A Short Frankfurt in Vienna* for reasons that I don't feel qualified to elaborate on, and it was not an altogether flattering appraisal of Dr. Freud's theory. I was taken with it, however, because it talked a lot about Mr. Hemingway, who I'd always had a keen interest in, along with the Dr. from Vienna. And I was *real* curious about any connection between the good doctor from Vienna and those little sausages of the same name.

I didn't learn anything about interpreting dreams from the book, but I did learn a good deal about psycho-sexual development. Least wise I learned enough to recognize that I have a powerful id working for, or maybe, against me. I guess that's a matter of perspective. My id I suppose is what got me in all the trouble with Roseabeth. And I am in trouble, or maybe it's Roseabeth who is in trouble, and that's why Preacher is forcing me to marry her. What I don't know is exactly what is so wrong about what we did. I've got to do some more brooding on it, that's for sure.

Well, as usual I didn't really have time to think the thing through; I was interrupted by some footballs outside in the stairwell. I sat up on the cot and watched and listened. Somebody was fumbling with the key in the latch; the latch snapped, and the door swung open wide and there stood Preacher with Mr. Winchester. He simply motioned for me to follow him.

"Come with me, boy." He started down the stairs, and I followed real close so as not to run the risk of him getting all aggravated with me again. When he stopped to look back for me I ran smack dab into the back of him. "Not so close, dammit!"

"Sorry!"

"You git ahead of me so I can keep an eye on you."

I passed him and asked, "Where am I goin'?"

"Hell, if you don't change your ways."

"I mean right now," I said.

"The sanctuary," he told me, pointing the way with Mr. Winchester. I knew the way so I plodded along trying to go neither so fast he'd think I was trying to get away nor so slow that he'd stick the barrel of the shotgun between my shoulder blades; that ain't a comfortable feeling. Once I reached the door to the sanctuary I stopped and waited.

"You wait in there," Preacher said, "Silas is comin' over. But don't git any funny ideas 'bout runnin' off somewheres. 'Cause there's nowhere on God's green earth that I wouldn't find you."

"You told me that already," I said.

"This time was jist for emphasis," Preacher explained.

"Oh, *emphasis*," I said. "Always a good practice to emphasize an important point."

"Now I'll give you 'bout ten minutes to git things square with your Uncle Silas."

"He's my dad."

"No he ain't," Preacher said.

"Yessir! 'Cause he adopted me."

"He's your step-dad," Preacher argued.

"He's also my legal father."

"It don't matter, dammit! I don't care one way or another anyhow. *Whatever* he is, you wait for him in there. And I want you to remember one thing."

"Jist one?" I said.

"You won't be in there alone."

"I know. I'll be in there with Silas."

"That ain't who I mean."

"Oh," I said. "Who else is gonna be in there?"

"The Lord," Preacher said.

"He's in there right now?" I asked.

"He's *always* in there, and you can bet your sweet tail that He'll be listening to every word you utter," Preacher said.

"Even if I'm not talking to Him?"

Especially if you're not talkin' to Him. Now git in there, and watch your mouth."

I slipped in and stood just inside the door as Preacher closed it behind me. If God really was in there I didn't figure He'd be all that interested in whatever conversation Silas and I had. I moved down the center aisle about halfway to the altar and sat down in a pew; it was real quiet. Somebody had put flowers all over the place, and up near the altar there was this little white arch with plastic roses all over it; under that arch I figured is where I was scheduled to exchange nuptial vows with Roseabeth.

Against one wall the sun was just beginning to show through the new stained glass windows, slanting down at an oblique angle and filling the sanctuary with all the colors of the rainbow in varying degrees of intensity. Another wall housed the same faded windows that had been in the church for as long as anyone could remember, maybe even longer. The wavy old panes in those windows had turned smoky over the years, and the world beyond them looked somewhat distorted and tainted. By looking outside in you'd get the same distorted impression because the glass was so old.

It was so quiet and all that it seemed kind of spooky. I could hear my own self breathing, and when I listened carefully I could even hear the beating of my own heart. And it was beating pretty good because I was still plenty nervous about my impending nuptials with Roseabeth. You probably understand that. Preacher had to have had a reason for bringing me down to the sanctuary; maybe he just wanted me to see the scene of my execution, like a man seeing his hanging tree beforehand. Or maybe he wanted me to confess my sins; that's why he left me in there alone with God. I'd have been more than happy to do just that if I had known exactly what it was that I had done that was, even by a Biblical definition, a sin. I brooded on it, going through the Top Ten one at a time.

I hadn't put any other gods before the God that gave Moses the Ten Commandments in the first place. Now I'm not saying that I'd never placed a few on almost equal footing, but that isn't the same as *before*. Moses didn't say a blame thing about equality, nor do most people as far as that goes.

I hadn't worshipped any graven images; I left that pretty much up to the Catholics. They had them all over the place.

I hadn't taken the Lord's name in vain, at least not on the previous night. Fact is: I didn't even *know* his name.

It was Friday night when it happened, so I hadn't violated the Sabbath, not by Baptists' teachings anyway.

I hadn't exactly always honored Silas and Mariko with my behavior, but God knows they were the most important people in the world to me and that I loved them beyond measure.

I hadn't killed Roseabeth, and I thought it was pretty well established that I hadn't killed Fanny either. At least I hoped that was well established.

I figured it took adults to commit adultery, so I was safe there.

I hadn't stolen anything, at least not since the tampons, and I'd already been punished for that.

And I don't recall bearing any false witness against anybody's neighbor, certainly not my own.

I didn't covet my neighbor's wife or his house, or his oxen, or his ass, or his manservant, or his maidservant. Hebrew Yuckum's kid did have a new English racing bicycle that I would have killed for, but Moses didn't mention anything about coveting bicycles so I figured I was safe on that one. Besides, Hebrew wasn't a neighbor; he lived clear across town.

It was Elvis rather than Moses that gave us the 11th Commandment—Don't Be Cruel—and that was one I'd tried hard never to break. There's enough cruelty in the world without me adding to it. And I certainly hadn't broken it with Roseabeth after the prom; I'd been nice as pie to everyone, *especially* Roseabeth.

"Hello, son," Silas said, appearing out of nowhere and about scaring the pants off of me.

"Silas," I said and turned to greet him. "I didn't hear you come in."

"I didn't want to disturb you; looked like you were doin' some powerful thinkin'."

"It was that," I told him. "Sit down." I slid over and he seated himself in the pew next to me.

"Boy, those flowers are somekinda fragrant; mighty pretty too," Silas said.

"I'd like them a lot better if they were for somebody else's benefit," I said.

"They are," Silas said.

"Roseabeth's?" I asked.

"And Fanny's." I gave him a bewildered look. "You see, Preacher has sort of a—double ceremony planned."

"Oh, great! Which comes first: Fanny's funeral or mine?"

"Yours—your *weddin'*, providin' nobody has an objection," he explained.

"Don't you?" I said hopefully.

"Do you?" Silas asked.

"Well, yeah, I think so. I mean I think I should have an objection. But I'm not sure; that's what I was ponderin' when you came in. You see, Silas, I'm not sure what it is that I did that was so terribly wrong."

He looked surprised. "You aren't?"

"No sir," I assured him.

He took off his ball cap and ran his hand over his head. "Reckon I should have taken this off when I came in. Not right—wearing a hat in church," he said, "except if you're Jewish or Roman Catholic."

I didn't know where he was going with this, but I wasn't about to let him go there. "Don't change the subject on me before we even git on it," I told him.

"What? Oh, oh, yeah, well, the subject—last night. You said you were broodin' on it when I came in."

I nodded. "Yessir, but I'm not certain of what I did wrong. And if I *did* do something wrong, I'm not sure I did it right."

"Well, there you are," he said. I just stared at him, waiting for him to continue. He finally did. "Now you *did* dance with Roseabeth; I heard about that."

"I won't deny it," I admitted.

"And you know Baptists don't much cotton to the idea of dancin'?"

"Yessir, I do know that, but I don't see why I ought to be forced to marry Roseabeth on account of *that*! Besides, nowhere in the Ten Commandments does it even say that dancin' is a sin. The Baptists made that up on their own; God had nothin' to do with it."

"That may be so, Son, but I don't think the dancin' is the real problem," Silas said and began to shift around uncomfortably in the pew.

"What *is* the real problem then, Silas?" He was just gazing out one of the old windows on the far wall. "Still don't want to talk to me 'bout sexual intercourse, do you?"

"My God, Son, would you watch your mouth?"

"What's wrong?" I asked.

"You can't talk like that in a church, Ezra!"

"What'd you want me to call it?"

"Why I don't want you to call it *anything*! I don't want you to even mention it," he said, taking a swat at a fly that buzzed by.

"What if I told you that that may have been what I did that got Preacher so riled up?"

"Then I'd say that Preacher jist might have a valid reason for your weddin' Roseabeth," he told me.

"And if I didn't?"

"Now if that's the case, I'd say he's exceedin' his authority." He pulled at his chin and looked at me. "Did you?"

"Have sexual intercourse with Roseabeth?" I asked.

"Ezra!"

"I dunno know; I *ought* to know, but I don't. 'Cause nobody ever told me nothin' 'bout sex when I asked about it."

"Now hold on there a minute, Ezra," he said.

"I've been waitin' for seventeen years for you to tell me somethin'. Now it's too late," I told him.

Silas shook his head and said, "Ezra, what you're talkin' 'bout is the kinda thing you git for yourself. Nobody told me anything either."

"Yeah, but you never had all this pressure. I'm the only kid in my class that wouldn't know a vagina if I saw one," I said.

"My God, boy, will you knock that off! We never taught you to talk like that; where'd you learn such language?"

"That's jist the scientific name for a pussy, Silas," I explained.

"I *know* that! And I know better than to go around spoutin' off the scientific name of *anything* in the sanctuary of the Baptist Church," he said.

"Silas, all I'm tryin' to do is show you that you don't havta be embarrassed 'bout talkin' to me 'bout sex. I know more 'bout it now. For instance—"

He reached over and covered my mouth and said, "Son, if you don't knock it off I'm gonna light right outta here faster than you can say Amen. Now I came by here to help you, if I can. But I won't sit here and listen to talk such as that. Now you jist tell me what happened last night. Agreed?" I nodded and he uncovered my mouth.

"Silas," I said, "if Roseabeth's not pregnant I shouldn't hav-ta marry her, should I?"

"There you go again," he protested. "I jist want the facts."

"Silas, listen, I figured it all out with Brinton and Phil. Roseabeth's period—"

"*Period!* Jesus Christ, son! Stop that!"

"Silas, her period was jist last week! We figured it out, so she couldn't of ovulated by last night."

"Ovulated! My God, Boy, stop it," Silas said mopping his brow on his shirt sleeve. "Periods and ovulatin'. You sound like some kinda sex maniac or somethin', I swear."

"Well, what do you call it?"

"I got sense enough not to talk 'bout such things, so I don't havta call them anything"

"Well then, what does *Mom* call them?"

"She doesn't talk 'bout them either, least wise not to me," he said, shaking his head. "Boy, you have got somethin' to learn 'bout sex all right."

"Which is exactly what I've been tryin' to do for the past few years," I reminded him.

"Well, the first thing you need to know is that sex is some-thin' you don't talk about," Silas explained.

"What? Sex is all anyone ever talks 'bout in the barber shop and pool hall," I told him.

"Ezra, they're *jokin'* about it," he said.

"Then it's okay to joke 'bout it, but not to talk seriously 'bout it with an experienced adult? Is that right?"

"That's right, son. Don't ask me why, but that's jist the way things are. And you havta admit that Mariko and I have been very open with you. With Doc's help we introduced you to information most kids won't even see until college—Greek culture, Oriental philosophy, metaphysics, psychology, philosophy and God only know what else."

"I appreciate that, Silas; I really do. But the one thing I was *most* interested in was something you and Doc wouldn't or couldn't discuss with me. I know you tried a couple of times, but you left so much out of it, that I jist got more confused."

"You seldom mentioned sex, Ezra."

"That's 'cause I didn't even know what to call it. By the time I figured even that much out, it was clear that you and Doc weren't going to tell me anythin' comprehensible."

"Ezra, sex isn't somethin' you talk about; it's somethin' you do."

"If you know how," I pointed out.

Silas took a deep breath and pinched the bridge of his nose. Then he looked at me and said, "Ezra, to tell you the truth, it's kind of a hard thing to explain; that may be 'cause I don't have a real good handle on it myself. And if I was to explain—say the mechanics of it—it might sound so ridiculous to you that you'd never even wanna try it."

"Gimme a try," I said, "so I'll know more 'bout what happened last night."

"Okay. So . . . now you know how your mom and I love each other, how we're always holdin and touchin' each other affectionately. You've seen us."

"Yessir. "Course I have; I think it's kinda nice."

"Okay. So—sometimes when you're with Roseabeth, say out parked somewhere, kissin' and huggin' some, do you ever—ah . . . you know?"

"Git a boner, a woody, an erection?"

"Dammit! There you go again. Now I want you to stop that right now," he warned.

"I thought we were gonna talk honestly 'bout it," I said.

"You thought wrong. I'm not sayin' another word. You know everythin' anyway with all your scientific knowledge. Besides I reckon you must know what happened between you and Roseabeth, and you're jist gonna havta be big enough to accept the consequences of your behavior. There's nothing I can do about that. If you didn't do anything, you let me know and I'll help you out of this mess. Otherwise, I'll see you at the weddin'. Mariko left your things with Preacher. Good luck, Son."

Silas, wait! I won't say anythin' else, I promise. Silas don't leave me here!"

He didn't stop until he got to the door; then he just glanced back at me and said, "Son, if it was *anythin'* else." Then he shook his head and walked out. I think he was relieved to get away. I realized then that I'd taken the wrong approach with him; I should have joked about my situation; that way we could have gone on for days or even weeks, thereby delaying the wedding until Roseabeth's *next* period, an event that would have proven conclusively that Roseabeth didn't have to get married after all.

And the flowers wouldn't be wasted because of Fanny's funeral. I guess I ought to give her a little more thought; she ended up in worse shape than the rest of us: dead and likely to remain so. That's another thing I didn't know much about—death—but at least people would talk about that, re-luctantly, but they'd talk about it because it was something we all had to face.

It was Doc, of course, who taught me about death, and it was Doc who taught me the ultimate value of life by forcing me to face the ever-present reality of the grim reaper's pres-ence in our own family.

11

FISH KILL

It was hot early that autumn when the fish kill occurred. School had let out for two weeks so us kids could help get in the cotton crop, but I wasn't entirely sold on the idea. It was one of those deals where the work was hard and the pay was low, but you were supposed to have such a good time doing it that you didn't mind the abuse. Never mind that you couldn't stand up straight for three days afterwards or that it took two weeks for your hands to heal from the spiny cotton bolls ripping into your skin.

I declined numerous offers to spend two weeks in a cotton field; however, so deeply ingrained in my being, in spite of my upbringing, was the Protestant work ethic that I volunteered to paint our house instead—for nothing. Unfortunately, my offer was accepted. Still, by doing the house I could work at my own pace, and I didn't have to sing unless I took a notion to. I didn't see much point in signing in a place where the acoustics weren't any better than in a field of cotton.

On Friday I'd promised to meet Doc at the river after I finished painting, so after washing away the top layer of paint from my face and arms I dug out my fishing gear, got on my bike and started pedaling for the river.

It was getting on toward evening, but still warm enough so the wind I generated by riding felt good because it kept me cool and dried any sweat before it could trickle down my back and soak my shirt. If I had ridden hard I could have covered the distance to the fishing hole in about twenty minutes or so; but I took my time, riding in the shade cast by the towering elms crowded alongside the road like spectators at a parade. There was a mat of gray shadows in front of me with the shadow of one tree connected to the next in an unbroken stream, laid out like a smooth passage of Faulkner's prose. I drew in deep, long breaths of the decay-filled air and watched as the limbs overhead brushed the sky with strokes that were considerably more delicate than what I was using on the house. After a while I arrived at the river and spotted Doc's old Pontiac sedan parked high up on the bank directly above our favorite fishing hole. I figured to find Doc dozing beneath the huge cottonwood below.

I leaned my bike against a tree, grabbed my stuff off the rack and stood there for a moment gazing down at the river which snaked off to the south and east in the cavity it'd dug for itself over the last million years or so. It was flowing by; ever so peacefully, its surface littered with flotsam and foam. Underneath, the current was pulling like crazy, same as always, and the fish were moving more since the intense heat of summer had passed. They didn't like the heat any better than the rest of us, but I don't suppose the humidity bothered them too much. By then the larger fish could be coaxed out of their deep lairs before nightfall to feed on frogs or worms that happened to be so unfortunate as to get into the river at the wrong spot. I'd even seen big catfish and gar feed on birds and small mammals. But the river was pretty quiet for the moment, just sort of gurgling, with a small wave slapping against the bank every now and again.

Doc was stretched out under the cottonwood where I'd received the lion's share of my ethical training. I kicked some dirt down the bank, and I thought it was curious he didn't stir. Because when I didn't aim to bother him I invariably did. And when I wanted to get some information—say something about maturity—he'd pretend to be asleep. Then it struck me that Doc was much closer to the river than usual and that one foot was at the river's edge with the water lapping away at his boot top.

"Hey, Doc," I called cheerfully, "you're gittin' your foot all wet." He didn't answer or even stir any. I stopped, swallowed hard and called, "Doc!" When he didn't answer I rushed down. His fishing gear, I noticed, was just resting beside him like it had been dropped, and he looked *too* relaxed, but relaxed in an uncomfortable position with one leg bent under him and his head stretched way back over an old log. I fell down beside him and cried, "Doc. Doc!" Then I lifted him by the shoulders and shook him hard, but he didn't move by himself, only when I shook him. And I knew he was dead then because his eyes didn't show anything but indifference, a look I never saw in Doc's eyes when he was living. He looked at me without seeing, his eyes blank and void of passion and concern. I pulled him to me and held him like he'd held me so many times before, and I cried, "Oh, Doc! Doc!" even though I knew he couldn't hear me. Then I held him away and his head fell to one side, and I laid him down and listened at his chest for any murmur of the heart, but there wasn't any. He was dead all right, but I couldn't hardly believe it because I'd seen him alive just a little while before when he'd told me that just because you paint a house white on the outside doesn't mean that what's inside is necessarily pure or good or right–or something like that. I think he was talking about some other house because I was painting our house beige. "Aw, Doc," I cried, "don't leave us. Please don't leave us. We need you here so much!" But he'd already gone.

I dug the keys out of his pocket, scrambled up the bank to his car and raced back to town. Silas and Mariko were in the front yard checking out my paint job when I got there. They saw me coming and watched as I tore up the street, slid across our driveway and into the front lawn before stopping. "Mom, Silas," I shouted as I threw open the door and leaped out. "It's Doc!" They looked at each other then rushed to the car. Silas slid in under the wheel to drive, and I climbed in between him and Mariko. "He's gone," I said. "He won't move; he's jist lying there." Mariko held me tight and patted my shoulder and kissed my head. She didn't tell me not to cry or that everything would be all right. She just held me and told me to go on and cry because that was all we could do and because tears had a wonderful healing quality about them. And she was crying too, and so was Silas. And I thought that it was good when someone in your family dies and everyone can cry and everyone can mean it.

When we got to the river Silas slid down the bank to where Doc was stretched out; he knelt beside him, held his wrist, listened at his chest and then looked up at us and shook his head. Mariko caught her breath, and then it was my turn to hold her. Pretty soon Silas struggled up the bank, carrying Doc in his arms. I opened the back door and Silas laid Doc across the back seat. Then he took Mariko and me in his arms and held us real tight for a long time. Finally he took a huge breath, sighed, and said, "We better go."

"I'd like to stay for a while," I told them. "I'll git Doc's gear and bring it home on my bike."

Silas nodded. "Okay," he said, " If we're not home when you git there jist wait for us. We—havta make some arrangements."

"Okay," I said.

"Be careful," Mariko told me.

I nodded and wiped at my cheek with the back of my hand. Then I watched as a thin cloud of dust rose behind the car as it sped away, growing smaller and smaller and finally disappearing down the narrow road. The dust settled back in the road or in a bordering half-picked field of cotton. Overhead the wind was moving through the branches of the cottonwood like an invisible hand, and the low sun was flooding the river with a soft yellow-orange light that intensified on the red clay banks, making them come alive with heat as if just pulled from a kiln. Across the river in a field of cut rye I heard the cry of a mourning dove, and from below came the sound of water rushing by. And when I listened real hard I could hear the sound of Doc's soft chuckling echoing up and down the river bottom and his low voice explaining to me how difficult it was to be decent in a world where so little monetary value was placed on intangibles such as decency and honor and kindness and integrity.

I'd stopped crying by then because while I knew how much I'd miss Doc, I thought about how much worse it would have been never to have known him at all. And I knew he'd tell me that I wouldn't be much good to anybody if I kept on moping about something there was precious little I could do anything about. So I decided to do something about the things that I could do something about. And I figured to start by gathering up Doc's fishing gear and giving it to somebody that could use it now that Doc didn't need it anymore.

At the river's edge I located Doc's tackle box, a can of bait, and the book he brought to read—*As I Lay Dying* by Mr. William Faulkner. I placed them in a neat pile, then picked up his rod and reel and began to reel in the line; I took a few turns, taking in the slack until the line quit coming. I figured he'd snagged a root or some piece of junk on the bottom. I tugged on the rod, putting more pressure on the line, but it still wouldn't budge. Then all of a sudden the rod nearly bent double and line started whizzing off the reel like it was hung on a locomotive. When I went to adjust the drag I found it dead-tight already, and I figured then that Doc had hooked into the very quick of the river itself and left me to land it. I was thinking it could be a huge old gar or a giant carp; the river was full of both. Whatever it was, I had to let it run to keep it from snapping the line. It would tire before long against such resistance, and if Doc had already fought it some, which he must have, it couldn't last too long.

It took out sixty, maybe seventy, feet of line, then slowed gradually and finally stopped. My heart was pounding away like a jackhammer; in the sudden quiet you could even hear it. I was excited and half afraid because I didn't know what Doc had hooked into. Then with my temples throbbing and my heart still pounding like I'd just finished a mile run, it occurred to me that this fish, whatever it was, had probably killed Doc. Doc's old system could no longer stand such excitement as I was feeling. That realization made me not afraid anymore, but calculating and vengeful instead. And I set about to even the score for Doc with all the skill and cunning of the world's most dangerous predator.

Whatever it was, was resting about eighty feet below me in a stretch of quiet water, gathering strength for another run, this time toward some tangled roots and branches that hung down into the river. In there he could wrap himself around something, tangling the line, and I'd never get him out. So I decided to turn him before he made another mad dash down river. I started him in real easy like, alternately pumping the rod and reeling in just a little line at a time. I'd coaxed him up river fifteen feet when he turned and made his final run. It was a poor effort. Doc and I ganging up on him was too much; against the heavy drag, spent like he was, he couldn't make any more headway. I turned him back and started pumping the rod again, figuring he'd still have something left for me when I got him to the riverbank. He kept tugging, but his heart wasn't in it; it was just a matter of foot-dragging by then.

As I kept pumping and reeling, he began to surface slowly about twenty feet below where I was standing, and I caught a glimpse of his great white belly as he rolled across the river's surface, spent, evidently accepting his fate. An old flathead or blue catfish it was, as long as I was and about as thick through the middle. I shook my head and blinked, hardly believing the size of him. His skin shone silver-blue and was marked with dots the size of nickels all the way down his body to his forked tail. His whiskers stretched to twice the width of his head; his eyes were like deep black holes, and his gaping maw could hold a man's arm and then some. He tried to turn when he saw me, but didn't have enough strength to make a solid effort so I kept him coming, more gingerly then because I knew from Doc's experience that he wasn't all done.

He let me pull him right up to the bank where he rolled over on his side and even closed his eyes. Then as I let just the smallest bit of slack in the line to reach down for him, that paddle of a tail swatted the river like an open hand and he flew at me with his mouth working like a buzz saw. I swung my hand away and caught him in the chops with my forearm; he left a row or two of his needle-like teeth embedded in my flesh. In the same instant, I jerked on the rod and lifted the brute clean out of the river. My forearm was bleeding from elbow to wrist from an ugly surface scratch and stung like crazy.

Cautiously, I then dragged him further up the bank and watched his mouth open and close periodically and his gills working uselessly in the thin air. He stared at me too, distantly, vacantly, maybe even helplessly, but at the same time, somehow proud. The fish made me think of Vardaman's mother, but I knew that wasn't what he was. I realized I'd finished off what Doc had started I don't even recall how many years before: I'd nailed Old Blue, the fish that had taken off Doc's finger. I peered down at him, helpless as he was, and tried to hate him. But as much as I wanted to, I couldn't do it anymore than Doc could have. Reverence for all life was a lesson Doc had taught me early on, and it had become second nature to me by then. All I could see was a poor animal, flopping around in the dirt and gasping uselessly for oxygen that he couldn't take from the stuff we humans breathe. He had no sense of what he'd done to Doc, only a sense that *his* life had been threatened by what we'd done to him. His instinct was for survival; he didn't have a notion of hate or malice or revenge. He was just trying to survive, like all the rest of us, given the limited tools God had given him and under some very difficult circumstances.

Keeping the line taut, I reached over and took the needle nose pliers from Doc's tackle box, snipped off the barbed end of the fish hook and removed the shank from the fish's mouth. The barb would either fall out in time or become covered with a kind of gristle and remain embedded in his lower jaw from then on. Even after I snipped the line he just lay there, flopping occasionally, covering his sticky skin with sand and dried leaves and twigs. After a while I grabbed him behind the head and gills and dragged him back into river, letting the flow of the current run across his gills and wash him clean. He gave his tail a strong sweep as I loosened my grip and he was gone. I watched for a moment, until the ripples he'd made with his final dive had passed away. Then I gathered up all the gear, climbed up the river bank and robe my bike home.

We didn't have a regular funeral for Doc; that's what he wanted, not to have one, or to be buried in a grave either. He said he didn't see any point in taking up good land with his old bones, land that could be used to grow something of value on. That was the idea anyhow; Doc never would have ended the sentence with a preposition. That was Doc's way: thinking about people even after he'd gone.

What we did was to have him burned up, cremated. Then Mariko put his ashes in a vase on the mantle. Come spring, the first really fine day, we were supposed to take the ashes and spread them in a field of ripening grain somewhere between the mountains and the river, didn't matter where really, just some field getting ready to burst open with new life.

In the meantime we had a memorial service conducted by one of Doc's former colleagues at the university, another religious liberal. Pretty much the whole town turned out for the service, not because any of them were like-minded when it came to matters of religion, but because most of them respected Doc for what he was—a good and decent human being. A few others were simply curious, and some, I suppose, came because it was such a lovely day.

There was a small Kiowa church on the outskirts of town; that's where the service was held. Doc had spent a lot of time there helping the people somehow reconcile what they were with what the rest of the country thought they ought to be. Doc had liked the place and had always felt as much at home there with the Kiowa tribe as with anybody else. They never asked him what or who he believed in; they just saw what he did, and they could tell pretty much from that what he believed.

The church was situated on a grassy knoll west of town; to the east the land fell of steadily, finally flattening out for good on either side of the river; to the west it ran flat for a while before it began to shoot up in jagged sections as the terrain turned into the hills and rocky knolls that made up the Wichita Mountains. Had it not been for the white carpet of ripening cotton covering the bottomland, the day could have been taken for high summer for all the green still showing everywhere.

The small church filled quickly; looking out an open window I saw people beginning to fill in the side of the hillock. I'd asked Roseabeth to come with my family, but Preacher wouldn't allow it. She'd managed to make it anyway, along with Fonda and what looked to be the rest of my classmates. I appreciated that they came; I realized they must have had some idea of what Doc meant to me, although I don't suppose that they ever understood Doc himself or what he stood for any more than most. I don't know why, but even Jason Clay was there, standing not far from my classmates and Roseabeth.

It was a lovely day, sad for obvious reasons, lovely because it was sunny and clear with only a few fluffy clouds in the sky. I felt good, secure, sitting between my mom and Silas, and I suppose the three of us made quite a spectacle—Silas favoring Doc's Irish side of the family, Mariko with her delicate Oriental features, and me being a fair combination of those two with a good measure of the Sac Nation thrown in. I knew I was different from most of my classmates, but I'd always thought of being different in terms of ideas rather than heritage.

Doc's friend was talking about him, but I had a hard time concentrating because I had my own memories of Doc to occupy my mind. So I just shut everything else down and let my mind run on like a movie projector, remembering exactly what I chose to remember. In a continuing newsreel in my mind I saw Doc doing nothing but good and decent things for as long as I could recall. Wherever there was an injustice, there too was Doc, even to extend of trying to make right what history had made wrong. History, he told me once, "was just the recorded narrative of people trying to keep from hanging themselves and everyone else." When people needed a hand, Doc was there, and he didn't ask any questions about what form of religion or government or economic system someone believed in before giving it. I recall Doc always helping the Kiowas and migrant farm workers that drifted in and out of our town with each passing harvest.

I saw him helping Alan in his fight with Jason and later helping Jason after his fight with me. It didn't matter that I was his kin and Jason had started the fight; all that mattered was that it was Jason that needed a hand. Doc had always fought for people who couldn't or who for one reason or another didn't know how to fight for themselves. Mariko told me how Doc had taken us in after my father was killed in the war and how bad it had been for him to have us there with him when people were so down on the Japanese. She told me all about the awful things he had protected us from. Doc enraged all kinds of people with his liberal politics and religion, but they could never make him quit his work. He was smarter than the lot of them, always turning their arguments upside down and inside out and showing in the Bible that everything he stood for was advocated by Jesus his own self. Deep down inside everybody knew Doc was right, that if Jesus was alive he *would* be on Doc's side, even though Doc himself didn't give a hang about being born again or saved. And that really infuriated people because they didn't understand why he was being so blasted decent if it wasn't because he was scared of going to hell.

If there was a heaven, Doc wouldn't care anything about going there either, I don't think. Because the people there wouldn't need any help, and the ones in hell would probably need all the help they could get and wouldn't be too fussy about where it came from. That's the way Doc was; just like Huck Finn: He'd go to hell for you. You can't ask much more of somebody than that. If he did wind up in hell, I just hoped that his notion of the place was inaccurate; he'd seen hell as a place where people only expressed themselves in shopworn clichés and heaven as a place where everyone spoke in beautiful metaphors all the time. If that was the case he really would suffer in hell, but at least he'd have had some preparation for it, having spent the last years of his life within earshot of me and my friends. If we didn't kill the language, we sure butchered it up some, and for Doc that was every bit as bad as original sin.

After the service we filed outside slowly where the sun was still beaming down ever so warm and bright and the ground was soaking up what seemed like gallons of salty tears. Everyone was hugging each other and patting one another and shaking hands and wiping away tears. And nobody was ashamed of crying and everybody seemed like they were all part of the same family, Kiowas and all. I knew how pleased Doc would have been; he always used to say that all humanity was just one big family in a very small boat with no paddle, except for whatever paddle we managed to make for ourselves.

When we got home I sat down near the tokonoma—a place of beauty—and looked at the vase that had Doc's ashes in it. It didn't really seem like Doc was in there at all; instead, he was outside the vase with me and in the hearts and minds of all those people who'd been at the service earlier. And it occurred to me that Doc wasn't really dead at all; we hadn't put him in a hole in the ground and covered him with dirt. Something of him was alive in everybody who knew him, a part of him that couldn't die so long as people lived the way he lived, so long as people *lived* a creed of decency instead of just reciting one. And I'm dead certain that that's the only kind of immortality that Doc would give a hang about, a kind of immortality that did some good for the living rather than the dead. In death, as he was in life, I'm sure Doc would be much more concerned with saving peoples' lives—from misery and ignorance and poverty—than he would be with saving their souls for the hereafter or whatever.

12

ID HAPPENED ONE NIGHT

So little time and so many questions left to get settled in my own mind. Even with all this thinking—the memories, the anxiety, the guilt, the madness and uncertainty—even with all that, I'm still not dead certain of exactly what happened. Or why. But I do know this: I liked it, at the time. And, to tell you the truth, which I've been doing for the most part, I'm looking forward to trying it again, naturally under more favorable circumstances. But I'm decidedly *not* ready to tie the matrimonial knot at this point in my life. That's not because I don't love Roseabeth; I do. At least I think that's what I did to her. And she's a looker for certain, but then so are Norma and Kathy and Patricia and Jackie and Jerry Ann and Valerie and Fonda . . . Lord the list could go on and on.

The thing that bothers me about marriage is that it's so permanent or that it's supposed to be; to me marriage means mating for life, like Canada geese and beavers. Doc used to tell me about these geese that made a habit of stopping over at his great granddaddy's farm in Rhode Island. Every fall, on their flight south, these geese would home in on that pond like they had radar and lay over a few days resting and filling themselves with corn from a nearby field. Then they'd fly off just ahead of the first real nor'easter. One year a hunter slipped in and shot a big gander, and every year after that for eleven years that gander's mate would stop over and search sorrowfully for her lost mate. She's wander about aimlessly, looking in the corn field and in the deep recesses of the pond, squawking, calling for her mate ever so pitifully. For eleven autumns she came back squawking, but she never got an answer.

I guess that's the way I want to feel about the woman I finally marry. Like I said, Roseabeth was mighty comely all right, but I'm not sure she'll be something to squawk about after eleven years. Not only that, but I'm not for certain that the daughter of a Free Will Baptist preacher and the son of a religious liberal could ever find happiness together, especially here in the territories, a place where a little doubt is considered to be treason.

So caught up was I in these ruminations that I didn't notice there was someone outside the door until I heard Preacher's voice.

"Ezra? You in there?"

"Yessir," I answered wearily.

"You decent?"

"Not accordin' to you," I told him, "but I am dressed if that's what you mean."

"Don't git smart, Boy. I wanna talk at cha."

"Come on in" I said, as if I had some say in the matter.

Preacher turned the key in the latch and stepped in boldly. He was packing his shotgun which, I suppose, was entirely appropriate under the circumstances. It had twin steel-blue barrels, a dark wooden butt and some fancy engraving around the chamber area. Preacher just stood there, staring at me, trying to make me feel real bad about what had happened. But I didn't. What I felt bad about was *how* it had happened.

"Well, Boy," he said, "What of you got to say for yourself now?"

I shrugged and began digging into the floor with the ball of my foot. Fact is, I didn't have a whole lot to say for myself, certainly nothing he'd want to hear anyway.

"Well, Boy?"

"Name's Ezra," I said.

"I know your name, Boy. Nice Biblical name too, but not too fittin' under the circumstances, if you know what I mean." I knew. He stood there waiting and just staring at me. "Well, Boy?"

"I don't know *what* to say for myself," I finally told him.

"You could start with I'm sorry," he demanded and emphasized the point by swinging the shotgun across my brow.

"Oh—oh, I am!" I said. "I'm *real* sorry, and I sure hope I didn't *hurt* Roseabeth any."

"Well, I reckon she'll make out all right long as she's cared for proper. But that don't make what you done right!"

"No sir," I agreed, "it don't." It didn't, however, make it any less enjoyable either. I had the good sense not to mention that to Preacher.

"Now I want you to understand one thing, Boy?"

"What's that, Preacher?"

"Now you ain't a bad boy, which ain't to say you're a good one either, but aside from takin' advantage of my angel, you ain't all that bad, but then you ain't no prize either, if you know what I mean."

"I have no idea," I told him.

"You're plenty bright, and I reckon you even got some potential. You got basically a kind nature about you, and I think you'd care for Roseabeth proper."

"I appreciate that, sir."

But I ain't so high on you that I'd hesitate one second to put a volley of shotgun pellets into your carcass if you was ever to mistreat Roseabeth in any way. *That's* what I want you to understand," Preacher explained.

"Why I have nothin' of the kind in mind, Preacher," I said vigorously. "But if we did have a little spat, I hate to think it would take the intervention of a shotgun to settle it; hardly seems like a charitable solution."

"I don't aim for it to be charitable, jist decisive," Preacher said and stroked his Winchester affectionately.

"I see. Shotgun diplomacy to go along with a weddin' of the same variety."

"The Lord's will."

"I git the picture," I said. Preacher did have a way of making a point.

"Good. I'm glad we understand each other. And consider yourself lucky—"

"Oh, I do. Roseabeth a *fine* girl."

"That's not what I'm talkin' 'bout."

"Maybe not, but she *is* a fine girl."

"I *know* that, the very best. But what I meant was that if I'd been able to git my hands on Mr. Winchester last night, we wouldn't be havin' this conversation right now. Or any other time, if you know what I mean."

"Well, sir, I'm certainly . . . grateful."

"That I couldn't find Mr. Winchester?"

"That and—and that you're bein' so . . . understandin' 'bout the whole misunderstandin'."

"So let it be did, so let it be done," Preacher said, looking up into the heavens.

"Matthew, Chapter II, verse four?"

"Son, that ain't even from the Bible. I made it up my own self."

"With God's help."

"Well of course, with God's help. Don't none of us do nothin' without God's help."

I let out a big sigh and scratched the top of my head. "Preacher, I was jist thinkin'."

"You know better than that, Boy'."

"More *wonderin'* than thinkin'," I told him. "What if—*Roseabeth* was to decide after some period of time that *she* preferred somebody else's company to that of mine?"

He squinted his eyes and moved real close to me and said, "Then I reckon that would mean that you'd done somethin' to bring 'bout her disfavor."

This man was certainly single-minded. "But *if* I hadn't, and she jist naturally took a likin' to somebody else?"

"Jist what kinda girl are you suggestin' my angel is?" Preacher asked. I took it to be a rhetorical question.

"Oh—oh, I didn't mean anythin' like that," I assured him.

"What *did* you mean?"

He poked me with Mr. Winchester. "Jist that . . . if I—I snored or somethin' like that. And *that* drove Roseabeth away. That's all."

"Well—don't," he commanded, and I added "Thou shalt not snore." To the original Ten Commandments from Moses and the one from Elvis, which brought the total to 12—one for each disciple. "One more thing," Preacher said.

"I'm all ears."

"I don't want none of my grandchildren to come out lookin' like Indians." He was getting into one of those areas that I was fairly sensitive about and clearly exceeding his authority. "Or Japs either," he said piling insult upon injury. "You understand?"

I just stared at him, beginning to boil inside, and knowing full well that he was pushing things way beyond my personal control. If his grandchildren being part Indian or Japanese was such a concern I didn't see why he was forcing me to marry Roseabeth at gun point. "No, no I *don't* understand," I said in a fit of vexation. "How does it work, Preacher? Can we put in an order down at Yeager's for a lily-white baby with rosy cheeks and lovely round blue eyes? Or is any baby that Roseabeth and I make goin' to be some combination of both of us? How does that work? Explain to me exactly how two different people can create a third livin', breathin' human being." He stood there clearly taken aback by my questions, watching me, his skin flushing to the color of a rose. "Come on, Preacher, I'm waitin' for an answer."

For a moment he was speechless. Then he explained: "As you must realize, Ezra, I'm not particularly well equipped to deal with questions that aren't of a theological nature."

"Then what good are you? There's never been a person in Mansfield other than Doc who ever had a theological question, and you wouldn't even speak to him!"

"You jist hold your horses there, Boy—"

Doc used to say: "You can lead a horse's ass to water, but you can't make him *think*." I know who Doc was talking about now. "Now here's a theological question for you, Preacher: God created man, right?"

"In his wisdom."

"And woman?"

"From the rib of a man. That's true."

"And sex?"

He glared at me. "Yes . . . I suppose He did."

"In His wisdom?"

"But he didn't intend for sex to be practiced outside of marriage," he argued doggedly.

"No?"

"Never!"

I narrowed my eyes and asked, "Were Adam and Eve married?"

He thought about it and said, "In God's eyes they were."

"But they weren't in *man's*! Because they didn't have a license from the state and no *preacher* had ordained their marriage *for* God."

"What are you gittin' at, Boy?" He was blanching now, and his voice, little more than a low snarl, came from some deep-rooted place in the darkest part of his soul.

"Jist this: That what Roseabeth and I did was all right as far as God's concerned; it's man who is puttin' the burden of guilt on a perfectly natural human act, an act created and ordained by the Creator Himself."

His gaze could of melted a glacier. He let the shotgun rest across the bend at his elbows and planted his thumbs in his wide lapels and said, "You may think it was all right, and God may think it was all right, but **I** think it was *wrong*! And I intend to make it right by seein' that you marry Roseabeth if it's the last thing I do. And if you try to wiggle out of it," he snarled, now bringing the shotgun to bear on my head, "that enlightened mind of yours is gonna git scattered all over three counties. Now do you understand *that?*"

I suddenly lost all my enthusiasm for debating the point and managed a faint, "I do." The phrase was probably good practice, under the circumstances. With that, Preacher wheeled around abruptly and stormed out the door, slamming it so hard that a vase fell off the desk and shattered on the floor. I'd only seen him madder once, less than 24 hours before. That was when Roseabeth and I succumbed to our passion, the night that *will* live in infamy, in these parts, and the night of Fanny Boltwood's *most* untimely demise. In short, it was prom night, the night of the *catastrophe* on Huckleberry Hill.

Reflecting on it, I fell back on the cot, folded my hands behind my head and let the memory of it bubble to the surface of my mind like boiling taffy. In retrospect, I couldn't help but smile, just a little.

The senior prom was just about the liveliest event of a public nature, aside from the weekly livestock auction, to take place in Mansfield. Everybody in town had at the very least an informal invitation to attend, and few, if any, declined the offer. Supposedly the event was put on to honor the graduating class, which was a fine gesture, but since only about half the class was actually graduating, Doc had maintained the prom was actually a ceremony of "reconciliation with society" for the participants, meaning it was high time we started paying our own way.

In any case, no expense was spared in an attempt to decorate the gymnasium to look like a South Seas island paradise, and that's pretty much what it looked like—a gymnasium decorated to look like a South Seas island paradise. While it may not have brought back vivid memories to the likes of Herman Melville, Paul Gauguin or Margret Mead, it wasn't too bad for a bunch of kids who'd never set foot outside the territories. It was truly amazing what you could do given enough chicken wire, plaster of Paris, crepe paper and tissues. The decorating committee, as usual, had done a slam-bang job, providing us with coconut palms, an outrigger canoe, graven images, sandy beaches and a horse tank—I mean, lagoon—full of catfish and rough old carp. It was about the most unique job of decorating you'd ever hope to see even if its authenticity was somewhat tainted by the overabundant use of the color pink. But there was a logical explanation for that: Heather Bunzel, the chairman of the decorating committee, thought Bermuda, which *does* have pink beaches, was somewhere in the South Seas. Heather's career goal was to become a travel agent, but to tell you the truth, she wouldn't be number one on my list when it came time to plan a trip somewhere.

Naturally everyone dressed to the nines for the celebration, me included, in a new Indian madras jacket, dark slacks, paisley tie and a new pair of penny loafers because Silas convinced me that Indian madras wouldn't go with cowboy boots. And I knew better than to wear sneakers. About everyone else was just as dazzling as I was, except for Rufus Ruffin, who attended in an official capacity and who naturally favored the little black suit worn by undertakers.

For as long as I could recall I'd had a date with Roseabeth to the prom. I don't actually ever remember asking her, but I

came to acknowledge her acceptance because she kept men-
tioning what she was going to wear and what a wonderful time
we were going to have. Personally, proms bored me to tears;
I'd been to two others, and I'd probably have gone to sleep at
last year's if it hadn't been for Jeb Porter throwing up in the
punch bowl. That livened things up temporarily, but it didn't
do the punch any good. Calling it "grog" instead of punch
didn't help either.

The affair formally began at seven sharp with a banquet in
the school lunchroom, which had been done up like a grand
dining room in the Waldorf, but any similarity between the
two, aside from the traditional salad, was purely coincidental.
Before the banquet the senior class and their dates had been
invited to a pre-party at Brinton Turkle's. Brinton wanted everyone to be "well-oiled" as he put it before we went to the
banquet. I didn't see much sense in it, because that's the condition Jeb Porter was in when he did the job on the punch the
previous year.

It was around 5:30 P.M. when I herded Silas' old pickup
into Roseabeth's drive and rolled to a stop. I killed the engine
and jerked on the emergency brake out of habit, even though
the brake had been busted for about a year. Habits are hard to
break, even good ones. Before going to the door I glanced in
the rear-view mirror and mussed my hair just enough to give
me a "devil may care look," a look I often strove for but, I'm
afraid, seldom achieved. Then I headed for the house, carrying an orchid for Roseabeth. On the way up the sidewalk I
caught a glimpse of Preacher, peering out at me like the Lord
Himself. I tried not to think about him, knocked on the door
and waited.

"Who's there?" Preacher called.

"Jesus!" I said quietly because I knew that he knew who was there.

"Who?"

"Ezra Casey," I called through the screen. "I've come for Roseabeth."

I waited until he decided to open the door. "Well, if it ain't Ezra Casey and right on time." He swung the door open wide. "And boy if you don't look fit to kill."

"I ain't planning on any killin'," I said.

"Git on in here, and lemme git a look at you." I stepped in and stood by uncomfortably as Preacher walked all the way around me, poking me now and again with his index finger. "Boy, if you don't look like Joseph his own self in that coat," Preacher remarked.

"I know," I said, "and it hasn't even started to bleed yet."

"And shiny new shoes. But . . . where's your boots?"

"Can't wear cowboy boots with Indian madras," I said.

"Boy, you don't look half bad when you're cleaned up." He ushered me into the sitting room and yelled up at Roseabeth. "Roseabeth! That no-count boyfriend of yours is here." Then to me he said, "No offense."

"What'd you say, Daddy?" Roseabeth asked.

"Come on down, Sweetie".

"Jist a minute, Daddy. Is Ezra here?"

"I said he was," Preacher yelled.

"*Was?*"

"*Is*, Roseabeth! Ezra is standin' right here in the sittin' room."

"Well, have him sit down, Daddy. What's that room for anyhow? You two can have a 'man-to-man' talk while I finish up. I'll only be minute."

I wasn't crazy about the "man-to-man" talk idea, so I was relieved when Preacher said, "Sit down, Boy." I wandered over to the couch and sat down into its cushiony embrace. "What you got in the box, Boy?"

"A flower," I said, "an orchid for Roseabeth."

"Well, ain't that nice?" It was a rhetorical question so I didn't answer it. "I don't suppose Roseabeth's ever had a orchid before."

"Not that I know of," I allowed. "I reckon there hasta be a first time for everything," I said and wished immediately I hadn't.

"Meanin' what?" Preacher demanded, making no attempt to hide his consternation and suspicion of my intentions.

"Well, nothin' ah . . . in particular, and . . . everythin' in general—first orchid, first date, first kiss, first dance—"

"First *dance!*" I was real glad he stopped me before I'd gotten myself in any deeper. "Now, I won't have you dancin', not with my angel," Preacher said quite emphatically.

"I didn't mean Roseabeth," I said.

"Who did you mean?"

"The—the Methodists and Presbyterians."

"All right then. So let it did, so let it be done. I jist want to remind you that Roseabeth has been raised to look on dancin' as a sin." Preacher glared at me with a piercing gaze.

"Of the first magnitude," I said. "I know dancin' is a sin and I don't intend to tempt fate, especially with Roseabeth."

"I'm relieved to hear it. "I'll hold you to your word," Preacher said.

Now I hadn't given anything so concrete as my *word.* All I'd said was that I didn't *intend* to tempt fate. And I didn't. But sometimes you lose control of a situation. I hadn't intended to participate in the events leading up to the incident and the disaster, but fate had me by the short hairs and dragged me right in. Sometimes things just happen for reasons of their own, so I didn't figure to make any promises I couldn't keep.

Hearing something rustling against the side wall in the stairwell, I turned and got my first glimpse of Roseabeth in her formal gown. I caught my breath and stared at her wide-eyed as she descended the last few steps like some rare butterfly, her metamorphosis complete and then some. Around her hem pink nylon net spread the entire width of the stairwell and covered yards and yards of flame colored taffeta that closed around her pencil-thin waist and then blossomed again as it approached her breasts. The taffeta clung to her torso like a second skin and ran to just below her arms, leaving her shoulder completely bare and pushing her breasts together and upward so they resembled a pair of lush, ripe melons. They bounced jauntily with the sway of her gown as she moved across the sitting room toward me. She stopped in front of me, curtseyed and spun around 360 degrees. "What do you think, Ezra?"

"They're beautiful," I mumbled.

"What?" Preacher growled.

"Beautiful," I said. "*Roseabeth* looks beautiful."

"Why thank you, sir. You look right comely yourself." She reached down and took my hand. "Come over here, Ezra. Daddy's gonna take our picture." I just stood there like a statue, staring at her breasts until I felt her tugging on my arm. They were like magnets; I couldn't take my eyes off of them. "Over here, Ezra! Daddy's got the Kodak." I stumbled along behind her, but my heart wasn't in it, and my mind certainly wasn't on it. I know I shouldn't have been thinking what I was thinking, but my mind seemed to have put aside everything I'd ever heard Preacher say about contemporary morality. I think my id was in *total* control. I saw this as a grand opportunity to get some feels off Roseabeth; her breasts were already half exposed, so it wouldn't be any trouble at all just to slip my hand down inside her gown. Looked almost *too* inviting; and something in my groin started to stir involuntarily at the thought of it.

"You wanna look *this* way, Boy," Preacher grumbled.

"Oh, yeah," I said, "I was jist—"

"I *know* what you was doin'," Preacher said.

"Don't jist stand there, Ezra," Roseabeth said. Then she took my arm, yanked it around her waist and slowly slipped her arm across the small of my back. Her touch sent a sensation of super-charged sexual energy surging through me that I had no control over whatsoever. I was well aware of just where such energy was most likely to manifest itself physically because I felt this uncomfortable tightness growing in my pants. I had a sudden reluctance to have this moment captured for all time in a snapshot, but it was too late.

"Smile," Preacher said.

I attempted to, but it was not my best effort. The flash suddenly exploded in my face, blinding me, and in that twilight of brilliance I felt Roseabeth's warm, sweet breath on my face. She was pulling us together for a "cheek-to-cheek" shot. That was too much. I tried to think of something else to stem the rising tide of my passion. Basketball: didn't work. I could only see Grace Farley up there in the stands behind the goal, spreading her legs out wide enough to accommodate a passing freight train. Football: no luck. I just saw Roseabeth prancing around out there on the old gridiron with her cute little fanny hanging out of that short skirt all over the place.

Finally, in desperation I said, "Roseabeth, what—what's your opinion of—of gravity?"

"What?" I think I caught her off guard.

"Gravity," I nearly yelled, "what's your opinion of it?"

"What in tarnation?" Preacher said, lowering the camera.

"I've got to know. I—I can't be goin' out with a girl who doesn't have a high opinion of it. Wouldn't be right when I'm so sold on the concept myself. It's like a—religion to me. I know I should of told you sooner."

"I declare, Ezra Casey. I don't know what has gotten into you!"

"What's your opinion of it?" I demanded. "I've got to know right now."

"Well, gravity is jist a wonderful thing in my opinion," she cried. "If we didn't have it things would be flyin' all over the place all the time and things that went up wouldn't ever come down. Does that satisfy your curiosity?"

It did satisfy my *curiosity*, but that wasn't nearly enough. So I wrenched myself from her grasp and moved to the center of the room where I started dancing and chanting an old Indian prayer that had been passed down from the Sac side of the family. Doc had taught it to me. It sort of went, "Heya—heya—heya." That kind of thing. I don't recall if it was for rain or not for rain, but since I was desperate I didn't bother with the details. "Heya—heya—heya," I chanted and kept dancing around in a small circle. I felt like a bloody fool, but I could tell I was doing myself some good. Roseabeth and Preacher were just staring at me, dumbfounded.

"He's gone crazy, Daddy. Ezra's plum lost his mind, and on the night of the prom!"

"What in tarnation are you doin', Boy?" Preacher yelled.

"Oh, he'll jist ruin everythin'!" Roseabeth cried.

"No, no," I insisted. "I'm fine. I jist wanted to show you this ancient dance of my people—-heya—heya. It's to drive the evil spirits away before a celebration—heya—heya—so ... so everybody *will* have a good time. No evil spirits around—heya—heya—heya—to mess things up. That kinda thing." I kept on dancing and chanting and actually began to enjoy myself. Until Preacher erupted.

"I don't allow no dancin' of *any* kind in this house!"

See what I mean about Fate having me by the short hairs? "Daddy," Roseabeth said, bailing me out, "you leave Ezra alone. He *obviously* don't feel well."

"He does look a bit flushed," Preacher admitted.

"It's this tie," I said, stopping my dance. "It's about to choke me."

"Here, lemme loosen it," Roseabeth said.

"Oh no! Don't touch me," I said. "I'll fix it in the truck. Come on." I grabbed the orchid off the couch and headed for the door.

"Ezra!" Roseabeth called after me, but I just kept going. Then she took out after me. "Night, Daddy."

"Night, Angel. You have her home by midnight, Boy. And don't you try nothin' neither!"

"Daddy! I won't turn into pumpkin', and it's prom night."

"One o'clock then, Boy, at the latest," he shouted loud enough for everyone in town to hear.

"Yessir," I called back to him from the truck and opened the door for Roseabeth. She began gathering her gown around her. "Think you can git all that in there?" I asked.

"Boy! You are in some mood tonight, the likes of which I have never *ever* seen before," she spat out.

"It's prom night," I said in my defense, "and spring. And you know what a young man's fancy turns to in spring."

"Yes, I do as a matter of fact: *Baseball!*"

"*Love*, Roseabeth. That's what Mr. Shakespeare said."

"Well your fancy has evidently turned to actin' like a bloody fool. I swear, Ezra Casey, when are you ever gonna grow up?"

"Roseabeth, you don't have *any* idea of how much I wish I knew the answer to that question," I told her and slammed the door shut on her gown.

"Ezra," she shrieked, "my gown!"

"Sorry," I said, opening the door and inspecting her gown. "It's okay."

"Okay? What's that spot there?"

"That?" She nodded and glared at me. "Just a little ... sludge."

"Grease!"

"It's ... similar to grease, yeah."

"How *could* you?"

"It was an accident, Roseabeth, and I'm sorry. But we've either got too much gown here or not enough pickup."

"You want me to git in the bed?" she snapped.

"No, I don't want you to git in the—back of the truck. Jist kinda gather everythin' together there as best you can, and I'll close the door." She started hauling in her gown like some kind of huge seine until it was finally clear of the door and all puffed up in front of her across the windshield. That cab was about as full of nylon net and flame colored taffeta as you'd ever want to see it. To get her mind off the gown I handed her the orchid as soon as I climbed in the other side. "Here."

"What's this?" she asked.

"Somethin' for you," I told here.

"Don't think for one second that this will make up for ruinin' my gown, Ezra."

"Jist take the thing, okay."

"Oh, Ezra, *must* you be so romantic?"

"Take it!" She grabbed the box out of my hand and started to open it. "Your gown's not *ruined*; it's jist a little spot. Nobody will even notice."

"Oh, Ezra, a . . . "

"Orchid," I told her.

"A orchid."

"*An* orchid."

"Whatever! It's beautiful, so delicate a flower." With that she turned and kissed me full on the mouth. "Thank you, Ezra. My very first orchid."

"I thought so."

"Here," she said, handing me the delicate beauty, "pin it on me."

I glanced at the orchid and then gave Roseabeth a quick once over. "Where?"

She tugged at the top of her gown then turned, lifting her upper torso toward me and said, "Here."

I gulped, found the pin and decided to take a stab at it. While lifting the gown away from her body my fingers actually brushed against the top of her breasts; she just looked at me and faintly smiled. After the orchid was in place she said, "Now there, isn't that nice?"

"Fantastic," I said and drove off toward Brinton's in a high state of libidinal anxiety. Sweat was trickling down my temples and my young heart was pounding out a chaotic rhythm like those noisy pistons under the hood. I'd never felt myself in such a state, except maybe when I got that first look up

Grace Farley's skirt. I mistook that for a state of Grace, but this was altogether different, because the situation was alive with potential.

The senior class was pretty well represented and pretty well-oiled when we got to Brinton's. Come to find out there had been a pre-pre-party at Phil Vandaver's place that only white Anglo-Saxons had been invited too, but I didn't care. At this rate the prom might be over by nine which was fine with me because I was already thinking about parking someplace with Roseabeth.

Aside from having an occasional sip of wine with my family, I didn't drink anything stronger than goat's milk. I'd heard too many liver stories to risk drinking the hard stuff, and I figured that when it came to making a fool of myself I didn't need any help. Roseabeth didn't drink either, to my knowledge, but she had on occasion expressed a mild interest in the "therapeutic benefits of alcohol." So when she accepted something called a frozen daiquiri from Brinton I wasn't surprised. To tell you the truth, I anticipated too that the drink might help loosen Roseabeth up a little. Maybe a lot. I know that was an awful thing to think, but by then that old id of mine was jumping up and down on the remnants of my mangled superego.

"What do you want, Ezra?" Brinton asked.

"Dr. Pepper," I said.

"Straight up?"

"On ice," I told him. Maybe I should have said "on the rocks." I wasn't too sure.

"Well, aren't you bein' darin'," Roseabeth teased. "Try a sip of this, Ezra. It's like a lime snow cone."

"Naw, it'll make my teeth ache," I said.

"You're such a prude, really no fun at all."

"Here you are, Ezra," Brinton said, handing me a drink, "Dr. Pepper on the rocks. I added a twist of lemon; hope you don't mind?"

"Naw, that's fine. Thanks." I tasted the drink; it was all right, but the lemon didn't really do anything for it.

"Chicken," Roseabeth said.

"Everybody's out on the patio," Brinton said. "Go on out."

The back of the house cast a lengthy shadow over the patio, a dark stone affair shaped vaguely like a spleen. Overhead some Japanese lanterns were suspended from chicken wire along with some tissue roses. The fragrance of Old Spice was nearly overwhelming, dominating even the smell of the freshly mown lawn. Roseabeth had on something called, "My Sin," which I found to be as stimulating as it was thought provoking.

"Hey, Ezra," Phil called, "get over here. Hey everybody, Ezra and Roseabeth are here." For all the nylon net you could hardly find a place to stand. And bare backs and shoulders. And bouncing young breasts about to leap out at you from every direction. It was like being in libidinal purgatory. "Don't you two look nice," Phil said. "Don't they look nice, Heather?" Phil had come with Heather Bunzel, and I figured he was lucky to have made it this far.

"I'll say they do," Heather gushed. "Why I've never seen Ezra look so . . . *debonair*, and Roseabeth that gown . . . has a spot it. Lookey there."

Roseabeth glared at me, but I managed to sidestep her elbow. "What are you two drinkin'?" I asked. "Roseabeth's havin' a . . . what is that thing, Roseabeth?"

"Same thing we got I bet," Heather said and giggled, "a frozen daiquiri, and it is simply—divine."

"What's that, Ezra?" Phil inquired.

"Oh, Ezra's havin' a Dr. Pepper," Roseabeth said. "Isn't he so ... *cosmopolitan*?" If I was I didn't know it.

I tipped my glass and said, "It's got a twist of lemon."

"Be careful of that lemon," Phil said.

"Isn't that simply marvelous?" Roseabeth said.

We sipped our drinks, standing there in the light of the retreating sun, laughing and making small talk. It was really kind of nice; with all the girls in their pretty dresses it was like a flower garden somehow come alive and floating all around you on the evening breeze. I loved the way the light was changing, growing ever so soft and golden as the sun settled lower and lower in the sky casting a wondrous sheen on Roseabeth's fair skin. The conversations were becoming softer too, hushed, like there was something special about the moment. Everyone was talking quietly in small groups; there was some gentle laughter, and it occurred to me how *mature* everyone was behaving, so far anyway. It was funny how you could dress kids up a little, give them a few adult privileges and see how grown up they became. But if you took a group of adults and put them in the same situation, sometimes they'd start acting like a bunch of kids—horsing around, getting louder and louder, carrying on in general like a bunch of fools, which was clearly behavior of an *immature* nature. I still found the whole business somewhat confusing. Before I could speculate on it any further Brinton showed up and reached for Roseabeth's empty glass.

"Another, Roseabeth?" he offered.

"Why, yes, if you insist, sir," she said, doing her best Scarlet O'Hara, "make it a double if you don't mind."

"Not at all. How 'bout you, Ezra?" I handed him my glass.

"Now a shot of run will make that Dr. Pepper a darn sight more palatable," Phil said.

"Naw, that's all right," I told him. "Besides, you know what alcohol does to people of my heritage. I might go crazy and start scalpin' people or singin' an Irish folk song." Brinton smiled and moved off with our glasses.

"I hope you wouldn't scalp *me*, Ezra," Roseabeth said and slipped her arm around my waist.

I smiled and said, "No, I wouldn't do that to you, Roseabeth."

She batted her eyes, pulled me close and whispered, "Jist what *would* you do to me then?" Lord, boy, look out, I thought. She's going to want to dance. "What, Ezra?"

I looked deep into her eyes and said, "Nothin' that doesn't come natural. I'm dead set against scalpin'; it's against my nature."

"I'm glad of that," she said and brushed her hand against my inner thigh. I'm thought it was an accident, but I wasn't sure. I gulped, tugged at my tie and looked into her lovely face. I'm not sure what I saw there because I'd never seen it before—playfulness, daring, intrigue, maybe even a kind of recklessness brought on by spring and the therapeutic benefits of the alcohol. She suddenly winked, squeezed my hand and said, "'Cuse me while I run to the ladies' room."

"Sure," I mumbled. "Okay. Fine." I watched until she disappeared into the house. Then Brinton showed up with the drinks.

"Where's Roseabeth?"

"Where do you think?"

"Oh," he said and nodded, handing me my Dr. Pepper. "Did you git a load of her tits?"

"Yeah, they're a little hard to miss actually."

He held up her daiquiri. "Another one of these and Roseabeth's gonna feel real compatible tonight, if you know what I mean."

I nodded and tried to give him a "knowing" smile. "Yeah, I know," I told him as he handed me her drink and walked off. But I didn't know if I really knew or not. Or if I really even wanted to know. What had me worried was this: What if the alcohol *did* make Roseabeth real compatible? Would I know what to do? Or how to do it? All I was really counting on was a few feels; now a whole new world was maybe beginning to open up to me, and I wasn't sure I was ready to leap into the breach. I had never even seriously entertained the notion of "going all the way" because I didn't have any idea of how to get there.

With these questions still racing through my mind Phil stopped by and said, "Boy, would I ever like to be in your pants tonight!"

"*My* pants?"

"Jesus, Ezra! Your shoes, *her* pants," Phil said and moved away, shaking his head.

"Oh," I said, relaxing. For a moment I just stood there, reflecting and staring into Roseabeth's daiquiri. Then I decided that if it was going to happen I wanted it to happen naturally; I didn't want to take advantage of her—for her panties to come down just because her defenses were. If I couldn't get it fair and square I didn't want to get it at all. I rushed to the kitchen where Ogden was throwing together what appeared to be a pitcher of daiquiris. "Hi, Ogden," I said. What are you up to?"

"Makin' more daiquiris," he told me.

"I thought so. A whole pitcher of them, huh?"

"They're goin' like hot cakes. Want one?"

"Nope. Jist curious." I watched him real close, waited until he left with the pitcher then started on my own batch, less the rum. I did shake a few drops on top to give it the right aroma and an initial bite. After that I didn't figure Roseabeth would be able to tell if there was rum in it or not. Ogden suddenly burst back in the door and grabbed a couple of empty glasses.

"Oh, I see you're makin' somethin' *special* for Roseabeth." He grabbed her glass and sniffed around the edge. "My, you do good work, Ezra."

"Let your light so shine before men that they may see your good works and give glory to their Father in heaven"...or something like that," I said.

"You can make *my* next one in any case," Ogden said.

I held up the bottle of rum and said, "So that's all there is to it, huh?"

"That's it. Easier than unsnapping a bra, huh?"

"No doubt 'bout that," I agreed as Ogden rushed out. I took Roseabeth's drink and followed him out to the patio where I found Roseabeth fortifying herself for the evening ahead by sampling every drink within reach. Ah, the best laid plans of mice and men. Or fate run amok. "Scotch and what?" she asked Brinton taking a sip from his tumbler.

"Here, Roseabeth," I said, grabbing Brinton's scotch and whatever and replacing it with her daiquiri. "This is yours." She accepted the drink and gave me her loveliest smile. Then she took a long pull from the glass and winked at me.

"Hmmm. Ezra, this is sooo good, and *potent*. Won't you take a sip, jist for me?" I frowned and shook my head. "It won't hurt you."

"Won't do me any good either."

"More than that stupid old Dr. Pepper. Least alcohol kills germs." She had a valid point even though she was unaware that her drink had very little alcohol in it. "Besides, it'll make you *feel* good."

"I feel jist fine," I said.

"Well, *fine* isn't good enough for the prom. I want you to feel real good, like I feel," Roseabeth insisted.

"Then gimme the damn thing," I snapped. She did so I took a big gulp. The thing actually tasted pretty good, but it didn't make me feel any better. And it made my teeth ache. "Okay, there! You satisfied?"

She just smiled what I'd have to call a wicked smile and said, "Not yet."

"You git me to drinkin', Roseabeth, I won't be held responsible for whatever happens."

"I won't hold you responsible, Ezra. For God's sake!"

"Your father will," I told her, "for your sake."

She took my arm and whispered in my ear, "Well, jist what are you plannin' on doin' anyway?" I gulped and my eyes widened. "Dancin' with me?"

"I don't know how to dance," I told her and noticed the heat was becoming unbearable.

"Why you *do*! That was jist the cutest little rain dance you did at my house that I ever saw," she announced.

"I mean I don't know how to dance regular," I argued.

"It's real simple, Ezra. All you gotta do is jist sorta . . . sway with the rhythm of the music. You begin to feel it after a while."

"How do *you* know how to do?"

"Maybe I been dancin' before. Or maybe I practice at home by my own self."

"Accordin' to Preacher it's still a sin."

"Not unless you git caught," she said.

"Or pregnant," I added.

"Oh, Ezra, you still don't know anythin'! Dancin' *don't* make you pregnant."

"I know that," I said. "Cows can't dance and they git pregnant."

"Cows? What's cows got to do with it?"

"Cows have got *everythin'* to do with it, Roseabeth. Boy, if you don't know that, you don't know as much as you think you do!"

By this time she'd backed me into the further reaches of the patio where the hanging branches of a solitary weeping willow separated us from the party. Looking deep into my eyes she took my hand and pressed it against what the women in town referred to as their bosom, what I thought of as breasts, and were what were commonly called tits in the locker room. "Maybe tonight, Ezra, I'll show you a little bit of what I know." I don't know what it was: Spring, the full moon that would show up in a few hours, the daiquiris, magic, but whatever it was we were caught up in its spell, and I decided not to fight it. I just stood there, watching her breast swell beneath my hand with her steady breathing. "Would you like that?"

I'd forgotten the question; hell, I'd even forgotten my name. "Like what?" I said.

"For me to show you a little something tonight," she whispered in my ear.

"Oh, yeah," I said, "I would. I'd appreciate that very much."

"Okay then, let's go."

"Right *now?*"

"To the *prom*," she said, moving my hand down to her side. "We'll go somewhere later." She smiled and her eyes sparkled like two mischievous diamonds.

"Okay," I agreed and followed her, hypnotized, as she fluttered across the patio like an aspiration sent to be a moment's—torment? I didn't know, and I didn't care.

The sophomore class served the banquet, the final prelude to the prom itself. The food, prepared by the regular staff of professionals, was uncommonly good and there was more than enough of it. Ham it was, sliced thin as a potato chip but not quite so brittle; string beans that more than lived up to their name; the aforementioned Waldorf salad, baked potatoes smothered in sour cream, and a side plate of grilled cheese sandwiches for the less adventuresome in the crowd. For desert there was an old mainstay of our chef's repertoire—peach cobbler buried beneath a mound of melting French vanilla ice cream. You could have about anything to drink—lemonade, iced tea, fruit punch, coffee, soda or milk. I chose milk and planned to wash down the whole meal with a cup of strong black coffee.

Graham Hickok, who, God willing was going to be an evangelist pretty much soothed whatever was left of our collective conscience by returning his personal rendition of grace before the ham had completely disappeared. I was understandably nervous, and I always ate a lot when I was nervous, provided there was a lot to eat which in this case there was. But Roseabeth, I noticed was eating like a bird, and for good reason. It didn't escape my attention that Brinton was passing a bottle around under the table, hooch of some description, no doubt. When the bottle made its way to Roseabeth she grabbed *my* glass of milk, moved it under the table and poured in God only knows what.

"Roseabeth, what are you doin'?" I protested.

"Shhh," she cautioned and said, "milk punch," like that made everything all right. "Try it." I did and just about choked to death on the spot. It was awful; it ruined the milk completely, and I doubt that it improved the hooch that much either. "How'd you like it?"

"Not much," I said, suppressing a gag.

"Oh, Ezra Casey, you're jist no fun at all."

"You already mentioned that," I said and gulped down her glass of lemonade.

Toward the end of the banquet there were a number of awards that had to be presented to the graduating seniors. Among them these: Most likely to inherit wealth: Brinton Turkle. Most likely to make a fool of himself at the prom: Ogden Burgatroid. I was relieved to hear that one. Most likely to marry well: Roseabeth Bascom. Most likely to fart at commencement: Phil Vandaver. Most likely to succeed: God only knows why, but that distinction was bestowed upon me, the first Japanese-Irish-Indian to be so honored.

As the presentation ceremony began to wind down, the soft strains of the "orchestra" tuning up in the South Seas island paradise next door drifted into the banquet hall. The squeak of the accordion mixed pretty well with the banging of the pots and pans coming from the kitchen.

The banquet finally completed, the lot of us began to meander into the island paradise where the orchestra greeted us with a rather catchy arrangement of *Moon Over Miami*, which was nice, but I believe the absence of the pots and pans proved to be somewhat detrimental. What Freddie Hondo and his wax musicians lacked primarily was numbers, the majority of the group having succumbed to a wide variety of ailments through the passing years. What was left was three part-time musicians, all of them very close to the overripe state of maturation, who played close to a dozen instruments among them, but none of them all that well. But what the group lacked in musical expertise, they more than made up for in volume.

Having failed to fill the dance floor with the initial number, they slid into a down-tempo rendition of *Stardust* which was met with the kind of indifference you all too often experience on the streets of a large city like Tulsa or Wichita Falls. The mood of the evening just wasn't quite right for dancing yet.

It wasn't long before most the boys—men?—started to congregate around the punch bowl and all their dates began to line up in the chairs across the gym like so many potted plants. The young girls in their summer dresses made as pretty a flower garden as you'd ever hope to see, each one a fresh bud, bursting with life and ripe for plucking. At the moment, however, the majority of the pluckers seemed more interested in spiking the punch than laying waste to the local belles. Noticing a tug on my sleeve I turned to find Phil Vandaver panting at my side.

"Reckon you'll git into Roseabeth's panties tonight, Ezra?" he asked.

"Come on," I protested, Roseabeth's a nice girl."

"Didn't say she wasn't. But nice girls like it as much as anybody else. You know what they say."

"No, I don't. What *who* says?"

"You now … *they*," Phil said and made a kind of all-encompassing gesture.

"Oh, *that* they," I said. "What do they say?"

He took a long pull on his punch. "To treat a lady like a whore, and a whore like a lady!"

"They say that?" I asked.

"It's common knowledge," Phil assured me.

I narrowed my eyes, mulling it and then asked, "I should treat Roseabeth like a whore then?"

"Well, *of course* you should treat her like a whore, a nice girl like Roseabeth," Phil told me and then shoved his way into the crowd surrounding the punch bowl.

I brooded over the idea in my own head. Maybe I *could* have done it, *if* I'd known how to treat a whore, which I didn't. I did know how to treat a lady, or at least I thought I did, but that didn't do me any good because I didn't know any whores, that I knew of. Something made me think of ole Stanley Kowalski. Why he treated both Stella and Blanche DuBois like dirt, and they were ladies, Stella evidently more so than Blanche, and he had his way with both of them. Maybe what I needed was a bowling shirt; but then my madras jacket was the equal of any bowling shirt I'd ever seen.

With the start of the *Hawaiian Wedding Song* a few couples filtered onto the floor and started swaying back and forth in what I took to be unison. I fought my way to the punch bowl, dipped out a couple of cups, then went to find Roseabeth. At that point I wasn't sure I needed any help, but I decided to try out my Stanley Kowalski on her. I found her just sitting pretty as a picture against the far wall beneath the scoreboard. When I got there I barked, "Roseabeth, what the hell are you doin'?"

I caught her off guard. She looked around, surprised and a little bewildered. But she recovered quickly. "Ezra Casey, don't you swear at me. I wasn't doin' a blamed thing."

"Well, you jist knock it off," I grumbled.

"There's not anythin' *to* knock off," she countered.

"That's what you think," I snapped. I had no idea where I was going with this nonsense.

She snapped right back at me, "Ezra Casey, I won't stand for this! You sound jist like that ole Stanley Kowalski. Now *you* knock it off unless you wanna spend the rest of the evening by your own self."

So much for what *they* say. I gulped and handed her the punch. "Here," I said, and sat down beside her. I don't know, but I don't think Brando was any better.

"That's more like it," she said, "thank you."

"You're welcome." In a second Roseabeth had settled down, and I was feeling real bad. She was gentle and just as pretty as a harvest moon. Sitting there next to me I could hear her sigh every now and again as she swayed with the music and finally nestled her cheek on my shoulder. "I'm sorry, Roseabeth," I said.

She just smiled up at me and said, "I just love this song, Ezra. Don't you?"

"It's all right," I said.

"Jist all right? Why the words say, I love you—or somethin' like that."

"Yeah," I said, "I love you too."

"Those are the words to the song, Ezra."

"Ooooh, I thought . . . "

"Oh, *you*," she said and poked me playfully, "you knew that. What am I gonna do with you?"

"I dunno," I said, wondering the same thing about her.

By then the townspeople had pretty well found their observation posts in the gymnasium and were looking on at the festivities with the faded image of proms long since passed rekindled in their memories like brilliant new stars. Most to the men had gathered in one corner where the coroner was, undoubtedly, telling one of his riveting off-color tales of yesteryear. His audience seemed to be in a state of near hysteria until Preacher Bascom joined the group. Then a thin veneer of respectability shown over the group like a coat of old wax on a hardwood floor. Even the orchestra responded to Preacher's arrival by slowing the tempo of the *wedding song* by about half.

Moments later Preacher hurried off with Rufus and Hilda Fartok in tow; it was a sure sign somebody had died, and on prom night. What a shame. With Preacher's departure things seemed to pick up.

The Methodists, who were already dancin', were soon joined by the Presbyterians, who couldn't be held responsible, while all the Baptists continued to sit around stewing in their doctrinal juices. Hell must have seemed a far ways off then, I suppose, because when I felt Roseabeth tugging on my sleeve and starting for the dance floor I only offered minimal resistance, although trying to hold steadfastly onto the conviction that dancing is a sin. But for the life of me I didn't know why. "Roseabeth, it's a sin," I said without conviction.

"Oh, hell with it," she said.

"But—"

"Ezra, what's the use of bein' a Free Will Baptist if you don't ever exercise your free will?"

She had a valid point there. So I gave in. As I followed her onto the dance floor a momentary hush fell over the crowd; even the band hesitated for an instant to contemplate the sacrilege I was committing with the preacher's daughter, but when God failed to nail us on the spot, things went on pretty much as before. I did, however, notice that nobody dared get too close to us in case He *did* decide to strike and took poor aim. Of course I didn't really know how to dance, but that was beside the point.

I just followed Roseabeth's lead and kind of swayed back and forth to *Graduation Day*, holding her close. The soft flesh of her back and her warm breath against my neck did something to the way I saw the world. Even through the layers of taffeta and nylon net I could feel her firm young breasts against my chest. Now and again she'd drop her head against my shoulder or fiddle with the back of my neck, running her fingers through my hair or just touching me ever so lightly. Roseabeth, lovely to begin with, was looking more and more comely all the time; if that was love, then I guess I was in it. Her cheeks were slightly flushed; her hair was just glowing in the soft light, and whatever was supposed to be holding up the front of her gown was doing a pitiful poor job. Every once in a while she'd take a huge breath that came just short of sending her gown to the remnant heap and me to the very limits of adolescent respectability. How long! How long was I to suffer the aching consequences of relentless adolescence and unrequited love? From the look of things, principally Roseabeth, maybe not too long.

It wasn't long until our dancing had degenerated to the point of standing in one spot and leaning against one another. We'd had a few more punches, and I'd reached the point where I didn't particularly care what people said about us, and as for Roseabeth, well, she was well beyond that point too. *Graduation Day* was beginning to unnerve me, so when Roseabeth suggested that it was time to go I was only too happy to comply. "Where to?" I asked.

She squeezed my hand and said, "Huckleberry Hill." Fantastic!

The night was as lovely as Roseabeth—clear, warm, quiet, except for the crickets and an occasional dog yelping off somewhere on the far side of the hill, and the brightest yellow moon just lounging up there, full and seemingly smiling against the vastness of space. With the engine already shut off I just coasted to a halt atop the hill and looked down on the river valley stretched out below us like some huge empty platter. There was a light on below us at Fanny's place, and every once in a while a car would temporarily illuminate the countryside, then disappear off somewhere beyond the horizon. Inside the truck, aside from what was happening to my body, I was aware of Roseabeth's breathing and the rustling of her gown against the dash and seat and windshield and even the far door. After a little while of just sitting I managed to say, "Well, here we are."

She didn't say a word; she just reached up, turned my face to hers and moved at me recklessly with her lips apart. Now I was way past to point of finding French kissing disgusting, but to tell you the truth, Roseabeth had never kissed me like this before. There was a sense of urgency and reckless abandon about it that I'd never before experienced, and it was fairly agitating. Not knowing exactly what to do, I tried to pull her more tightly against me but ended up fighting that nylon net like a floundering fish; the stuff seemed to be rising with the height of our passion. I pushed through the stuff the best I could and found her mouth again with mine and started to caress her back and shoulders. Then I let my hand slide around her until I cupped a breast outside her gown. She kind of groaned or something and said, "Ezra," in a raspy voice.

I was as far along with her as I'd ever been, and I decided to go ahead and go for it. If the mere *thought* of doing something was just as bad as actually doing it, like Preacher said, I figured I might just as well go ahead and get my money's worth. Still fighting that net and trying to hold a kiss at the same time, I slid my hand down the front of her gown and finally felt the wonderful softness of her breasts. She sort of groaned again and said, "Ezra, please—don't—stop." So I didn't. Nor could I have had I wanted to. With a sudden move of her hand she reached behind her, released a hook and her zipper, and the front of her gown suddenly plummeted forward like the drawer of a cash register. In the shimmering light of that full moon I pulled away and gazed at the unique beauty of a woman's body. Then, with my hand quivering like it used to do when I was a little kid opening a Christmas package, I reached out and touched her with my fingertips, then felt the fullness of her with my palms. She responded by breathing more deeply, sighing now and then and making little cooing sounds like a dove. There's no way that I could ever explain what I felt because . . . because the whole thing was so magical. I simply had no idea that a woman's body would be so—different, so positively wonderful. I would have gladly stopped right then and probably would have remained dazed for weeks to come had Roseabeth not begun to tug at my tie and unbutton my shirt.

"Oh, Ezra," she said breathlessly, "I want to feel you against me."

"Okay," I said, "but you're choking me."

"I'm sorry. But I'm tryin' to *loosen* it."

I coughed and said, "Lemme do it." As we separated her gown shut up between us like it was spring loaded. I actually lost sight of her behind that flaming taffeta jungle. "You over there, Roseabeth?"

"Yes, I am, but this gown is a royal pain," she cried.

"It *is* awfully crowded in here," I agreed.

"Why don't we git in the back?" she suggested. "We can put down that old blanket we use on picnics."

I groped under the seat and found the blanket. "Okay, I got the blanket right here," I told her.

"Okay then," Roseabeth said and slid out the door opposite me. I got out and stood there watching her as she shed her gown as naturally as a bird taking up flight. She put her gown in a corner of the bed of the truck and said, "The blanket, Ezra."

"Oh, yeah," I said and reached over the fender to spread out the blanket. She climbed in the truck bed, wearing nothing but a pair of frilly white panties. She settled herself down on the blanket and looked at me. "Roseabeth, you are incredibility beautiful," I said.

"Well I don't have any way of knowin' whether you are or not, standin' there in your Sunday best. Git in here, Ezra!"

I undressed and left everything but my saggy BVDs in a heap beside the truck. Once in the bed, Roseabeth rose up on her knees, took my hands, and then pulled me down beside her. Our bodies sort of fit together naturally, like pieces of a puzzle. When we kissed every nerve seemed to tingle in fits of fantastic awe and wonderment. She was soft as silk against me and as warm and luscious as the summer night. "Do you love me Ezra?" she asked me between kisses.

"I think that's what I'm doin'," I told her. Then I kissed her again, and my head began swimming with the magic of it all, and I lost track of exactly what was happening. There was just this surge of energy, passion I guess it was, filling the night with darkness and light and sounds and all. All at once, Roseabeth's leg was across my thigh, and as I pulled her to me she seemed to float over me like some kind of a vague spirit that was feather like and soft and lovely. And she was rocking back and forth on me, and then, I swear I don't recall how it happened, but we were both lying there as natural and Adam and Eve and she was over me with her head thrown back and I was touching her everywhere and kissing her and she was moving on me. Then suddenly, I exploded as Roseabeth began screaming and the stars were blinking on and off in the night sky and the moon was stretching every which way and its light was filling the earth with shafts of honey-dipped gold. Stars were streaking across the sky in a rush, leaving a tapestry of fragmented light glistening against all that blackness. Finally, amongst all that delicious chaos I made some sense out of what Roseabeth was carrying on about.

"We're movin', Ezra! I think we're movin'!"

"Huh, what? Roseabeth are you all right? Did I hurt you any?"

"No, you didn't hurt me, Ezra. You didn't even—dammit, Ezra, the truck is movin' I tell you!"

Now things were beginning to register. "Movin'! Right. Oh, Jesus, that damned brake."

"It don't have one," Roseabeth said.

"No, it has one; it jist don't work. And we must of knocked it out of gear!"

"Well, don't jist sit there: Do somethin'!" she demanded.

"I am," I said, "I'm lookin' for my pants."

"They're back *there*," she screamed, pointing a good ways behind us. "Do somethin' else!"

276

Considering the fact that my pants weren't even in the truck, this was all too swift an administration of Divine justice as far as I was concerned. Spontaneous retribution was more like it, and I didn't like the concept one little bit. With all those worlds up there in the sky to choose from, I don't know why God had to be watching this one. I glanced over the side of the pickup and said, "Oh my God!" Until that moment I had never realized just how steep Huckleberry Hill was. As I tried to step onto the running board and from there into the cab we hit a huge pothole and I tumbled back into the truck on top of Roseabeth and her discarded prom gown.

"Ezra, my gown!" she screamed.

"Forget the gown!" I countered.

We were bouncing crazily down Huckleberry Hill at a good clip and gaining momentum. I crawled forward and looked through the rear window and windshield. Lights were on in Fanny's place, and I could make out a car or two shining black against her white frame house. Straight down the hill we were headed, zeroing in on an aluminum gate stretched across the entrance to her property. Beyond the gate we'd have a clean shot at the screened-in porch where Fanny would often relax in the cool of the evening with her Bible and a cold drink. I hoped most sincerely she wasn't out there now. Seeing that a crash was inevitable I grabbed Roseabeth and pulled her down next to me with my back against the cab so I'd act as a cushion between her and the truck upon impact. She was struggling, showing her hysterical side, so I had to hang on for dear life.

"Oh, Ezra," she cried, "we're gonna die! That will jist ruin *everythin'.*"

Death was a distinct possibility; still, I thought she was a little short on optimism—until we crashed against the gate.

Then hell started coming apart at the seams. The gate just exploded, sending shreds of aluminum through the sky like a volley of tiny missiles. The truck careened sideways, scraped the gatepost with an awful ripping sound and plowed ahead raised up on two wheels. So far we were still alive, and the gate had slowed us up a little. Then, on level ground, we slowed some more before finding the wet ground beneath Fanny's nasturtiums which slowed us more, but not enough.

As we tore into the porch I felt like a sandwich with Roseabeth's naked body providing some mighty fancy trimmings. The wind sailed right out of me as my back and shoulders flattened against the cab. I heard some yelling; Roseabeth was crying until a potted Yucca plant fell from the porch ceiling and caught her in the butt, then she started screaming and the rest of the porch came down behind us as we plowed ahead. Some two-by-fours went flying as we crashed through a set of French doors into Fanny's sitting room, upsetting tables and chairs and vases and books and I don't know what all. We finally ground to a halt with Fanny's caged canary swaying perilously above us. That bird was singing like it had good sense, but everything else became frightfully quiet. In the silence I heard Roseabeth's quiet crying and the joints of the house creaking and groaning a delayed protest. Then with the dust still settling all around I became aware of some other movement in the house: Fanny, I suspected.

"You all right," I asked Roseabeth and removed the tip of the Yucca plant from her fanny. She could only nod; her eyes were still open wide with fright. I raised up slowly and peered through the cab of the truck, and what I saw took my breath away and saddened my heart. Fanny was lying across the hood of the truck; her eyes were open, but she wasn't seeing anything with them. That was clear. Her fragile neck was twisted at an obscene angle; her face was flattened against the windshield, and it was clear there was no life left in her small body. What moments before had been the "best of times" for me had suddenly degenerated into the worst. And Charles Dickens' "epoch of incredulity" had not yet reached its full bloom. The worst was yet to come.

Before I could even start feeling real bad about Fanny I glanced off to my left where I sensed some movement, and saw Hilda Fartok rising up from behind an easy chair. When she spotted me in my altogether, needless to say, she fainted. She was prone to do that. She hit the floor with a dull thud, and then I heard the unmistakable voice of Rufus Ruffin.

"What the goddamn hell was that? The son-of-a-bitchin' sky fall in or somethin'?" I watched him rise up from behind the overturned couch and reach down to give somebody a hand. "You all right, Preacher?" There was only one preacher in town that people called "Preacher," and that was Preacher.

"Oh hell," I said to myself. "Ooooooh hell!" I'd of gladly exchanged places with Fanny on the spot, no questions asked. Fanny, of course, was the person who had died earlier. That's why Rufus and Preacher were there; I was relieved to realize that I hadn't killed her. But the soothing effect of that realization didn't provide much of a balm against the slings and arrows outrageous fortune had dealt me this time.

Preacher finally got up, still half-dazed, dusted himself off and looked around finally letting his gaze settle on the truck. "Now, I believe that' Ezra's truck? Ain't it?"

Roseabeth looked at me panic-stricken. "Is that Daddy?" she whispered.

"It's *actually* Silas' truck, I believe, Preacher," Rufus said.

"But Ezra was drivin' it. And he was with Roseabeth!"

"Oh, God!" Roseabeth whimpered.

"Don't worry," I told her.

"Don't worry!" She curled up in a corner crying, and I can't say that I blamed her. Between the two of us we had Roseabeth's panties and her formal gown to put on. I opted for the gown and reached for it.

"Who's that?" Preacher snapped.

Rufus was moving around the truck now. I managed to force a smile as I wrapped the gown across my vitals. Roseabeth I noticed had managed to cover herself with the blanket, and I decided I'd rather have that than the gown but didn't fig- ure this would be a good time to negotiate a trade. As Rufus approached I widened my smile and said, "Evenin', Rufus. Preacher."

Rufus grinned real-wide like and said, "Preacher, I believe we caught the boy here with his pants down." Rufus, for all his faults, had quite a sense of humor.

"What's that?" Preacher demanded.

"I can explain this," I said, rationally.

"Where's my angel?" Preacher yelled, irrationally.

I couldn't find the words to tell him that his "angel" was in the back of the truck with me as naked as the day she was born. I cleared my throat and said, "Roseabeth, you mean? Why . . . she's jist fine."

"*Where* is she?" he yelled again even more irrationally. I was beginning to see how Roseabeth came about her hysteri- cal side even though she bore no physical resemblance to her father.

They were peering in the truck now and could plainly see Roseabeth curled up in the corner, shivering under the blanket like a frightened child. Things were just about as bad as I'd ever seen them; I couldn't imagine how they could possibly get any worse until Roseabeth suddenly raised up, dropped the blanket and yelled, "*Daddy, I have sinned!*" at the very top of her lungs. That's how.

I cursed my naturally optimistic nature and then Roseabeth: "Dammit, Roseabeth. We didn't commit any sin. Now stop being hysterical!"

"I am *ruined!*" she screamed this time.

"Roseabeth!" I leaped out of the truck opposite Rufus and Preacher. "She doesn't mean that. She—she's jist upset—I got this grease on her gown, you see."

"You son-of-a-bitch," Rufus yelled and grabbed a poker from a rack of tools next to Fanny's fireplace. Preacher grabbed a shattered two-by-four and started stalking me from the other side.

"Roseabeth! Please!" She collapsed in a heap and started sobbing. Rufus took a swipe at me with the poker and managed to catch the nylon net as I started running. It began to unravel in chunks behind me as I plodded through Fanny's flattened nasturtiums. Once clear of Rufus I stopped and tried to reason with Preacher. "Preacher, sir, if you'll jist give me a chance to explain. What happened here was an—accident, you see. We—was ..." Preacher narrowly missed me with the two-by, and I saw there was no use trying to reason with a Free Will Baptist preacher whose only daughter was stark naked in the back of my truck and still screaming about me ruining her.

There are times when the only rational thing to do is to run like hell; this was one of those times. So I gathered what was left of Roseabeth gown around me and tore out across the countryside with Preacher and Rufus in hot pursuit of their naked prey. When things calmed down some, I intended to tell them what really had happened. I'd have told them then if they'd stopped trying to kill me—and if I'd known.

13

MOMENT OF TRUTH

Si's wreck of a pickup is screaming down old State Highway Nine, west, heading out of town. He's in the cab, herding the thing along with the moral support of Mariko. I'm sitting in the back, attempting to catch my breath, pick pieces of glass out of my elbows and kneecaps with one hand and filling in the last few pages of my Big Chief tablet with the other. My new black suit is ruined, but where I'm headed, I won't need it. I will, of course, if Preacher catches us, but for my funeral, not my wedding. I hope most sincerely that this wreck of a truck and my tablet hold together long enough for us to make Houston; that's where I'm shipping out, provided, like I said, Preacher doesn't catch us first.

Speaking of Preacher, I've got to fill you in on what happened back there while it's still fresh in my mind, not that it's the kind of thing you could ever forget in a million years but because there's a lesson in it for somebody, possibly me.

The end began when the cock in the barnyard across the way from the church crowed three times; there was no doubt in my mind for whom the cock crowed: ole *Watakushi*. Nothing short of a miracle or a natural disaster would keep me from being wed, not entirely of my own volition, to Roseabeth in little more than an hour. Now I might not have minded it so much by and by—in a few years maybe. As it was, however, I barely had a chance to uncork the bottle of life's sweet wine and was consequently anxious to try another sip or two prior to committing myself for life to a single variety. I will admit that Roseabeth had a fine bouquet, but, there were so many others out there, none of which I'd had a chance to sample, that I felt the *rational* thing to do was to try a few others before settling down with just one.

The *irrational* thing to do was to use a shotgun as a mean of persuading me otherwise; but given such a persuasive factor, the *rational* thing to do was to accept the wine being offered and hope it didn't go bad somewhere down the line. That way at least I'd get out of the situation alive which left me more options than I'd have otherwise. And it would probably make Mariko a lot happier too.

Having come to such a wise decision as that, I wandered over to the desk and surveyed the clothes Silas had brought me for the ceremony—my new black suit, white shirt, dark tie, black socks and a little red carnation. I didn't much care for it to tell you the truth, but Silas said this way I wouldn't even have to change clothes for Fanny's funeral which was scheduled to take place right after mine. Still, I didn't like it; black didn't suit my personality; it was too hot to wear black in the spring, and I didn't see why I had to wear black when Roseabeth was going to wear white. If she was as pure as that color suggested there wouldn't be a wedding taking place at all. At least not one in which I was playing such a prominent role.

Anyway, there I was, obviously physically mature at long last, but in no way ready to accept the responsibility of being a husband, much less a father. I didn't figure I needed anyone else depending on me when it was so clear that I couldn't even depend on myself. And life had done no more to prepare me for the role of husband and father than it had for that of companion and future mate. I wasn't ready for it; clearly I wasn't; I needed more time, but if I had erred so badly, I was willing to face the consequences of even my uninformed judgment. No, I wouldn't run out on Roseabeth if she was ruined or pregnant or tainted or whatever it was that she was as a result of my unbending libido. I would do my duty as a decent and grammatical, more or less, human being.

In a kind of fathomless resignation I plopped down on the cot and pulled my T-shirt over my head. *I* needed a shower which is what Roseabeth was getting (something thrown together on a moment's notice, needless to say), but all I had was a pitcher of well-water and a porcelain pan to wash up in. Getting up, I crossed to the bureau, poured some water in the pan and started to work up a good lather on my torso with a bar of Lava. As I began to rinse off a rock hit the window. "Great God Almighty!" I said to myself, "they have decided to lynch me." Then I reasoned that they wouldn't dare because that might leave poor Roseabeth as an unwed mother, and there was *nothing* worse than an unwed mother to the good people of Mansfield. Even so, I was relieved about the lynching; life hadn't prepared me for that either.

I started for the window; just before I reached it another rock hit, this time crashing through and sending a shower of broken glass across the entire floor. "What the heck?" Stepping ever so carefully I continued to the window, looked out and saw what was going on: My blood brother, Jason Clay, was beneath the window in the churchyard, apparently looking for another rock.

"What the hell, Jason?" I shouted. "You're gonna pay for that window." He looked up and signaled for me to keep quiet, like maybe there was something sneaky going on. "Like hell I'll be quiet! Preacher's runnin' 'round here with his shotgun. If he thinks I'm tryin' to escape he'll fill us both full of buckshot."

"Dammit, Ezra, will you shut up? I've gotta talk to you," Jason demanded.

"I got nothin' to say to you," I told him.

"Yeah, you do," he insisted, "you jist don't know it."

"Okay," I yelled, "go to hell! There, I've said it; now git outta here."

"*Ezra!* This is...*important!*"

"Who for?" I demanded.

"Both of us!" Jason shot back.

"Us? You gotta a mouse in your pocket or what? There's no, '*us*' as far as I'm concerned, Jason!"

"Ezra, dammit, *listen!*" His sense of urgency caught me up short momentarily. "Look, I'm sorry, okay? I apologize for everythin' I've said and done to you over the years. I was wrong; I was bein' a shit, and I wanna make up for it. But I was a kid back then, immature, you know?"

"Yeah," I guess," I said thoroughly confused. This clearly wasn't the Jason Clay that I had come to know and not particularly care for.

"Look, I can't talk like this," Jason said. "I'm comin' up."

"What? What for? Are you crazy?"

"In a way, yeah," Jason said.

"Preacher will shoot you dead," I warned.

"Not if I'm climbin' *in*," he said as he started up the trunk of the oak whose sweeping branches extended out over the roof of the church. Besides he and Rufus went down to git Fanny."

I had no idea of what he *really* wanted, but I'd have sooner trusted a rattlesnake or a politician; no I take that back—not the politician. Jason came crawling over the roof and pulled up outside the widow. "Well," he said.

"Well what?" I asked.

"Well, open the window, Ezra!"

"Well, okay," I said absently. Then I opened the window and started backing away from it.

"Look out, Ezra, the glass ... "

"Oh! Damn! Ahhh, my feet!" I'd managed to locate the worst of the breakage with my bare feet. "Damn! I *knew* I shouldn't have listened to you."

"You can't blame *this* on me," he said climbing in.

"'Course I can," I argued. "I've blamed everythin' bad that happens in Mansfield on you for years."

"So has everybody else," Jason said, "and it's not fair. Now git over here and sit down." Before I could move he picked me up bodily, carried me to the chair, set me down and found a stool to hold up my feet. Then he went to work, picking out the glass and cleaning my bloody feet with the wash cloth from the bureau. "What'd you think you were? One of those ... whatchamacallits from India?"

"Fakir," I said.

"Yeah, one of them."

"I'm not fakin'," I told him.

"I know," Jason said, "this here's real blood, even if it is Indian blood."

"Don't you start on me Jason," I warned.

"I'm jist foolin' with you, Ezra. Can't you tell that?"

"No," I said. I'd never know him to fool anyone before, so how was I supposed to know he'd suddenly developed this wild sense of humor?

"That feel any better?" he asked. "I think I got all the glass out."

"You think!"

"You'll havta walk on them to tell for certain."

"Now that's a hell of a way to find out if your feet are all full of glass," I said.

"Okay! I got it all," he said after taking another quick look.

"You did?"

He nodded. "Yeah."

"You're sure?"

"Pretty sure."

I stood up, gingerly at first. "Okay," I said, "it does feel better. Thanks." For a moment we just looked at each other through a long uncomfortable silence. "You said you had somethin' important to tell me."

"I do," he said self-consciously, "somethin' 'bout Roseabeth." He looked right at me, making eye contact.

"Roseabeth?" I said.

"Yeah," he said and let out a long breath. Then he shook his head and said, "Ezra, you—you *can't* marry her!"

"What do you mean, 'I can't'? I havta after what happened last night. Preacher's makin' me marry her."

Jason sighed heavily. "Ezra," he said, "do you even *know* what happened last night?"

He had me there; there was just so much of it, and I wasn't dead certain about any of it. Still, I said, "Well, ah, yeah, we—we sorta—made out, I think. What's it to you anyhow?"

"It's *everythin'* to me, Ezra, 'cause *I'm* gonna marry Roseabeth!"

I gulped and said, "You are?" He nodded. "Does *she* know it?"

"'Course she knows it; she *wants* to marry me."

"She does?" I said woodenly.

"She sure does," Jason said.

"I don't believe it," I argued for my vanity's sake. "Roseabeth loves me!"

"No, she don't," Jason said, "she *likes* you all right; she likes you a lot, Ezra, but she *loves* me."

"You're crazy! Where'd you ever git such a notion as that?" I demanded.

"From Roseabeth," he said confidently. *Too* confidently.

"From Roseabeth?"

"Ezra, I been seein' her for a long time."

"Behind my back!"

"Not exactly. You knew we'd been together a number of times. You even saw us."

"Yeah, but—but Roseabeth said that—that she was tryin' to *convert* you."

"She did try," Jason admitted, "at first. Then we got to likin' each other and I guess you could say that I ended up . . . convertin' her."

"Into what?"

"A woman," he said frankly. Definitely *too* frankly.

"You mean …you mean to tell me that—that you and Roseabeth have been—you know—what I mean."

He nodded and said, "We love each other, Ezra. It comes natural."

"Then, then I—I didn't *ruin* her?" I asked, somewhat relieved and disappointed at the same time.

"Ezra, neither of us ruined her. Boy, the way you talk."

"But—but how can you want to marry her after—after what I did."

Jason smiled and tried to explain: "I've talked to Roseabeth, Ezra. And I hate to be the one to tell you, but you didn't do anythin' to Roseabeth."

"I didn't?"

"Close, but no cigar."

"But—but I *tried*, Jason, I'll be honest with you: She sure let me try."

"That was my fault."

"Huh?" I was beginning to get the distinct impression that love did something to logical thinking. "How was it *your* fault?"

"We had a little spat—okay a *big* spat. I was mad 'cause she was goin' to the prom with you, so I took Fonda out the night before the prom and made sure that Roseabeth saw me with her. So to get even with me she was gonna let you have a little fun with her. But from what I understand, things got a little outta hand."

"A little outta hand!" I thought for a minute, mulling it all over in my mind trying to reconstruct what had happened and what hadn't. Then I said, "You mean to tell me that I'm *still* a virgin?"

"As far as I know," Jason said.

"Dammit it all! And Roseabeth isn't pregnant or ruined or even *mad?*"

"Roseabeth is jist fine, a little nervous maybe, and awfully sorry about the fuss she put up, the trouble she got you in. But she was hysterical. You can understand that."

"Yeah, I can," I told him, but I wasn't happy about what she put me through.

Jason looked at me a little nervously. "She don't wanna marry you though."

"You mentioned that."

"Sorry."

"It's okay," I said reflectively. Never in a million years would I have expected my savior to appear in the person of Jason Clay, but there he was, in the flesh, and about, I was confident, to get me off the end of a *very* large hook. He walked slowly to the bureau, wet the cloth and began to wash his hands.

"There's more to it than. . . what I've told you so far, Ezra," he said without looking at me.

"What more *could* there be?" I asked nervously.

"A lot," Jason said, "And I reckon I owe it to myself to admit it to you."

"Admit what, Jason?"

He turned around and said, "It's true. I do love Roseabeth, but even if I didn't, I wouldn't of stood by and let Preacher force you to marry her, or anybody else against your will."

"You wouldn't?" I said, genuinely puzzled. "Why not?"

"'Cause of what you did for me."

He *really* had me this time. The only thing I could recall doing for Jason was busting his head open and dislocating his shoulder in our final confrontation. Secretly and somewhat sorrowfully, I hoped things never got so bad for me that I'd consider a severe beating a *favor*. "What'd I do, Jason?"

He glanced at me for a moment, gulped and stared at the floor. "You—you made things a hell of a lot safer for me."

"I *what?*" I was under the impression I'd made things safer for everybody else.

Looking at me, he went on with some difficulty, "When—when I got that plastic plate put in my head, where—where my skull was busted, the doctor told me that I—I couldn't fight any more, that—that I could be killed easy as anythin'."

"I'm sorry 'bout that, Jason. I really am. But you—"

"That meant . . . that I didn't *havta* fight any more, never again, that—that I didn't havta prove myself to anybody ever again, not—not to my old man or my buddies or the creeps in Yellville or even to myself. *Nobody*. I was free!"

"I thought you *liked* to fight."

"No! Maybe there was a time when I thought I did, but I didn't. Not really. I hated it, *hated* it, but I was scared, scared of my old man, scared of not livin' up to my tough reputation and of one day gittin' the hell beat outta me. But I couldn't see no way of gittin' out without *lookin'* like I was scared. I couldn't let anybody know that. Don't you see?" He started pacing then and just let it all roll out of him like a molten stream of lava. "I never hated *you*, Ezra, not 'cause you're Indian or Japanese or whatever the hell it is that you are. What I couldn't stand was that you were always so *safe* with Doc and Silas and your mom always frettin' over you. There was just so much love in your family, even with everythin' so messed up lookin' at it from the outside. And for me there was nothin' but fear. My folks never wanted me, and they didn't bother to hide it neither. If I hated you, it was 'cause I wanted what you had. I reckon that's why I bullied you for so long, 'cause—'cause you knew what it was to be loved, to be cared 'bout and safe. And I didn't 'cause—'cause nobody ever loved me . . . "

"Until Roseabeth," I told him and swallowed real hard. Jason walked to the window and looked out because he didn't want me to see him break. I didn't care if he saw me or not because I felt so rotten. Probably I couldn't have done anything about his dark world, had I known it even existed, but had I known, I might have at least understood his behavior as I now understand it. A few pieces of what it meant to *live* life were finally beginning to fall into place for me, a sign of maturity of some sort, I suppose. I looked at Jason standing there in the bright afternoon sun, but I didn't say anything because I didn't know what to say. There was nothing really meaningful I could tell him, nothing that would take away the sting of all those years of abuse. Finally I managed, "I'm sorry, Jason." That was all.

Turning from the window, he took a deep breath and forced a slight smile. "Then you won't marry Roseabeth?"

"No," I said, "I won't marry Roseabeth."

He hurried over and grabbed my hand. "Dammit, Ezra, *thanks!* And—and don't worry, you'll find someone . . . why, Fonda would marry you I bet. Or Heather! She'd probably marry you in a minute."

"Now hold on there jist a minute, Jason," I said. "I don't feel like I'm ready to . . . leap into another—situation of such proportions jist yet. I—"

"I know. You'll need some time to git over, Roseabeth."

"That's right," I said, and thought ruefully that I'd need about another three seconds to get over *poor* Roseabeth. "I'll git through it all right; don't you worry 'bout that. What we havta do right now is figure out a way that will *keep* me from marryin' Roseabeth without one or both us gittin' shot. 'Cause, pardon my sayin' so, Jason, but I don't think Preacher is all that knowledgeable 'bout your more admirable qualities."

"I don't think he is either," Jason agreed, "so here's what I think we ought to do: You know that part of the weddin' when the preacher asks if anybody has any objections to the weddin' takin' place?"

"Don't you think that's cuttin' things a little close, Jason?"

"Don't worry. What can Preacher do when I tell him that the ceremony can't go on 'cause Roseabeth loves *me*, not you?"

"He could shoot us." I said.

"No. I jist step in, trade places with you, and you stay on to be my best man. I've already got a license and everythin' 'cause me and Roseabeth were gonna elope anyway."

"Now that's a right beautiful plan all right," I agreed, "but, I'm not dead certain Preacher will go for it. For one thing, and I hate to keep harpin' on this, but you're ignorin' his shotgun. And for another, I think he'd dead set on my marryin' Roseabeth whether *she* wants to or not. He thinks I got . . . potential."

"Well why would he want you to marry her if you got somethin' like that?"

"It's not a disease, Jason . . . never mind. I jist don't think your plan will work."

"You don't honestly think he'd shoot one of us, do you? A good man like Preacher, a Christian!"

I looked him straight in the eye and said, "Lord, Jason, don't you know there's nothin' more dangerous in this world than a good man with a shotgun who's convinced he's absolutely *right* 'bout something? Remember the Crusades?"

"No. What's that?"

"Never mind. Jist take my word for it: Even the best of men can be downright awful when they git somethin' all screwed up in their heads. They won't even give another body a chance to say their piece."

"Then what we gonna do, Ezra?"

"Well, we'll *try* your plan, but jist in case it doesn't work, we'll need somethin' else to fall back on, besides the floor," I said.

"Okay," Jason agreed.

"So, you git hold of Silas. Tell him the whole story and to have his truck ready for a quick getaway, like I said, jist in case. And you think of a way to get Roseabeth outta town, if need be."

"I'll think of somethin'," Jason said.

"And git hold of Silas."

"Okay," Jason said.

"Okay, good luck, Jason. I wish you and Roseabeth nothin' but the best. I hope she can—can ... make your world safe and..."

"Ezra, I know what you mean. Thanks." I nodded and half smiled as he crawled out the window and disappeared down through the branches of the oak.

The church was chock-full of people when Preacher ushered me into the sanctuary through the rear door. Ordinarily, the groom wouldn't receive such preferential treatment, but in the case of shotgun weddings, Preacher made special allowances. I cast a sidelong glance at those assembled and frankly was amazed at how you could draw such a crowd on such short notice. Out there amidst all the suppressed smiles and undercurrent of snickering, I failed to spot Jason, who, I assumed would seat himself conspicuously since he was to have such a prominent, even if unrehearsed, role in the festivities. As I passed Mariko and Silas on the front row, Silas nodded toward the stained-glass window on the west wall and spoke under his breath. "Truck's under the window, the one with the disciples on it."

"Where's Jason?" I asked out the side of my mouth.

"He'll be here. Don't worry," Silas said.

"Don't worry!"

"Shhh," Preacher warned. Then he positioned himself with his head held high before the altar; his black Bible was in one hand and under the flowing dark robe, his shotgun was in the other.

Hilda Fartok was doing an injustice to some lovesick melody on the old Hammond organ, and the combined fragrances of the flowers, perfume and aftershave turned the sanctuary in a kind of olfactory diner. Looking around and still not seeing any sign of Jason, I glanced over my shoulder and mouthed the words to Silas, "Where the heck *is* he?"

Silas shrugged and mouthed the words, "I don't know. Last time I saw him he was goin' to git his car washed."

"Damn," I said too loudly and felt the good reverend nudge me with the business end of Mr. Winchester.

"Watch your tongue, boy," he warned.

As the rear door of the sanctuary opened with a bang, Hilda slid into the *Wedding March*, a sound that sent cold chills darting around my spine like minnows in a bait bucket. Roseabeth suddenly stepped into a golden path of sunlight that was slanting across the aisle and started toward the altar. She was wearing what had to have been her mother's wedding gown, and, from what I could tell, her mother must have been on the portly side and a good deal shorter than Roseabeth. And time hadn't been kind to the silks and satins of the gown, turning their once bright brilliance to a subtle shade of off-white that was not very far from yellow. Then Roseabeth wasn't all that pure either; nor was I, nor was anybody else there either, I suspected. Everybody, I suppose, had a tinge of yellow in their past.

Even so, Roseabeth did look lovely, moving down the aisle with all the grace and dignity of a great swan. As she got closer I could see her eyes scanning the church for Jason through the thin veil. Just as she reached me, Silas stepped forward to serve as my best man. He poked me and said, "Ezra, you've got on *white* socks. I brought you some dark ones."

"I know," I said as Hilda continued to maul the *Wedding March*.

"Then why didn't you wear the dark ones?"

"You know better that than," Roseabeth said, getting in a last lick.

"I *know* I know better," I said defensively, "but I couldn't put dark socks on my bloody feet!"

"What did he say about bloody feet?" I heard Mariko whisper.

"I cut my feet on the glass," I explained.

"What glass?" Silas asked.

"From the window that Jason broke."

"So Jason broke that window," Preacher said. "I'll take care of him later."

"It was an accident," I told Preacher. "He was tryin' to hit me and ...it's hard to explain."

"He was tryin' to hit Ezra, Daddy," Roseabeth said in Jason's defense. To tell you the truth, I didn't much care for her tone.

"Then Ezra can pay for the window," Preacher said. " Now everybody be quiet; this here is a *sacred* ceremony."

Hilda began to pick up her pace and volume so I took the opportunity to quiz Roseabeth on Jason' whereabouts. "Where's Jason?"

"I dunno; he'll be here. Don't worry."

"Don't worry!" Where'd I heard those words before? "Why didn't you tell me about him?"

"'Cause I didn't think you would of—"

"Have."

"Would *have* understood," Roseabeth said.

"Well, I wouldn't of!"

"*Have.*"

"Okay."

"That's why I didn't tell you," she told me.

"Well, a fine fix you've got me into now!"

"You? You're always thinkin' 'bout yourself, Ezra Casey. I declare—"

"What are you two bickerin' 'bout?" Preacher said tight-lipped as Hilda began grinding to a long overdue close.

"Nothin', Daddy," Roseabeth said and gave him a gooey smile.

"Well stop it. This ain't no time to argue, " Preacher demanded.

"That's right," Silas agreed. "That comes *after* the weddin'"

"There ain't gonna be a weddin'," I said.

"The *hell* there ain't," Preacher snarled.

"Yessir," I agreed, "of course there's gonna be a weddin'." I didn't elaborate any further.

Hilda's final few notes drifted off somewhere into the nev-er-never land of used up musical notes as a senseless kind of tranquility fell over the sacred proceedings. Preacher cleared his throat, pushed out his chest and began: "Dearly Beloved, we are gathered here in the presence of the Almighty God and this assembly here of the Holy Many to join this man—"

"Man?" I said.

"Ezra!" Roseabeth said and poked me.

"I'm still jist a boy," I protested.

"Boy," Preacher threatened, "if you don't settle down you're not *never* gonna git to be a man neither." I settled down momentarily, but remained highly agitated because of the circumstance and because Preacher had used a *triple* negative. Preacher went on. "We are gathered here to join this . . . *man* and this woman in Holy Matrimony." He paused there so I took the opportunity to take another look around. No Jason. He was cutting things pretty close if you ask me. I hated to be critical, but the role of the sacrificial lamb was not one that I was too anxious to play. You probably understand that. Preacher started up again. "If there be anyone here among you who would state why this man and this woman should not be wed, let him step forward and state such an objection or forever hold his piece." I glanced at Silas then at Roseabeth, who had just scanned the congregation. Still, no sign of Jason. Roseabeth planted an elbow in my side.

"Say somethin', Ezra," she whispered.

"What?"

"*Anythin'!*"

"Silas," I said, grasping at straws.

He stretched his neck and looked around. "I'd run like hell if I were you."

"Very well," Preacher said, "so let it be did, so let it be done. Ezra, take Roseabeth's hand."

"Which one?" I asked.

"It don't matter; jist grab one!" Preacher demanded.

I took the left one, reluctantly and then said, "Reverend?" I gave him a kind of meek well-meaning smile.

"*What now?*" he snapped.

"Now, *I* don't have any objection to marryin' Roseabeth; I most surely don't, but, maybe you ought to find out how *she* feels 'bout marryin' me."

"Roseabeth will do what I tell her," Preacher said.

Before we could debate the merits of free choice, I heard the roar of Jason's twin glass-pack mufflers, the sudden squeal of his tires and finally, his locked wheels sliding through the gravel in the parking lot beside the church. I breathed a heavy, and I might add, premature sigh of relief. Everyone in the church turned around and looked at the rear door. Jason all of a sudden burst in the sanctuary as spruced up as I'd ever seen him and came rushing up the aisle yelling, "*Stop the weddin'!*"

"What in tarnation?" Preacher growled. "You git outta here; this here is a sacred ceremony!"

"I don't care 'bout that," Jason said, stopping next to Roseabeth and taking her hand from mine. "Roseabeth don't love, Ezra; she loves *me!*"

"Like hell!" Preacher shouted, wild-eyed.

"I do, Daddy," Roseabeth cried, "it's true!"

"Like hell!" Preacher said.

"And *I'm* gonna marry her," Jason insisted.

"Like hell!" Preacher roared, this time unveiling the shotgun and Roseabeth along with it. Then he looked at me, his eyes burning with a kind of witless rage, and yelled, "This is *your* fault!"

"Like hell!" I said.

"You're the one that led my angel from the path of righteousness."

"Now wait a minute," I pleaded. Preacher swung the shotgun at me; Roseabeth's veil was still dangling limply from the twin barrels like some unfortunate bird of prey. "I didn't do *anythin'* to Roseabeth."

"You didn't?" Silas said.

"No! I tried," I explained, "but evidently, I didn't do it right. Didn't Jason tell you?"

Silas was chuckling. "How could you not do it right?"

"*I dunno.* You sure never told me how to do it right," I pointed out.

"Silence!" Preacher screamed. "I want silence!" There was, to tell you the truth, a good bit of speculating going on among the town folks about the situation. And rightly so. It wasn't every day that you saw someone volunteering to exchange places with the groom who was about to exchange vows with the bride at a shotgun wedding. Not even in Mansfield, where I was single-handedly making the extraordinary commonplace, did you often see such a thing,

Over the chatter I heard Silas trying to reason with Preacher. "Why don't you just let the kids do what they want, Preacher? The union of Ezra and Roseabeth is not one that was made in heaven, and you know it."

"Daddy, I *know* who I love," argued Roseabeth. "And Ezra isn't ready for marriage; he so ... *immature.*"

"Now wait a minute," I protested.

"No, No!" Preacher roared. "That boy *ruined* you."

"No, he didn't," Roseabeth yelled, "*Jason* did!"

"Now wait a minute," Jason said.

"What?" Preacher demanded and trained his gun on Jason.

Jason gulped and cried, "*Roseabeth!*"

"Daddy!" Roseabeth screamed.

Silas poked me and said, "I'm gonna git your mother and git the hell outta this madhouse. You know where the truck is. We'll be waitin'."

Just then Preacher raised the shotgun heavenward and let go with both barrels into the ceiling. Good thing Michelangelo hadn't painted it. The blast filled the room with blue smoke and the acrid smell of sizzling gunpowder. As if tormented, Preacher screamed, "silence!" while little pieces of plaster and flakes of paint rained down on all of us like pieces of broken sky. He had managed pretty much to get everyone's undivided attention. He was standing there, looking down on us from his elevated position, his eyes bulging from their sockets and the veins near his temples about to burst. Clearly, the shit was *very* close to hitting the fan. He glared at the lot of us and said, "You mean to tell me that *both* of these boys ruined you, Roseabeth?"

"Boys will be boys," Silas said, attempting to inject some levity into the situation now that the sanctity of it had all but gone to seed.

"Daddy, they didn't *ruin* me," Roseabeth cried.

"No, sir," I agreed wholeheartedly, "I tried to, but—"

"Oh Ezra, shut up," Roseabeth snapped. "Daddy, Jason's the one, but I'm not ruined. I—I'm a woman now, all grown up. You havta face that."

"No, no!" Preacher snarled. "*They* done it!"

"What are them things for anyhow?" Jason abruptly cried. "And who the hell are *you* to tell us how to live our lives?

"That's not the way to handle Daddy," Roseabeth said.

It was a decidedly different track than I'd have taken if I was going to debate the issue with Preacher, but Jason was committed to it, and there was no stopping him now. "You ain't God; you can't pass judgment on Roseabeth or me or Ezra. And how the hell did Roseabeth git here unless you *ruined* her mother?"

"*I never touched her mother!*" Preacher suddenly screamed incoherently and the place became silent as a tomb. There it was: the moment of truth. All the pieces suddenly fell into place.

Roseabeth was stunned; she blinked and mumbled quietly, "What—what'd you say, Daddy?"

Preacher looked right through her; he looked right through the lot of us.

"He's not your daddy is what he said," Jason told her. Roseabeth clutched Jason's arm and they began to back away slowly as Preacher grew very silent, cocked his head and somehow looked at us as if we were a great distance away.

Preacher stood there for a moment longer with his rage building like steam in a covered kettle; as he gazed into the ceiling where a beam of sunlight shown through the shattered roof, I heard him whispering, praying I suppose, but not for anybody's salvation. "Lord, have mercy upon me for I know what I must do to right this terrible transgression against me and Thee. Give me a steady hand, a keen eye, and a cold heart so that I might see Thy will be on earth as it is in heaven. So let it be did, so let it be done." He reached under his robe.

"He's reloading!" somebody screamed, and then all hell broke loose in the house of the Lord. Jason ran up to Preacher and gave him a violent shove that sent him stumbling backwards until he fell headlong into the baptismal pool. Then Jason turned, grabbed Roseabeth's hand, and as they rushed up the aisle Hilda started banging out the *Wedding Recessional* in a tempo that pretty much matched the fast-paced action of the less than Holy matrimonial proceedings.

Until I heard Silas yelling for me to get out, I hadn't been able to move; everything seemed to be happening around me in a dream-like fashion. When I tried to run it felt like my feet were stuck in heavy molasses. I couldn't move. Only when I saw Preacher clawing his way out of the Baptismal pool, shaking off water like a hound dog and cursing to high heaven did I come to my senses. I started running up the aisle and saw Silas at the window across the way. "Over here, Ezra!" We're ready to roll. Look out!"

Glancing over my shoulder I caught a glimpse of Preacher leveling the shotgun in my general vicinity, so I dived between the two closest pews as a fiery blast of the Lord's breath shook the entire sanctuary and ripped into the pew just above me, sending splinters and dust flying every which way. Preacher's eye wasn't too keen, but his old heart seemed to be plenty cold. He was shooting to kill.

People were screaming and scurrying all over the place like a bunch of cockroaches caught in the light. The organ reached a final crescendo of chaotic musical rhetoric then fell abruptly silent as Hilda did the same thing, hitting the floor with her usual thud. Everything got real quiet then; all you could hear was Preacher sloshing his way up the center aisle, slowly, like he was stalking game. Sometimes he'd stop, turn, and you'd hear someone gasp or whimper. Then he'd move on, like he was looking for someone in particular, which, of course, he was: ole *Watakushi*. I managed to stay ahead of him by rolling under the pews; the line of pews that ran perpendicular to and directly in front of the stained-glass window with the 12 disciples is where I was headed. That's where Silas and Mariko would be waiting. Beneath the pews I could see Preacher's huge feet in the aisle, sloshing steadily forward, one wet step at a time.

"Ezra, justice is seekin' you, boy. You gotta pay for what you done to my angel. You can't run from sin, boy, or justice. Stand up! Stand up for Jesus. I got justice right here waitin' for you. Stand up, repent, let me wash your sins away."

"Don't you do it now, Ezra," some friendly voice called. "He's gonna *blow* your sins away."

And me along with them, I figured. I don't think I need to tell you how far things had gotten out of hand. Preacher was completely berserk, raving about God's laws and my sin and whatever had or hadn't happened between him and his Mrs. way back when. I could finally make some sense out of why Preacher was always so down on so natural a part of the human experience as sex. Clearly, he was nuts, driven that way more by demons from his own past than by anything I'd ever done. That was nice to know information, but likely to do me more harm than good at that moment. It only meant that he'd probably get off with a few years on probation if he *did* kill me, a fact that didn't drive me crazy with delight. You probably understand that.

"Boy! Come on out now. Where are you?" he called. "Mr. Winchester and me and the Lord wants to have a little visitation with you."

I was almost to where I was going. As Preacher came up the aisle I rolled directly under the pew next to the window and held my breath as he passed ever so slowly by and continued up the aisle. I toyed with the idea of saying a prayer of some kind, but then figured if we were both praying to the same God, Preacher would have the inside track so I decided against it. I was on my own. When he passed by, I raised up slowly, resting my hand on the pew in front of me. The pew creaked under my weight, and I saw Preacher turning my way and raising the shotgun. I grabbed a Bible off the pew and let it fly, catching Preacher in the side of the face and knocking him off balance. He fell backwards, raising the shotgun and sending a blast of buckshot into the window. Diving through the opening, I found myself in a shower of broken glass, fragments of a shattered rainbow that fell toward earth and landed in the rear of a battered old Chevy pickup along with a kid whose libido wasn't in much better shape.

Silas lit out, his knobby tires tearing up gaping pieces of green grass as he spun off the church lawn heading in the general direction of Main Street and the only highway leading out of town.

Framed there in the broken window behind me was the receding image of a good man driven into the witless rage of a snarling animal by a perverted view of one of God's most beautiful gifts.

As for my own self, I had no intention of becoming perverted by sex, but I sure did look forward to the *opportunity* of become perverted by it. What I didn't know was how and where in the world I could ever manage even that, certainly not here in territories where things had gotten so civilized.

"Hey, Ezra," Silas called out his window and slowing down some now that we were out of harm's way, or appeared to be. "Where to?"

I brooded on it momentarily and then said, "The South Seas!" Mr. Melville, I knew, had fallen on hard times there and *savages* had taken him in and treated him real amiably. And that's better treatment than I was getting from civilized folks here in the territories. And in Samoa I could get mature in one night, if I wasn't already too late. So I told him again, "Yeah, the South Seas; that's where I wanna go."

As the truck surged ahead I knelt down and started to strip off my suit; I wouldn't need it in all that sunshine and surf. Then I looked up and saw Mariko smiling at me through the rear window. I could always count on her to understand, even if I didn't.

The End

ABOUT THE AUTHOR

David W. Christner was born in Sweetwater, Tennessee and raised in a small farming community situated between the Washita River and the Wichita Mountains in southwestern Oklahoma. In his youth he attended church, picked cotton, plowed fields, harvested wheat, hauled hay and moved irrigation pipe. After a stint with the U.S. Navy in Vietnam and Norfolk, VA, he settled permanently in South County, RI, just across Narragansett Bay from Newport where he had attended Officer Candidate School. Speculations on the cosmos, sex, war, religion, injustice, environmental exploitation, aging, women's issues, the homeless and capital punishment have formed the thematic content of the plays and novels he has written so far. Christner is an award-winning playwright. In addition to the U.S., his plays have been produced in Australia, Japan, Belgium, India and Canada. "Red Hot Mamas" was recently translated into Russian and Italian for pending productions. Christner is the theater critic for the *Newport Mercury* in Newport, Rhode Island. "Huckleberry Hill" is his third novel.

11145146R00189

Made in the USA
Middletown, DE
14 November 2018